Geist

Mark Kelly

Winnipeg, Canada

Developmental editor: Craig Gibb
Proofreader: Francisco Feliciano

Published August 2022 by Deep Hearts YA, an imprint of Deep Desires Press and Story Perfect Inc.

Deep Hearts YA
PO Box 51053 Tyndall Park
Winnipeg, Manitoba R2X 3B0
Canada

Visit deepheartsya.com for more great reads.

Geist

Chapter 1
Ghosted

Sitting safely in McDuffie's Irish Tavern, I had a perfect view of the two maniacs standing across the street. They were part of a cult, that I was sure of. They were loud, they were harassing everyone in their path, and they were breathing my air. I wanted them gone.

A short, grungy looking woman with big boots and an oversized army jacket held up a sign that said *DEMONS ON EARTH* in big red letters. She looked a little feral, which meant she was an authority figure. Definitely not the leader, but someone with power. Next to her was a ratty-looking boy about twice her size, trying and failing to hand out pamphlets to passersby. No one looked at them, no one grabbed a pamphlet, and one man almost did a twirl to avoid the boy. I had been staring at them for maybe ten minutes straight before remembering why I was at McDuffie's in the first place. I looked down at my phone. Still no new texts.

"Goddammit," I whispered.

I put on my headphones and turned on my ancient iPod. Flipping through a dozen songs, I pretended that the crazy woman was lip syncing to each one. Ironically, "Take Me to Church" by Hozier fit almost perfectly. It was like watching my own personal drag show, except the stage was the outside of a dilapidated corner store and the drag queen was a militant religious zealot. After a while, Yvonne walked over from the bar, holding a pitcher of lemonade. I pulled off my headphones and looked up at her as she refilled my glass.

"Any word from him, Ash?" she asked.

"At this point, he's either going to say he can't make it or he won't text me at all." *Don't be so damn pathetic,* I thought. I lifted up my head and ran my fingers through my hair. "His loss. Any guy that doesn't want me is either straight or an idiot."

"That's redundant." Yvonne let out a dry chuckle. She wasn't buying it, clearly. "But you're right. It's his loss. You're a cute boy. You're a tall athlete with youth and abs and a metabolism that hasn't been decimated." She said that with such contempt it felt like she wanted to kill me. "I think I lost the plot. Anyway, just because you can't find a husband the second you graduated from high school doesn't mean you don't have a million other things going for you."

I averted my eyes. "That's a lie. I've been out of school for weeks and I'm still not married. That means everyone hates me and I'm going to die alone."

Obviously, everything was said sarcastically, but that didn't mean I didn't also believe it. The first real boy to ever offer to go on a date with me decided to leave me alone in a sad Irish pub in the middle of inner-city Chicago during peak stabbing hours. It really said something that my closest friend was a thirty-something waitress-slash-violinist that hung out with my grandma.

On the bright side, most of my frustration was getting diverted toward the cult that set up shop outside. The grungy woman outside had gotten so fed up with people ignoring her that she decided it was time for a megaphone. She bellowed into it as if preaching to a five-mile-long congregation. As pissed as she looked, she was probably living for it.

"God's world is in danger!" she screamed, in a voice exactly as obnoxious as I hoped it would be. "He gave us all a chance to live our lives in His image! And now the Geist are destroying everything He has worked for!"

"Oh, well, there goes my theory that they were just a pyramid scheme," I mused, absolutely transfixed on the lunatic. "You know what cult they're part of, Yvonne?"

"The Brotherhood of something stupid. I have some neighbors that are part of it, and I forget the name every time they try to save me. Which is a lot, by the way," she droned. Her bored look suddenly vanished. "In fact, I think the big one holding the sign lives down the hall from me." She squinted a bit. "Oh yeah, that's James."

"He ever tell you what a Geist is?" I asked, smirking.

"Oh yes." Yvonne covered her face with her braids, doing her best impression of the girl from *The Ring*. "They're ghosts that want to feed your soul to Satan."

"Spooky." Cue eyebrow raise. "And do you ever tell him how goddamn stupid that is?"

"Constantly."

We both laughed. She turned on the TV above me to drown out the screeching, then headed to another table. She gave an overly elaborate martini to a white-haired woman in a long, silky dress. Yvonne headed back into the small kitchen, but the white-haired woman raised an eyebrow at me and took a sip of her martini. She looked like she fit in more at an opera house than a dying tavern, but I wasn't one to talk. While everyone else in the restaurant was in boring tees or whatever they wore to work that morning, I was tarted up in a tight jacket and strategically ripped jeans because I thought a boy liked me, like a fool. I was even wearing my favorite necklace. The Celtic knot in the shape of a crescent moon that my brother Zack made me to distract me during my grandma's cancer scare. It didn't exactly have the best memories attached to it, but it made me look mysterious and edgy and that was all that mattered.

I checked my phone again. Still nothing. Slouching down and hiding my phone behind my glass, I stupidly reopened the hookup app, just in case he messaged me on there instead. While there were dozens of profiles, his had vanished from my phone. He must have blocked me. I was ghosted. Bottom line, cut and dry, ghosted. The app's patented notification sound pinged. My heart soared until I realized it was a message from a man in his fifties, this one complete with a photo. I knew better than to open it.

Before I closed the horrible app, someone caught my eye. Right next to my profile picture was a sexy, shirtless torso. I instantly clicked it to get a better look, for investigative purposes. Abs! Pecs! A goddamn man! A long scorpion tattoo covered one of his thick arms. Then I saw the profile name. "Discreet." I shoved my phone back into my pocket, swirled a little whirlpool in my lemonade, and sighed. I had been eighteen for all of two months and I already hated being an adult.

Almost on cue, my phone rang. Unsurprisingly, it wasn't my date. It was only my grandma. I was half-tempted to answer it and just hold it outside so she could have a long conversation with the screaming cultists. But I knew better. The first twenty times I did jokes like that didn't go over well. I answered like a normal human instead.

"Hi, Faye," I groaned. "You'll never guess what happened."

"Well, you're not dead, so that's a good sign." She said that so matter-of-factly I had to laugh. "So is the date going well? Is he handsome? He better be handsome. I told you you're too young to date an ugly boy."

"Well, he's off being handsome somewhere else, I guess, because he never showed up." I started playing with the condensation on my lemonade. "Better disappointed now than later, though, you know?"

"Oh, damn him. I told you all men were horrible," she huffed. "You want me to come and pick you up? I'm at my condo right now. I can just swoop on by in no time at all."

"It's fine. I'm staying at Dad's tonight. I'll just get a taxi or something."

"Are you sure? You're not in the best neighborhood." She cleared her throat. "Because Yvonne just sent me a picture. You told me he was taking you to a movie, not the South Side!"

I glared at Yvonne from across the tavern. She had her phone camera pointed directly at me. I stuck out my tongue at her, and she did the same to me.

"Yeah, okay, maybe I'm at McDuffie's. But, bad neighborhood or not, I'm a cross country star. I can outrun anything that comes my way." I tried out my perky voice again. "If I wanted, I could run all the way home."

"Ashton Matthew Murphy, if you even joke about that, I'll write you out of my will," she hissed. I had to laugh again, even if she had been making that joke since I was five. "There's not a city on Earth where a boy can run home safely from the inner-city, but that goes double for Chicago, triple for being on the South Side, and quadruple for being almost nine o'clock!"

"Faye. It's only seven. And I'm getting a cab."

"Thank you." A little quiver appeared in her voice. It frightened me. I knew exactly what was coming. "You're not allowed to joke about stuff like that. I don't—"

"Please don't mention Zack."

We both went quiet. The grungy woman across the street continued her tirade, but my grandma's silence was louder. I shifted uncomfortably in my seat, but I kept my spine straight and my head high. As Faye always said, "It's better to look good than feel good," and I was not about to let anyone see me squirm. Not Faye, not Yvonne, and definitely not the elegant white-haired martini drinker.

"Sorry," I sighed. "I love you."

"I love you too, sweetie." Her quiver left.

"I'll also tell Mom that you love her." I smirked.

"Don't you dare."

We made little kissy noises and hung up. I almost checked my phone texts again, but at that point, I lost any faith in the date. The screaming outside stole my attention again. Someone else joined the grungy woman to pass out fliers. This one was a frail girl with jet black hair down to her shoulders and dyed pink bangs. She was much more eager to hand out fliers than James, who had his eyes firmly on his phone. When someone walked on by without taking one of his fliers, the grungy woman smacked the back of his head. My eyes almost popped out of my skull and it took everything I could not to run out into the street, snatch the megaphone from that woman, and hurl it into traffic.

Yvonne headed to my corner again and sat down next to me. Somehow her smile was both comforting and condescending. Before I could think of a snarky quip to make myself look calm and collected, Yvonne detached a long blue tube from her keychain and handed it to me.

"What's this?"

"It's mace," she said. "I know that look in your eyes. If you're going to harass the Brotherhood, the least I can do is to give you some protection. Your dad's gonna find a way to blame me for everything tonight so I might as well help you burn someone's mouth shut if they threaten on you."

I would have preferred the Medieval kind of mace, but I figured the regular kind would have to do. Hopping up from the table, I gave Yvonne a quick hug, and headed out the door into the moonlight. With the wind at my back and Yvonne's mace in my hand, I was ready to take out some rage on a cult.

Without waiting for the light to change, I strode down the crosswalk. The grungy woman's cries grew louder, and my strides became longer. Within seconds, I was standing right beside the grungy woman and her two lackeys. She came closer to me, megaphone still glued to her mouth.

"The spirits of—"

"You know, with normal cults, they try to recruit people with parties and fake workshops," I started. The woman kept trying to interrupt back, but I just kept going. "They have classes about life and happiness and enlightenment. It's not until you're emotionally compromised and massively in debt that they make you drink the Kool-Aid. You all, meanwhile, start with the crazy. You're on the street corner screaming about something only people crazier than you will believe. And you're assaulting your own minions in public, which obviously isn't kosher. So, I guess what I'm trying to say is—" I glared at the grungy woman. "Ghosts? Really?"

The exhausted look on her face really made my crappy day better. She stepped closer to me, holding the megaphone like a spy holding a silenced pistol. Even with her oversized boots, I was still way taller than her, and I would have bet that the massive coat was covering a twig body.

"You think you're the first person to get cute with us today?" Her voice dropped. "We're doing God's work! And if you don't realize that, you're just another useless NPC that's going to get killed by the Geist."

I zoned out a bit as I tried to figure out what "NPC" meant. The lackeys both tried to look away and get back to handing out fliers. At least the girl with the glasses did; James just kinda looked at his phone and held a pamphlet out in front of him. The woman kept perfect eye contact with me. In her rage, the woman's neck veins turned red, but I remained as cool as I could.

"You know what, you're right. Maybe if I could just take a pamphlet or two…"

I leaned over to James and took a pamphlet from him. And another. In fact, I took the entire stack from him and then took the girl's stack, too. James was so distracted by whatever was on his phone that it took him a while to process what I did. Before the grungy woman could say anything else, I had all of their fliers in my hands.

"Yeah, there we go, some for the whole neighborhood. You're welcome."

I walked into the corner store, not turning back. If she was yelling at me, the door shut before I could hear it. My smile faded. No one was looking. I didn't need to fake anything anymore. Some boy by the coolers had his back to me. The clerk in the corner glanced up at me but went back to reading his magazine. I walked down the aisle of the tiny store, ignoring all the chips and poorly-made trinkets, and headed straight for the candy.

In the long run, the date didn't matter. College was only two months away. There was no point in dating a guy who'd dump me two weeks into freshman year, at best. In a few months, I'd be far away from fake cults talking about ghosts. Far away from McDuffie's and its slowly-dying charm. Far away from my parents arguing over whose house I was staying at. A date would have been a nice distraction, but it would have been just that. A distraction. I pulled my headphones up and put on some Fleetwood Mac to lighten my mood. It didn't work.

"Pardon me, are those pamphlets up for grabs?"

I turned around and jumped back. The same white-haired woman from McDuffie's stood in front of me, gazing at me with a glint of mischief in her dark eyes. Her beautiful, youthful face belied the washed-out colors of her body. I took another step back. She reached her arms forward and grabbed one of the pamphlets from my hand. It took me a while to even remember I was still holding those.

"You look distressed," she cooed, slipping the pamphlet into her brassiere. "I couldn't help but notice you were alone back at the bar. Girl troubles?" My brow furrowed. "Boy troubles?" she chuckled. "Well, I'd be an absolutely awful woman if I didn't help a young lad out, now wouldn't I?" The woman reached into her clutch. She pulled out a twenty-dollar bill. "How about I treat you to something sweet?"

"I'm fine. I don't need any help." I forced a smile and grabbed a pack of lemon drops from the shelf. "People make promises, then they break them. Human nature."

"Oh, poor, little, rich boy, you're too young to be that cynical." She shook her head. "Tell me, what in the world is up with your little music player?"

"Excuse me?"

My forced smile disappeared. I took another step back, half-tempted to reach for Yvonne's mace. The woman inched closer, swaying her wrists with her movements.

"I'm sorry, I must be coming off as completely terrifying," she laughed. "It's just that not many people carry those things around anymore, and yours looks positively ancient. There must be some reason that you keep that clunker with you."

"It has all my music."

"That's all?" She jutted her jaw. "No sentimental reason?"

I looked around. The cashier was off in space, drumming his fingers on the counter and sighing. The boy by the coolers still seemed preoccupied with the soft drinks. I looked back at the woman. She played around with the bill in her hand.

"It was my brother's."

"Ohhhhh," she purred. A crooked smile crossed her face, like I said exactly what she wanted to hear. "Where is your brother? That looks like it'd be really important to him. You'd think he'd always have it with him."

I opened my mouth. No words came out.

"Oh, now I see," she chuckled.

The woman crumpled the twenty and tossed it to me. It fluttered right past me and landed on the floor. I knelt down to pick it up and tried to thank the woman. But she was gone. The only other people in the store were the boy and the cashier. The white-haired woman vanished without a trace.

I paid for my candy, shoved all the remaining fliers in the bag, and left the store. The Brotherhood was gone from the sidewalk. Best case scenario, I embarrassed them enough to leave their cult. Most realistic, they just went home. And I was ready to head home, too. I slumped onto the side of the store and called for a ride back to Dad's house.

With a few minutes to spare, I pried open my bag of lemon drops and slid my phone into my pocket. In my shuffle, I dropped my iPod. The iPod broke away from my headphones and bounced onto the sidewalk.

"Goddammit," I mumbled.

The boy from the drink cooler walked out of the store, knelt down, and picked up my iPod. He looked a little older than me, with dark skin that glistened in the streetlight and a crew cut only a little longer than his thick stubble. His tight, short-sleeved hoodie exposed a scorpion tattoo going down his arms. I screamed internally. It was the exact same tattoo that "Discreet" had. He handed my iPod to me, smiling.

"Thanks," I mumbled, shoving it back into my pocket. I

poured some lemon drops into my mouth, hoping the sour taste would calm my loins.

His smile was gorgeous, and it showed off his pronounced canines. I smiled back, but tried to hide it. The boy leaned on the side of the store with me. He was on the other side of the doors, but still close enough to talk. I ate another lemon drop and looked toward the street, hoping that my ride would come quickly. The boy rummaged through his bag and pulled out some kind of gross energy drink. In tandem, he drank and I ate, all while stealing glances at one another.

"I've got the same iPod," he finally said. "It's pretty old, but it gets the job done."

"Yeah, mine just has thirty hours of ska on it."

"Really?"

"No, ska is for forty-year-olds who still wear flame print," I coughed.

He smirked and rolled his eyes. My ride home was still missing. I tapped my foot. The streets looked empty, though. No pedestrians, no cultists, and no creepy white-haired woman asking intrusive questions. Just a lonely street corner, with only me and "Discreet."

"I'm Ash, by the way."

The boy smiled. He walked closer and leaned against the wall right next to me.

"Gabriel."

I held out my lemon drops. He plucked one out of the bag and plopped it in his mouth. His face contorted for a second, but he quickly got used to the sour flavor. I laughed, accidentally going from a cute chuckle to a gross snort. I stopped immediately, but the second he heard it, he started laughing. I blushed. *There's still time to cancel the ride,* I thought, and I looked at my phone.

The silence broke when a familiar yell echoed through the

street. Within seconds, I saw the source. The grungy woman was back, along with James and the frail girl. Gabriel stopped laughing. I sighed and looked toward the street again, wondering where the hell my ride was.

"This is all your fault. Both of you," the grungy woman grunted toward her lackeys. "The Brotherhood would be better off without you."

The woman smacked the frail girl on the back of the head. She recoiled, and Gabriel pushed himself away from the wall and stormed forward.

"Dinah!" he howled. "Enough!"

Dinah sneered. My heart sank. Gabriel started arguing with Dinah in such a low growl, I couldn't hear anything. But I didn't need to. A few streetlights away, a taxi rolled down the road. Just enough time for another fight.

"You know them?" I asked, walking closer. I tried to look more bemused than pissed. Didn't work. "Wait, better question: you're with them?"

"Yes," Gabriel said, nodding. He saw my pissed bewilderment and went on the defensive. "We're a part of the same church."

"Don't talk to him, Gabe," Dinah spat. "He's just some diva that thinks we're a cult."

"Also, he stole all our fliers," said James.

"Oh, like you can't print more." I mumbled, then turned my attention back to Gabriel. "So, you believe in ghosts? What else do you believe in? Vampires?"

It took me a long time to think of what to say next. Maybe criticize him for being "discreet" on a hookup app, or just flat-out call him stupid. But after everything, I was tired. From the look on his face, Gabriel was too.

I sighed. "Never mind."

I just walked away. I didn't look back at the Brotherhood. All I did was hop into the cab. The driver tried to make small talk, but I told him where to go and left it at that. We started rolling away from the street corner. In the corner of my eye, I got one last glimpse of the Brotherhood. Dinah and Gabe were arguing, with the other two lackeys silent on the sidelines.

The driver weaved through the bumper-to-bumper traffic. The streets gradually became less dilapidated the further we got from McDuffie's. He tried to make a little more small talk, but I just stared out the window. We drove up the highway's entrance ramp. I pulled up my headphones, turned on my music, and closed my eyes.

The car swerved, and my forehead slammed against the window. A red pickup skidded into our lane and continued to move from side-to-side. I blinked a few times, then looked around. The highway was practically empty. While the traffic heading into the city was still flowing, the only two cars on our side of the highway were my car and the truck. Never in my life had I seen a road in Chicago so barren.

My driver apologized, then got in the lane furthest from the truck. I rubbed my head, closed my eyes, and tried to rest. Slowly, my music grew quieter, and my headphones slid to my neck. A cold chill went down my spine as I felt lips touch my ears.

"Don't worry about the Brotherhood, love. If religious zealots frighten you, you're lucky you weren't alive a thousand years ago."

My heart stopped. My head jolted sideways. Suddenly, the entire car was clouded by smoke. Through the thin haze, the white-haired woman smirked at me from the other side of the back seat. I screamed, slamming the back of my head onto the window. She took a long drag from her pipe, keeping her puckered smirk the entire time.

"Oh, don't scream. He can't hear you. You're in my aura." She blew her smoke right into the front seats. The driver didn't even wince.

The pickup swerved into a closer lane, speeding up, then slowing down again. My heart followed suit, beating eight times a second before stopping, then starting up again. A million other questions bounced around in my head, but there was the only one I could let out.

"Where did you come from?"

"Darling, I've been sitting next to you this whole time. You didn't notice me? Well, aren't you a foolish boy?" she chuckled. She then pulled a metal blue tube out of her brassiere and wiggled it by my face. I checked my pockets. The mace was gone.

Every synapse in my brain broke down. I gawked at the woman, unable to even speak. All I could do was hyperventilate her second-hand smoke. Whatever she was smoking, it definitely wasn't tobacco or weed; it almost smelled like ammonia. The woman yanked on my headphone cord. My iPod jumped out of my pocket and right into her palm. I snatched it back before she could do anything else to it.

"Anyway, so there I was in that godforsaken bodega, thinking my investigation went cold once again, when I remembered that I completely forgot to ask you the most basic question! Some detective I am."

The smile left her face and all that remained was the cold glower of the most terrifying woman I had ever met. That's when I noticed something wrong with her face. One of her eyes was almost completely black except for a shining silver iris. My face was reflected in her eyes, and I saw a little boy trembling. Smoke ricocheted off her perfectly smooth skin. Her face came closer to mine, as if a curtain was opening.

"What do you know about Father Abram?"

Before I could even think of an answer, the driver screamed. My head turned back to the road just in time to see the pickup swerve back into our lane. The tail of the truck collided with the front of our car. Horrible, metallic screeches filled my ears. A thick, crunching sound came from inside the hood.

Every second became an hour, and I could see everything happen around me with perfect vision. The white-haired woman, completely stoic, pulled my necklace out from my shirt. She rubbed her thumb and index finger across it and a static shock flowed throughout my body. She stuffed my necklace back into my shirt, leaned in, and whispered into my ear.

"Ashes to ashes."

The driver let go of the wheel. The car spun out, changing direction within a split second. While the red pickup slid to the left lanes, we headed right into the median. The car raced toward the edge of the highway, crashing right into the guardrails. In an instant, we flipped. My head hit the ceiling, and everything went dark.

An eternity later, I opened my eyes. Everything was clouded by a thick, black smoke. A rising heat crept up my body. The white-haired woman left no trace of herself. I tried to look through the smoke into the front seat. The driver was still firmly in his seat, limp and dangling. A stream of red dripped down to the roof.

I tried to move my arms. Every bone in my body felt broken and every part of me seared in pain. Nothing moved. Not even my neck. All I could do was try to keep my eyes open. A light shined through the smoke. Briefly, I thought it was daylight. But when I felt the heat sizzle my skin, hope faded. I closed my eyes again, for one last time, and I waited for a bang.

But I never heard the bang, and the heat was gone instantly. My heart rate slowed, and I tried opening my eyes. My entire body was numb, almost like there was a needle stuck in every single nerve down my spine. My eyes were burning and I tried to focus them, but all I saw was blue, then red, then blue again, then red again. And suddenly, a fuzzy blur of purple, brown, and white.

"Sweetie? Sweetie?"

My vision cleared. Red and blue lights brightened and dimmed around me. And right above me, the blur of purple, brown, and white swirled together until they formed a girl. Her full face and big eyes made it hard for me to guess her age, but she couldn't have been too much older than me. Her dark skin was offset by her short, white hair and her silver eyes. The same silver eyes surrounded by black that the woman in the car had.

A jolt of pain coursed through my chest. I felt like I was hyperventilating, but I wasn't breathing. From the tiny opening between my lips, I gulped in the burning air. The girl lifted my back from the ground, putting me in a sitting position, and kept her hands on my face to keep my eyes on her. She ripped off her purple cardigan and wrapped it around me. Wind flowed into my lungs. I could feel the pain fade away from my body. It was slow, but I could feel again. I felt fine. As if nothing was wrong.

Chapter 2
Long Walk Home

I stared at the girl in front of me. Seeing her strange eyes and hair, I slowly pieced a few things together, until one question went through my mind.

How did I get out of the car?

I opened my mouth to speak to the girl, but no words came out. I tried again, and only a strained wheeze left my lips. I wanted to ask her what happened. Why I was in a burning car one second and safe on the pavement the next. But every time I tried to speak, yet another strained gasp came out of my mouth.

"Shh, shh, shh. Don't strain yourself. Just breathe. Ain't nothin' you gotta do but breathe," she whispered. Her slow, Southern twang was oddly soothing. "You've had a bit of an accident. You're probably feelin' a bit strange right now, but it's gonna be fine." She paused. "I'm Clementine. Clementine Leigh."

Her silver eyes reflected the blue and red lights in the distance. I glanced to the left, and a flash of panic crossed the girl's face. She tried to keep my eyes on her, but I turned my head anyway. Squad cars. Ambulances. A fire truck. My heart raced. There wasn't just a crash; there was a fire.

I was on the side of the highway, sitting in the middle of an exit ramp, while two charred cars surrounded by emergency vehicles blocked three lanes of traffic. The cars were so blackened, I could barely tell which was the taxi and which was the pickup. Paramedics went back and forth between the fire truck, the ambulance, and the cars. There were two long black bags across the ground, and it took me all of five seconds to realize what those were. Before I could push myself up, Clementine put her arms around my waist and tried to keep me on the ground.

"What's your name, darlin'?" The warmth in her voice wavered.

I coughed. "Ash." My voice sounded raspy, as if I hadn't spoken in days.

"Ash, I need you to listen to me. Something very bad happened." Her hands shook as she held me down. "No matter how bad you want to, no matter what you hear coming from over there, don't look. I know we just met, but you have to trust me."

Despite all the paramedics around me, the only person looking at me was a small, frail woman with the same eyes and hair as the woman who once again disappeared. She at least helped me sit up, still doing her best to keep me from looking directly at the crash. Once again, I tried to talk, but all that came out was a croak.

"Ash, sweetie, I'm going to get you out of here."

She helped me to my feet. My legs were stiff and unyielding. Clementine kept her hand on my shoulder, making sure I didn't fall on my face. My heart was beating so rapidly I could almost feel it against my ribs. It took everything I had to keep breathing and walking. Clementine gently guided me away from the scene.

The thought crossed my mind again. How did I get out of the car?

Clementine kept on pushing me away from the scene. Finally, gathering enough strength, I stopped dead in my tracks.

"T-tell me what's going on," I stammered. "Where's the other woman? How did I get out—"

I looked back at the scene Clementine didn't want me to see. Paramedics everywhere. A man with the Jaws of Life opening up what used to be a taxi. My eyes widened when I realized he was cutting open the door I was sitting next to. I broke away from Clementine and hobbled over to the taxi remains. It only took me a few steps to get a clear view of what was going on.

After one cut of the metal, an arm flopped out of the car. A passing paramedic's face wrinkled when she saw how bloodied and scorched the arm was. I didn't move. I stared directly at the scorched arm. The skin was so badly burned it was barely recognizable. It was red, black, and purple all over, with only small slivers left that looked normal. My eyes watered, each lid slowly filling with tears as the revelation came closer to me.

I didn't get out of the car.

Clementine caught up with me and tried to pull me away again. For a brief moment, I followed her again. But eventually, my legs gave out. I fell to the ground and covered my mouth with my hands. Trembling, I stared at the ground as Clementine clasped my shoulders. She was saying something, but I couldn't hear it over the voice in my head screaming one thing over and over again.

I died.

I let out a muffled scream into my hand. And still, no one but Clementine noticed me. Everyone else was busy looking at what used to be me. That, and the two other bodies lying on the road. Absolutely nothing made sense. My brain couldn't focus on anything except for the arm.

Clementine pulled me up off the ground. She ran her hands across my back and gave me the tightest hug I'd ever had. I pointed my head toward the sky. My breath became sporadic. Tears slowly blurred my eyes until the skyline in the distance looked like stars.

"I'm sorry," she said. "Cry as long as you need to. Don't feel pressured to do anything else."

A single tear finally left my eye. "Am I—am I really dead?"

For a long time, I kept my head toward the sky. Clementine kept her arms around me, slowly rubbing my back. Eventually I gathered the courage to look around again. The paramedics around us continued their cleanup. In the one clear lane, a few drivers rubbernecked, but still kept on driving. The bags on the ground all looked the same, and I couldn't tell which one was my body, which one was my driver's, and which one was the bastard that killed us all. No sign of the other woman.

"You were given a second chance," she whispered. "Whoever left you here, they—" it took her a second to find the right words "—they helped make sure you were able to come back."

Clementine turned me away from the scene of the wreck again. Away from my body, the scorched cars, and the paramedics. We walked along the edge of the highway, barely a foot away from the cars racing by. And each time one passed, I shuddered, and Clementine held me tighter. Slowly, we made our way down the exit ramp, and I couldn't feel a thing. I was dead. I just kept my head forward, then put one foot in front of the other.

Clementine and I walked down the streets of Chicago. I didn't know where she was leading me. I didn't even have an idea what time it was, but it must have been getting close to midnight. I tried to pretend it was normal. Even as Clementine and I walked along the sidewalk, I imagined nothing was wrong. Still alive, safe at home, without the ghostly woman next to me.

I shook my head before my denial went too deep. Tears formed in my eyes again, but I wiped them away. A group of men walked right by us. Like opposing magnets, they separated and walked around us. Not a single one acknowledged us.

In the window of a darkened restaurant, I saw my own reflection. Even if no one else could see me, the window still showed me something. My hair was snow white and ash gray.

My eyes became black and silver. Just like Clementine and just like that awful woman.

My eyes crept down. Under Clementine's cardigan, I was wearing a thin white robe, with the right breast wrapped over the left. Something shimmered on my neck and I saw that I was still wearing my necklace. I touched it, and it felt warm. Almost as if it had a heartbeat. I ripped my hand away from it and faced Clementine.

"I'm like you. I'm like—" I couldn't find any words. "What am I? What are you?"

"Guess the, uh, the person that did this to you didn't explain much, huh?" Clementine bit her lower lip. "In the grand scheme of life, there's a system after death that you were chosen to be a part of. When people die, you're gonna be there to greet them with a smile and lead them to the next stage. We're called—"

"Geist," I breathed.

Clementine's eyes fluttered.

"So, you do know at least a little." Clementine averted her gaze. "Guess you must'a heard about us from the other people."

The Brotherhood was right. The crazy cultists yelling about ghosts on the street corner, the ones I mocked only hours before, were right. And I was one of the ghosts they were screaming about. I collapsed onto the sidewalk, shaking.

I was dead, but I wasn't dead. My body was incinerated after a crash, but I had a new body, one with creepy white hair. Possibly invisible, but one person could see me. I was a Geist, which was either an evil spirit or a kind middleman of death, depending on who I asked. And all of this was that awful smoking woman's fault, or maybe it was the pickup driver's, or maybe it was mine.

Something slid from my robe. Out of a pocket I didn't even know I had, my iPod bounced against the concrete. I reached out to grab it, and my heart skipped a beat. It felt almost warm, just like my necklace. I gripped the edges of my iPod so hard, my knuckles turned purple. I still had my necklace, and I still had my iPod, and I still had my brain.

"I'm going home."

I stood up and started walking toward the entrance to the subway. Clementine stuttered and started running after me. I quickened my pace. All the trouble I had walking vanished as I slipped into the CTA. As other people swiped their Ventra cards to get through the turnstiles, I hopped over the turnstiles unnoticed.

"Ash, wait! You can't!" she yelled. She ran through a small crowd of people, who parted like the red sea for her, only to rejoin once she made her way through. "Ash!"

I was already to the top of the steps by the time Clementine reached them. A warm breeze hit my face once I got to the rails. A train was waiting for me, its doors wide open. People trickled in and out of it, still unable to notice the white-haired boy running toward it. I didn't care. All I wanted to do was get home and prove to everyone that I wasn't dead.

Before I could get through the door, a hand grabbed my wrist. Clementine, despite looking dainty and being half a foot shorter than me, was shockingly strong. As I tried to break away from her grip, "Doors closing" pinged from the intercoms, and the doors slid shut.

"Wait!" I pounded my fist against the door as the train pulled away. "Let me in! Let me…"

The train left the station. Everyone was gone. The only people left on the platform were the two invisible weirdos. The Geist. I gritted my teeth and glared at Clementine.

"Why'd you stop me?" I hissed. I threw my hands up in the

air and looked toward the tracks. "You know what? Fine. If I'm dead, I might as well just hop on the tracks and run after it, right?"

I hopped down onto the tracks. Clementine kept a calm face. She closed her eyes and sat down, carefully draping her skirt over her legs in order to show as little skin as possible. But as the train kept moving ahead of me, I didn't chase it. I stared at it until it went completely out of sight. I looked down at my feet again and kicked one of the rails.

"Sorry."

"It's alright, hon." Clementine tucked a stray coil of hair behind her ear. "No one ever takes this news well."

With the warm air breezing past us, I took a deep breath. Even if my body burned up in the crash, my new body felt just like my old one. Same arms, same legs, same lungs. The only things that were different were white hair and creepy eyes. Everything else felt familiar. I looked up at Clementine and tried to force a smile.

"So, I really died in that crash, huh?"

Clementine smiled, too, and it looked just as forced as mine. She nodded. Without thinking, I started to play around on the tracks. Jumping from rail to rail, making sure I didn't touch the third one. I wasn't too sure how my new body would handle six hundred volts of electricity. It was almost like I was dancing, but much too sporadic and senseless. I made sure not to twirl too intensely, though, because I wasn't wearing anything under the robe. Clementine chuckled a bit. Her smile turned a little more genuine.

"I guess the Geist who gave you their Legacy Spark didn't tell you anythin', huh."

"I don't even understand half the words you just said." I shot the most blasé and confused facial expression I could muster her way. "But no. There was a creepy smoking lady who said some weird cryptic shit to me, then she disappeared. All I know about Geist is that there's a weird cult that thinks you're a bunch of soul-eating demons."

"Well, I can safely say that we're so much more than that," she huffed.

Clementine scooted a little closer to me, dangling her feet over the edge. She seemed mesmerized by my movements around the tracks. I wasn't necessarily sure whether to call it a dance or a very long and fluid bout of fidgeting. Either way, it was keeping me grounded.

"When people die, their spirits don't automatically move onto the next life. They're trapped. That's what Geist are here for."

"Alright, so, that's great and all, but I literally do not believe in an afterlife."

"Well, start believin'," she shrugged, "because this is it."

Something escaped my mouth. It couldn't have been a laugh. Not with the day I had. But it sounded like it. Clementine must have thought it was a laugh, too, because she let out a chuckle. Her smile suddenly felt real. Nothing forced about it, nothing sarcastic. It was weird.

The smile quickly vanished when a bright light illuminated the station. I turned around, only to be greeted by an oncoming train. I shrieked and ran back toward the platform. In my haste, I stumbled a bit. My big toe hit the third rail. In almost an instant, I felt a shock that felt so intense, my heart almost burst through my chest. Clementine gasped and hopped up to her feet. The train was coming back quickly and I was immobilized by a scorching pain I couldn't even imagine.

Clementine waved both her hands. It could have been my imagination or my eyes exploding from the pain, but it almost looked like there was a whirlwind forming around her. A giant gust of wind pushed me away from the rails. My chest collided with the platform hard and all the wind got knocked out of me. My vision stopped spinning for a second as Clementine pulled me back onto the platform. I rolled onto the safe, electricity-free wood of the platform and coughed.

"Did you just—you're gonna—you're gonna have to explain that part—" my vision started to blur again. "—too."

"Hon, there's a lot of weird stuff about Geist and I only know about half of it," said the five blurry Clementines swirling above me.

The train skidded to a halt. A few more people trickled out, unwittingly avoiding us. My vision cleared slowly and my breath returned to me. Whatever this new Geist body was made of, it was sure resilient. All the pain was gone. Clementine laid down right next to me. Once again, I was staring up at the starry sky.

"So, there's no going back, huh?" I mused. "I just lost everything. My family's gonna hear I'm dead any minute now."

Clementine rolled onto her side. This random woman who found me on the side of the road, possibly the only person on Earth that could actually look me in the eyes, put her hand in mine. My eyebrows furrowed for a moment, but I saw the starry look in her eyes and I didn't break away.

"You feel this? You feel my hand squeezing yours?" She tightened her grip a bit. "That means, even after that, you're still alive."

Clementine guided me away from the tracks. I had no idea where she was taking me, but for some absurd reason, I trusted her. If I were to believe the Brotherhood, she was about to drop me into a portal to Hell. But despite everything, I still did not believe in Heaven or Hell, so I was more willing to trust her than the cult.

As we headed through the somewhat run-down neighborhood, Clementine stopped when we reached a small, open area right underneath the station. Another train pulled into the station A strange glimmer waited for us right next to a support beam. From the looks of it, it was a lily, somehow growing right out of the concrete. The lily was glowing a delicate white light, and my eyes lingered on its calming glow for much longer than I wanted them too.

Clementine leaned down next to the flower. She pulled something round and silver out of a pocket on her dress and gently pressed it against the lily. The lily almost shivered and its white light turned a deep purple. The sound of shifting stones echoed around us, but the people walking along the sidewalk didn't seem to hear a thing. What looked like a hole opened up a few feet away from the lily, but as it expanded, I saw stairs forming. Black, marble-like stairs going down into the darkness.

Of all the weird things to happen to me that day, for some reason, a set of stairs magically popping up only elicited a slight "Huh."

Clementine reached for my hand, and I accepted it once again. Together, we walked down the cold stairs. It wasn't too long before we reached the bottom, and I still had a pretty good view of the world above when we got there. But around me, all I could see was the dark marble. Clementine reached forward, and as my eyes adjusted to the darkness, I could see her grab onto a doorknob made of the exact same material as the strange stone surrounding us. She hesitated, then let go and looked up at me.

"I know we just met. And I know you're scared of what you are." She took a deep breath. "But I'm gonna be here for you every step of your journey. No matter how hard it gets, I'm gonna be here."

Everything that happened to me ran through my head. My

entire life, everything I had planned for my future, gone. The people who loved me were going to bury what remained of my scorched body. Visions of my family crying over me clouded my head, along with the face of the smoking woman, laughing.

I grabbed the knob and opened the door myself, instantly blinded by the white light coming from inside. When my vision cleared, I was greeted by the foyer of a grandiose and well-lit Victorian mansion. My eyes widened as I tried to make sense of what I was looking at.

"Well, Ash," started Clementine. "Welcome to Zinda Mansion."

Chapter 3
An Amazing, Fleeting Moment

I tried to sleep that night. For a couple hours, I felt at peace. And then, barely any time later, I woke up to see a dark and unfamiliar ceiling. For an amazing, fleeting moment, I forgot I wasn't really alive. And a few seconds later, after I remembered I was in a new room, everything came back to me. I shoved my face into my pillow to try to suffocate any sobs. *Please,* I thought, *just get back to sleep. Just let me have a few hours away from this.*

There was no getting away from "this." I was dead. Or rather, a "Geist." I gathered that I was sort of a Grim Reaper that people couldn't see, except there was a gang-like cult that knew about me. I sat up in my bed. The vintage alarm clock next to my bed said it was already 5:30 AM, but I stopped trying to get back to sleep. *This is it. This is forever.*

The ceiling above me did not resemble mine at home. My old room was pale blue, while my new room was completely white. From the curtains to the carpet to the bed itself, it was spotless and sterile.

I walked over to the small closet door next to my bed and slid it open. Nothing was in the closet. Not even a T-shirt or a pair of socks, just a bunch of hangers. Clementine was nice enough to find me a set of pajama pants before bed so I wasn't freeballing it around the mansion, but that was it. All I had were the pants, my weirdly warm necklace, and the weird death robe I was "reborn" with. I looked like a hobo or an indie musician that made acoustic covers of rap songs. Faye would have killed me if she saw me looking like that. "It's better to look good than feel good," which was very appropriate because I neither looked nor felt all that good.

A myriad of doors littered the walls outside my room. Far too many doors for just Clementine and me. I wondered just how many Geist lived in the mansion, because I saw neither hide nor hair of anyone else when Clementine showed me to a room the night before. Every door I walked by was closed. No sound was coming from behind them. I headed down from the third floor to the second. At the very end of the hallway was a mezzanine with two grand staircases that led down to the foyer.

White tile covered the floor of the giant foyer, which matched the white walls, the white doors, and the white ceiling. Everywhere in the mansion looked like a goddamn hospital. To the left and right of the entrance were two archways. On the left was what looked like a large dining room; on the right was a grandiose living room. The only color in the entire mansion seemed to be the giant stained-glass windows far above the entrance.

A vibrant spectrum of lights filled the pure white foyer as daylight flew through the stained-glass windows. I didn't understand where the light was coming from, or how the entrance of the mansion was only about a dozen feet down in the Earth but the mansion itself was several stories tall. The mansion seemed so normal on the inside. No moving staircases or talking doorknobs, just a completely normal Victorian mansion underneath Chicago that seemed to exist on a plane outside of reality, complete with electricity and running water.

I probably would have questioned it more had I not been sleep deprived, so I instead squinted and shielded my puffy eyes from the mysterious light. I stepped down the staircase, hoping that there was a coffee machine somewhere on the ground floor. I touched the railing. The banister was thick, made of sturdy wood, and was well polished. I paused, putting both hands on the banister, then propped my butt onto the banister and slid.

The second I got to a curve, I flew off the banister and fell face-first onto the first-floor tile.

It took me a while to get up from my face plant. My nose felt a little weird, and when I touched it, I felt a giant bend in it. I yelped, but almost instantly, I felt a pop, and the bend was gone. After that, I felt no pain. I only contemplated my life. Everything I ever did up to that point led me to a one-story fall onto my face. I rolled onto my back and kicked myself off the floor.

"Is there any flight of stairs in this mansion doesn't look like a damn curly fr—?"

My toes brushed up against a set of claw marks on the floor. My brain stopped working for a second as I looked down at three long, jagged lines going from where I was standing toward a set of large, black doors in between the two staircases. For a brief moment, I tried to tell myself they could be literally anything other than claw marks. Maybe someone tried to move furniture and carelessly scraped the tile. But the marks were almost too winding, too irregular, and too animalistic to have been anything but claw marks.

Every caveman instinct in my head screamed at me not to go through the scary doors. Plus, they probably didn't lead to the kitchen. I turned tail and headed into the dining room instead.

Ornate chairs surrounded a sleek white table that could seat at least twenty people. Oddly, the room still felt empty. Just like almost every other room in the mansion, it was all white, with white walls, white chairs, white curtains, and white tile. The only decoration in the room was a vase in the middle of the table filled with lilies. They were, of course, white.

I walked through the dining room and saw it was connected right to the kitchen. The kitchen was more modest than the decadent dining room but still fit right in as a room in a giant Purgatory mansion. A kitchen island sat in the middle of the room with an oven built right into it. And in the corner was a perfectly pristine and high-tech coffee maker.

Clementine made an off-hand comment the night before about helping myself to anything in Zinda Mansion. This, of course, meant that I used all the creamer she had in her fully stocked fridge and a good portion of her sugar too. It only occurred to me as I was pouring my coffee into a cutesy mug with a frog on it that it was kind of weird that ghosts had a fully stocked kitchen. And, for that matter, that I could drink coffee and it wasn't just falling right through me and onto the floor.

But I was far too depressed to think about logistics of what a Geist was. My hands were shaking as I sat down on the kitchen island and drank the coffee. As the caffeine flowed through my body, everything from the night before flowed back into my brain. Ash Murphy died via vehicular manslaughter after a hitchhiking Geist said something about "Father Abram," and I was whisked away by a nice Southern Belle to live in a lavish underground mansion while everyone I loved had to see my burnt-up body.

I wondered exactly how far into the mourning process my family was. It hadn't even been twelve hours. Images flowed into my head of my parents and Faye, all miles away from each other, wailing into a phone at the same when they all got the news. I wondered exactly which one was going to be forced to examine my body to confirm it was mine. It was far too early for them to bury me, but my funeral was pretty easy to visualize. Betsy, John, and Faye would form a perfect triangle around my tombstone. Not making eye contact with one another, doing their damnedest to stay as far apart from each other as possible.

The fantasy came pretty easily. It was exactly what it looked like when my brother died, after all. The only difference was that Zack's funeral had me.

Reality came crashing back to me when another Geist entered the kitchen. The dank smell of weed filled the room when a tall woman stumbled toward the fridge. From the neck up, I would have honestly mistaken her for a model, if not for the noticeable lip scar. But below that was the body of a wrestling diva. Her white hair had a choppy bob cut, and she dressed sloppily, wearing an ill-fitting pair of jeans and a partially-buttoned flannel shirt. From the way she smelled, I assumed this was the outfit she went to bed in, assuming she went to sleep at all.

She didn't even bother to look at me. She just opened the refrigerator door and pulled out a beer. It took her maybe ten seconds to down the entire thing. I watched her the entire time, absolutely fascinated. Then she halfheartedly tossed it into the trash, closed the door, and slumped back toward the dining room. It wasn't until she was halfway out of the room that she realized I was here, because her bloodshot eyes darted right toward me. The uncomfortable stare-down lasted much longer than it should have, and then she just stormed out the room without saying anything to me whatsoever.

"Clementine!" she bellowed. "There's a meth addict in our kitchen and he's stealing our coffee!"

A cacophony of yells echoed through the mansion. I tried my best to down my coffee before whatever nonsense was coming my way arrived. By the time my coffee mug reached the sink, the drunken Geist came back into the kitchen, along with a very tired Clementine who was still dressed in her nightgown and headwrap. I thought for a second that her nightgown had a cute orange pattern on it, but then I realized they were clementines. Because that was her name. Clementine yawned when the other

Geist pointed at me with a strange mix of contempt and confusion in her eyes.

"Vee," Clementine yawned. "This is Ash."

Vee rolled her eyes, which seemed to get less bloodshot by the second. Her sobriety must have been coming back to her at light speed.

"Great. So, this is what you were doing last night? Picking up another stray?" hissed Vee.

Clementine's face scrunched when Vee said another. She quickly regained her composure and did her best to seem well rested.

"Yes, Ash and I met late last night." Clementine did her best to stand up straight and appear as tall as Vee. "I'm fully expectin' you to be a wonderful and courteous roommate while he's with us."

Vee snarled. "Is he good at anything?"

Both of them looked at me expectantly. My mouth dried up as I completely forgot every talent I had.

"I did cross country in school," I mumbled. "And I like to bake, I guess."

"There we go." Vee snapped her fingers and started headed out of the room again. "Make me some brownies and we're golden."

Vee headed back upstairs. I headed a loud door slam from the mezzanine, and suddenly it was quiet again, and everything smelled a lot better. Clementine turned to me, her eyes looking very tired

"Under no circumstances are you allowed to bake her marijuana brownies in my kitchen."

She sighed for a very long time before forcing a smile back on her face. Clementine made herself a cup of coffee, not even looking at any cream or sugar.

"So, I was thinkin' today I could show you around the mansion," she started. "I have a tour all planned out, and then—"

"Clementine," I interrupted. "Do you think, uh," I stammered. "Maybe we should start with the Geist basics."

She stared at me for a hot second, then nodded without changing her expression. She brought her coffee to the dining room. Clementine and I sat across from each other and I waited intently for her to start teaching me the ways of the Geist.

"Okay. Basics." Clementine tapped finger against her mug. She took a big gulp. "You're dead."

"Duh."

"But before you died, someone shot somethin' called a Legacy Spark into your Memento. Your Memento is something that makes you a Geist, and it can be anythin' at all, but it's usually somethin' very near and dear to you. I'd say it's the source of your power, but that's oversimplifyin' it a bit."

Far be it from me to complain, but I wasn't too sure if "source of your power" was about our weird immortality or her weird ability to create a mini-tornado. Probably both, so I wondered if I would be able to create mini-tornados, too. Either way, there were bigger fish to fry.

"And you're positive that you don't know anything about the Geist that did this to me? Pale woman, inhumanly long hair, talks like someone that did too much theater in high school?"

Clementine shook her head. "Sorry, hon', but I don't even know who gave me my Legacy Spark."

I put my fingers up to my necklace. It still felt warm to the touch. In some ways, I felt like I should have been thankful to that woman that gave me her "Legacy Spark." In other ways, my death was her fault and I hated her. Clementine took a huge swig of her coffee.

"After she gave you her Spark, when you died, the Legacy Spark in your necklace helped give your spirit a new body. A new body that's eternally youthful, invisible, and has the power to guide the spirits of the dead to the afterlife."

"Eternally youthful?" I paused. "Mind if I ask how old you are?"

"I do." She glared at me. "This body is a bit weird, in a lotta ways. You saw me do my little wind magic last night," she chuckled, "but in a lot of ways our bodies are a kinda product of our thinking. We can eat and sleep and drink, but it's mostly only cuz our mind says we should. Our bodies are real and physical, they're just a bit off. Johanna—you'll meet her later—she ain't gotta sleep. Matter of fact, I don't think that lady's slept since she became a Geist."

I stared at her blankly for a bit. "Wait, I'm getting mixed signals. Are we ghosts or zombies?"

"Neither, we're Geist. But if I had to pick one, we're ghosts." She grimaced. "They're more dignified." She shook her head and continued on. "Anyway, important thing you might have already noticed: you can't go too far away from your Memento." Clementine leaned over, unclasped my necklace, and put it on the table. "Take a few steps."

I raised an eyebrow at her, but I did as I was told. I took a few steps, looked back at her, then took a few more. My face collided with something hard. I cursed and shut my eyes. I opened them again and saw I ran into nothing at all. I reached my hand forward and felt what I hit. Right in front of me was an invisible wall.

"You can move seven feet away from your necklace, then you're stopped in your tracks." She looked back down at my necklace. "It's a gorgeous necklace. If you're stuck with keeping one thing glued to you, you're lucky it's something so striking."

I sat back down, still rubbing my nose from its second injury of the day. Clementine put the necklace around my neck again. She reached into her cardigan's pocket and pulled out a silver pocket watch, which must have been what she poked the lily with to create the spooky, magical stairs. She unlatched the watch and showed me the little clock on the inside. Roman numerals circled the timepiece, with two hands pointing to the hour and the minute. A tiny ring of numbers sat above the VI with a miniature hand showing off the second.

"This here's my Memento. It was my daddy's watch." Her eyelids closed a little. "He used to work on the railroads. We were goin' through a lot of financial troubles and my mama told him to sell the watch, but he gave it to me instead. He said a lady like me needed something special. Every time I look at this, I remember my daddy." She stopped paying attention to me for a few seconds. "He deserved so much more than he got." She looked back at me, her eyes wide again. "The Mementos are also what help us bring spirits to the afterlife. We're like walking butterfly nets."

"And, uh, when exactly do I need to start reaping?"

Clementine put her mug down and pushed it aside. "Whenever you're ready, hon."

I closed my eyes and took in a deep breath. "Okay. So those are the basics, then." I looked around the white dining room before focusing on Clementine again. "You said you wanted to show me around the mansion, right?"

Clementine headed back to her room for a bit to get dressed. When she came back, all decked out in a cute sundress and lace stockings, she was ready to be my tour guide. Clementine started our tour with one of her favorite rooms in the mansion: her library. The room was even bigger than the foyer, and every inch of it was lined with bookshelves. It was like in *Beauty and the Beast*, except it was honestly a lot more depressing.

Clementine showed off a special section of her all-time favorite books, most of which were yellowed and probably read dozens of times. She pulled out one in particular that looked like she might have gotten it from Hatshepsut's estate sale. The door creaked open again. I turned around and saw a familiar woman stand by the doorway. Vee strode into the room, much more gracefully than when I first met her. Clementine looked less than thrilled to see her.

"Vee, you're supposed to be on patrol," she said. "Why are you still here?"

"Well, I was half-way out the door when I realized I desperately needed to read some porn. That's actually a lie. I haven't even started packing yet."

Vee walked over to a set of shelves filled with very thin paperbacks. She delved through a few of the books until she found one to her liking. She walked back to Clementine and me, holding her book. The title was *CEO Mothman's Adventures in Go-Go Boy Land*, and on the cover was a picture of the Mothman in a business suit next to a muscular man in nothing but a neon-green jock strap.

"This one's one of my favorites," she said, almost shoving the scandalous cover into Clem's face. "I've read it thirty times."

"Vee, you have a job to do."

"Yeah, a job I'm doing two days in a row, because your boyfriend's stupid writer's retreat put our whole schedule out of whack and now suddenly you want a vacation off too!"

"This is the first day I've asked off in over ten years and you ask for a day off almost every—" Clementine bit her lip and took in a deep breath. "Please just get ready as soon as you can."

"It's not like they're going anywhere. What's going to happen if I'm late? Will they die again?"

Clementine sighed and put her hand on her face. Vee prodded me on the shoulder with her calloused palm.

"So, is this guy, like, permanent?" Vee laughed.

"If he wants to stay, then yes," Clementine said.

"As long as that means I work less, he's my guest." Vee closed her eyes and threw her hands into the air. She put her arm around my shoulder and gave me a little noogie. "Welcome to Zinda, Carson."

"It's Ash," I said.

Vee shoved me away and left the room without another word. Clementine picked up her book with such an intense grip that the cover crinkled like tissue paper. She slammed the book into a random place on a shelf. Her hand stayed on the book for a while, still keeping that tight grip on it.

"So how many people live here, exactly?" I asked.

"Four. Five, now." She let go of the book. Her chipper attitude returned. "Anyway, let's keep at it."

We headed out of the library. Vee's door was ajar. Clementine peeked inside, huffed, and pushed the door open. Vee moaned about getting ready to leave, then slammed the door. We skipped past a few empty bedrooms and extra bathrooms, along with a special room Clementine said was a surprise.

My room was near the very end of the third-floor hallway. Clementine took me into the room that was right next to the stairs: her own bedroom. It was the most adorable bedroom I had ever seen with pink wallpaper, frilly curtains, a hoard of tiny tchotchkes on the dresser, and two full-sized canopy bed with yellow drapes and a nightstand separating them. It was somehow the only room in the entire mansion that didn't scream "death."

"I know it doesn't look it, but it's the same size as your room. We'll get your room lookin' as pretty as you want in no time."

The third floor also held a workout room, which I knew I needed to hit up once in a while. If I was going to have to deal with the Brotherhood, I needed to get a lot buffer than them. Next to that was a small room with shelves of records, cassette tapes, and CDs, along with everything needed to play them

Clementine opened the door to a tiny indoor garden that smelled absolutely awful, but did not let me inside. She said that only Vee tended to the garden, she only grew one plant, and there were better things I should be doing with my time. A small art studio and an even smaller billiards room sandwiched my room. The largest room was full of musical instruments. A giant piano was the centerpiece of the room, but I was more interested in the glittering guitars, shiny brass instruments, and polished violas hanging from the wall.

The final room of the third floor was at the very end of the hall, directly across from my bedroom. There was not much in the room. No shelves or windows or trinkets. In the very center of the room was a massive table with a glowing map of Chicago on it. Dozens of colored crystal skulls were scattered around on the top of the map. I took a closer look at it. All of the skulls on the board were moving, millimeter by millimeter, around the city.

I found the location of the mansion on the map. A bright circle of light surrounded the area, and three skulls were inside the circle. One was royal blue, one was dark purple, and one was teal. The blue skull had an engraving on the top of it. It was an exact replica of my necklace. I checked out the purple skull, and it had a pocket watch on its skullcap. The teal skull slowly shifted away from the purple and blue skulls while a red skull came closer.

"The grid tracks every Geist in the city, even the ones we don't know about." She pointed to the skulls outside of Zinda

Mansion. "The teal skull is Vee. As you can see, she's finally going off to work." The contempt in her voice was honestly hilarious. "The red skull's Johanna. She's probably on her way home, so maybe you'll get to meet her in a bit."

There were dozens of skulls on the board, each with a different color and engraving on the top. The city was filled with Geist that roamed around town with other Geist, made little invisible adventures, and occasionally did whatever eldritch deeds Grim Reapers were supposed to do.

The fourth floor was filled with rooms that had no real purpose, at least to my knowledge, and was mostly used for storage. One room had a pulsing generator inside, which explained the electricity but opened up so many other questions. Another had supplies for every kind of domesticated pet imaginable. Clementine listed more than twelve different animals they'd kept over the years, including a munchkin cat named Mr. Diddles and a kunekune pig named Pignatius. There was one room that was completely filled with sad, deflated balloons. I asked Clementine what that room was for and she looked really uncomfortable.

"We're getting rid of that one, I promise," she said.

"No wait, I wanna know—"

"Moving on," she said as she slammed the door and walked away.

Clementine made up for the lame fourth floor by taking me to the attic. We climbed up one final staircase and came up to a room that looked like the inside of a clock tower. Rusty gears lined the ceiling, all of which were making the "clock" tick. The clock in question, though, raised some questions I didn't really feel like asking. A large window at the end of the room had a perfect clock face on it, giving the illusion that the room really was the inside a giant clock tower that Cockney peasants depended on. A tiny lounge area was set up to be able to "look" out of the clock, not that there was anything to look at. The clock, much like the stained-glass windows around the building, was opaque and only let in a dim light from the "outside." Just as I was taking in the uncanny nature of the room, a loud creaking echoed from a few floors below.

"Johanna's home."

The two of us walked down the first floor just in time for the front doors to open, and an ethereal woman glided in. Johanna carried herself much more maturely than the other two women in the house. Her posture was straight and every step she took was the exact same length and angle as the last. Her white hair was long and flowed behind her like a miniature cape. She exuded an air of mystery and wisdom, possibly because she dressed like a ghostly nineteenth-century schoolmarm.

Johanna did not react when she saw me. All she did was blink. She did make eye-contact, though, so she was already higher than Vee on my list of favorite Geist.

"Is this Ash?" she hummed to Clementine. Her voice was light and distant, as if she was actually talking to someone else across the room. She had a faint accent I couldn't pin down but sounded vaguely European.

"Hi, yes, I'm Ash Murphy," I answered. "You must be Johanna."

"Johanna Hutchinson. It is nice to meet you." Johanna shook my hand. Her grip was so limp, I felt like I was holding mud. "Welcome to Zinda Mansion. Will tomorrow be your first day collecting souls?"

"Wh-what?" I stammered.

"Johanna," interjected Clementine. "I figured that Ash needs a little more time before he gets goin' with all the Geist business. He's still gotta get his sea legs with all this."

"I understand. I am sure another week of preparation will suffice," she said. With that, Johanna left us behind and walked up the stairs. Half-way up, she turned back around and looked down at us. "Ash, if there is any advice you need with regards to your place in this world, please feel free to come see me."

I kept my eyes on Johanna as she walked up the stairs. I didn't really know what to make of her, but at least she knew my name. Nothing in her voice pointed to any hidden meanings to her words, meaning that she was either naturally sincere or really, really shady.

"Wasn't there one last room you wanted to show me?"

"Good golly, how could I have forgotten?" Clementine laughed. "It's the absolute best room in the mansion!"

Clementine and I walked back to the second floor and went to the special door that she didn't let me see on the first trip. Clementine put her hand on the handle, but didn't open it. Her eyes sparkled when she slowly turned the knob.

"Before I open it," she said, stopping her turning, "I wanna know what you think it is. Guess."

"Personal movie theater!" I exclaimed.

"Nah, we ain't got one of those."

"You have a room full of balloons and you don't have any place to watch movies?"

"I told you, we're getting rid of that one."

Clementine opened the door. I gasped. Clementine's special secret room was a gigantic sewing room with more clothes than an outlet mall. On the left, dozens of different reams of fabrics lined the walls. On the right, what seemed like a mile of different articles of clothing hung on racks. The back wall was covered by mirrors and right next to the door was a large sewing station with a half-finished dress propped up on a mannequin. I was practically drooling.

"This is my favorite room in the house, my workroom." Clementine pushed the unfinished dress back, as if to hide a weak point in the perfect room. "When we're done here, your closet will be overflowing with new clothes. Everything in here is made by yours truly, except the shoes. Still don't know how to make shoes."

"You made all of these from scratch?"

"I've been making clothes since the early '80s. When I first started, I couldn't make a T-shirt, but now I make pretty much anything." Clementine perused through a few of the dresses near the front of the room. "But my mama, she would make clothes for the whole family, along with all the neighbors."

Clementine stopped talking. I glanced over to her and saw her mouth twitch downward, then perk back up when she pulled out a short blue cocktail dress. We walked down the wall of clothes with Clementine pulling out a few shirts, pants, and jackets along the way. She pressed a few of them up to my chest to see if I fit them.

I was fascinated by the clothes in Clementine's collection. I had never seen clothes like the ones she made. Everything looked horrifyingly impractical in all the best ways. It explained how Johanna managed to dress like that in the twenty-first century. While a lot of the shirts and pants looked like everyday clothes I could walk down the street in, everything else had an extravagance to it that could turn heads so fast, necks would break. Some looked like they were taken from Parisian runways, others looked like they were taken straight out of those melodramatic video games I played as a kid. There were animal furs I had never seen used in fashion, clothes with thousands of crystals sewn in, and stunning dresses that could probably pay off the national debt. The men's section was smaller than the women's, but that was like saying Texas was smaller than Alaska. It felt it would take years to sort through everything.

"If anything catches your eyes, feel free to try it on."

"I'm trying on everything. We got time for that?"

"All the time in the world, Ash," she chuckled.

For the next hour or so, I tried on more clothes than I had ever worn in my life. Clementine and I set up a miniature fashion show by the wall of mirrors. Clementine averted her eyes every time I took something off, but sometimes I got too excited and stripped before she could turn away. A leather jacket with belts going down the arms, a shirt made entirely out of zippers, pants with weird mesh areas I was almost positive was some kind of fetish thing. I spent a really long time parading around in black slacks and a calico cat fur coat. I liked it until Clementine said I looked like a "spooky gigolo." Then I loved it.

As much as I would have loved to parade around the house in some of the weirder stuff, I decided I needed something more practical. So, I put on some lace-up boots, a sleeveless top, some nice black jeans, and then tied a thin flannel shirt around my waist. To finish it off, I stopped by Clementine's accessory corner, picked out a nice pair of black studs, and shoved them into my ears. I checked myself out in the mirror, just to make sure everything matched. Even if I was still dealing with the objectively worst twenty-four hours of my life, at least Clementine's clothes made me look stunning. I looked good, and I deserved to look good.

The person looking back in the mirror didn't look like me. At first, I wrote it off because I suddenly had new hair. But after looking at how my new clothes fit me and how my face looked with the earrings, I saw Zack. Whether intentionally or not, I gravitated toward clothes that my brother would have worn. A long sigh left my mouth and I sat down on the floor. The man in the mirror who looked just like my older brother did the same. It hadn't hit me until that moment that Zack and I both died at the same age.

Clementine gathered the clothes I liked and folded them in a pile. I shook my head and pretended I was just gawking at my marvelous physique in the mirror. Clementine tossed the pile into a basket. She handed the giant basket over to me and we both headed toward the door.

"If you ever want to try on more clothes, come right on in," she said. "This entire mansion's yours now, hon. Everything in this room is just as much yours as it is mine."

"Thank you."

"Don't mention it, Ash. You can't very much go around town naked, can ya? It's improper, even if no one will notice."

"Not just that. Thank you for being with me all this time. You didn't have to. I've never really—no, nevermind."

Clementine looked confused, but she didn't press on. Clementine and I took my new clothes to my room. As each article of clothing filled my closet, I slowly saw a little bit of life permeate the room. Clementine organized everything perfectly and cleanly, as if each sweater and jacket was her baby. She gingerly hung each outfit on a wooden hanger, and I imagined she'd beat me if I ever tried to use a wire hanger for her precious garments.

A little jingle permeated the room. I looked around, trying to think of where the ringing could be coming from. There was no way that was a phone. Clementine reached for her pocket. That ghost had a phone! Clementine pulled out an ancient-looking flip phone.

"You've got to be shitting me. Is that a damn phone?"

"It's prepaid," she chuckled. "We're all smart enough not to mess with phone companies. Hard enough getting' runnin' water around here."

Before I could open that Pandora's box, Clementine flipped the phone open. She walked out my door and whispered into her phone in the hallway. I hung the last pair of jeans in the closet and slid it shut. Then, like a good Catholic-raised gay, I leaned against my wall, stuck my ear toward the door, and listened in on Clementine's private conversation.

"How many people?" she whispered, obviously miffed but still polite and Southern Belle-like. "No, last night I specifically said 'intimate.' Fifty people ain't intimate. You wanna turn this little get-together into Ash's quinceañera." The voice on the other end was muffled but still bombastic enough for me to hear it from several feet away. "I don't think I can come over to help, Winona. He's probably real fragile right now and I don't know if it's smart to leave him alone. It hasn't even been a full day." More of the bombastic voice. "I'll—I'll see how he's doing. Maybe I can slip away for a few hours."

Clementine snapped her phone shut. I dashed over to my bed and pretended I was doing something completely innocent and not invasive. Clementine walked back into my room and smiled.

"So, for lunch, I was thinking I could make some—"

"Actually, Clementine, if it's alright with you, I think I need some alone time."

Clementine seemed a bit taken aback by that. Almost literally, in fact, as she pressed herself up against my wall. My response didn't get the reaction I expected, because her smile scrunched in a way that certainly wasn't comfortable.

"You sure about that, hon?"

"Yeah, don't worry about me. I think I just need time to breathe for a while."

Clementine nodded and didn't fight it. Her shoulders slumped as she headed out my door, but I knew she'd be fine. She had way more important things to do than babysit me. I didn't need someone to monitor my every move just because something bad happened. I already had to deal with that enough after Zack died. All I needed was time to think.

I plopped down on my bed and looked up at my unfamiliar ceiling. I knew whenever I woke up and saw the strange ceiling, there was no more pretending I still had my old life. Every day was going to start with a slap in the face and a reality check. Just what I needed.

Chapter 4
Pray

Clementine took a while to leave the mansion. She spent about ten minutes going over everything I could possibly need and what to do if there was an emergency. I made sure to tell her I would be fine. Nothing could go wrong, because I was already dead. I left out that last part. She then spent a long time talking to Johanna, and as much as I would have loved to eavesdrop on that conversation, I let them be. Clementine then left to deal with whatever this Winona person needed done and I was alone with my thoughts again.

My parents were definitely crying right now. Maybe scheduling a funeral. Wouldn't be open casket, that's for sure. No one needed to see me looking like a sliced open fig. I wondered who broke the news to Yvonne. Probably Faye. No one else spoke to Yvonne.

The first hour alone went by so slowly that I almost wanted to run off, find Clementine, and beg her to come back. I headed to the kitchen to make myself lunch. I wasn't hungry at all, but I knew that if I didn't force myself to eat, I was going to starve. Or not. Clementine said I only needed to eat because my old body did. For all I knew, I could have just spent my afterlife eating packing peanuts. Either way, I made a roast beef sandwich and shoved half of it down my throat before eating just got tedious. I spent the rest of "lunch" staring at the half-eaten sandwich as if it was going to start talking to me or something. Like one of those sandwich puppets with the olives for eyes.

I slapped my cheeks before the sandwich actually did start

talking to me and I threw it away. Looking through the kitchen, I realized that Clementine actually had a lot of fun baking gadgets. With no one else in sight, I went to town and started baking. The pantries had everything I needed, and more. Everything was generic brand and the vanilla was fake, but I knew it was too early for me to complain about that. Without a second thought, I grabbed everything I could and started making a batch of chocolate chip cookies.

I continued working on cute little baking projects even before the cookies were out of the oven. Sadly, macarons were out of the question, because Clementine didn't have almond flour on-hand. Of course, I should have expected that, because no sensible person just had almond flour on-hand. Only crazy people just happened to have almond flour lying around somewhere. Instead, the kitchen became Brownie City.

Time turned into an illusion. What started as a one-man brownie factory ended up more like an *I Love Lucy* rerun. The only reason I stopped baking was because I used up all of the baking chocolate we had. The clock on the oven said it was eight o'clock. I had been dead for more than a full day. Five batches of brownies sat across the counters, each one looking sloppier than the last.

"Uuuugh, where the hell is Clementine?"

It didn't take me long to make the kitchen spotless. It almost looked even more sterile than when I first got there. I waited for something to happen. Maybe Clementine finally coming home or Vee getting back from whatever patrol she was on. But even when the eight turned into a nine, the mansion stayed dead.

Boy, I wondered who had to look at my body in the morgue and say "Yup, that's Ash." Oh, it was definitely dad, since he had to do it with Za—

I needed to leave before my imagination re-killed me. I

stood up and ran upstairs. My iPod was sitting by my bedside and I snatched it up. Then I headed toward the music room and grabbed the first pair of headphones I could find. They were ratty and one of the earpieces was louder than the other, but it was good enough. I blasted the music as loudly as possible to drown out my thoughts. Not like I had to worry about damaging my eardrums anymore. Without a second thought, I went back downstairs, burst out of the front doors, and stepped away from Zinda Mansion.

The second I left the underground, the steps leading down disappeared, leaving only the lily to show that there was anything there at all. Stepping into the night air, it felt like I was alive again. Chicago never seemed bigger to me than it did at that moment. I walked away from Zinda Mansion, entranced by the city around me. I didn't understand why I felt the way I did. The sky was its usual gross gradient of yellow-to-black. The light pollution of the city made the stars invisible, leaving a cream-colored glow around the skyline. The streets were still littered with cigarette butts. The air was just as stagnant as ever. But, somehow, everything felt new.

No one turned their heads toward me as I walked down the street. People would step aside without noticing anything. I had no idea where I was going, but I needed to walk. Eventually, I would head back to Zinda Mansion and no one would be the wiser. Just a little walk to clear my head and pretend the last twenty-four hours hadn't happened.

While I didn't know my way around the South Side too well, I had been to McDuffie's more than enough times to know the neighborhood around it. And then I paused. I wondered if Yvonne was at McDuffie's that night and whether she was acting as a waitress or as a performer. In the back of my mind, I hoped she was performing. It had been so long since I had seen her play the violin. McDuffie's was only a few blocks away. But no. I was going to keep walking and not even glance inside.

I stopped by the corner and waited for the green light to turn red. I wondered exactly why I cared about traffic laws, but getting hit by a car would really sting. In the smoggy, yellow moonlight, cars kept streaking by way too fast, and the light refused to change. Each time I scrounged up the courage to jaywalk, another car sped on by, barely a foot away from me. My heart raced, and I looked away. Almost instantly, I saw a boy sitting on the stoop of an apartment. My eyes bulged, and when I saw scorpion tattoo peeking out of his rolled-up sleeves, I took a few steps back. It was that closeted Brotherhood guy who possibly-maybe flirted with me before my crash. Graham? Greg?

I started hyperventilating and turned my back to him. The light had been red for some time. I ran forward, almost losing my balance and toppling to the ground. I took a quick glance back to the stoop. Gavin? Was it—No! Gabriel! It was Gabriel! But he was gone. Gabriel ninja-ed himself out of there, which was either really good or really, really bad. Shoving him to the back of my mind, I kept walking.

In the distance, I could see McDuffie's dim sign flicker in the darkness. My excitement grew. Pangs of guilt flashed through my head, but they were drowned out fairly quickly. Maybe a peek wouldn't hurt. Just a little look inside for five seconds and see if she was playing.

I slogged over to the wide windows of the tavern. McDuffie's looked exactly like it did the day before. At most, ten people stood inside the bar. An old woman with stark white hair sat on a bar stool downing a full pint in one gulp while the aging bartender played with the beer taps. A few men, all in their mid-thirties, sat close to the stage area, drunker than former child stars. Yvonne was nowhere in sight, and I let my forehead slam against the window.

The old woman turned around and looked right at me with her terrifying black-and-silver eyes. She wasn't old at all. In some ways, I should have been surprised to see Vee getting drunk at McDuffie's. In other ways, she wasn't the first Geist I found there. For all I knew, McDuffie's was just straight-up haunted. Vee continued to stare right at me, neither of us saying anything, until she finally let out a giant burp that shook the glass.

My wonderment immediately subsided. Eyes half open, I sauntered through the door of McDuffie's and sat down at the bar. The second I got close to her, my arm hair stood on end. The entire bar felt like it was at least ten degrees colder than it should have been. We began eyeballing each other, but she turned her attention back to her booze pretty quickly. When she got to the bottom of the glass, she stared at it for a bit. As she did, the black in her eyes cleared and, as if by magic, her eyes were a normal shade of brown.

"Eh, Jordan!" she slurred toward the bartender. "What part of 'drown me' was lost on you? My glass's been empty for so long I'm about to get an AA chip!"

The bartender looked at her from the corner of his eye. "Vee, ain't no man on Earth gonna sleep with a woman like you."

"No man on Earth deserves me," she cooed.

The bartender swiped the glass and filled it up with more beer. He handed it back to her, and Vee made a cutesy kissy face at him. He rolled his eyes and turned his back to her. Meanwhile, I was staring at her, wide-eyed and mouth agape.

"He talked to you."

"And?" she asked in-between gulps.

"And you're a Geist!" I stuttered. "We're dead! We—"

"And we can turn our invisibility on and off anytime we

want, for whoever we want," she said, as condescendingly as a kindergarten teacher. "Watch."

Vee blinked and her eyes turned dark again. She finished her entire glass, slammed it against the bar, and then tossed it right at the bartender's feet. He didn't even flinch when it shattered right next to his exposed toes.

"See? Spooky. Didn't Clementine teach you anything? Eventually, you might learn how to toggle it so only a few people can see you. But those are some pro strats right there." Vee rummaged around in her pockets, still not looking me in the eye. She reached into her shirt pocket and pulled out a self-rolled cigarette and a lighter. "Mind if I smoke?" She lit the joint and took a huge puff. A cloud of weed flew into my face, burning my eyes. "How did you two even meet? Judging by those tight-ass jeans, she must've found you haunting Boystown. Was there a fire at a *Drag Race* viewing party or something?"

My mouth dried up. I glared toward the stage. It was still empty. Vee took another puff of her joint and blew more smoke at me.

"How long have you been dead?" she asked. "You even seen a ghost yet?"

"You mean besides the two of us?"

Vee chuckled. She twirled her stool and faced me directly, then leaned in. I scooted back a bit, but she kept creeping forward until I was almost lying down across three stools. She stared down at me, putting her cold face so close to mine, my eyes felt like they were about to freeze.

"What about the Brotherhood?" she asked. "Seen them yet? They've been known to target poor, innocent-looking Geist so they can exorcize them."

A small puff of smoke left her mouth when she removed her joint. I grabbed it out of her fingers and tossed it into a half-empty glass of water. Her eyes became bloodshot, and I wasn't sure if it was because of the weed, the booze, or the intense rage.

"I can take care of myself," I said.

"Well, you better watch out." She pushed herself away from me, straightened her back, and looked me dead in the eye. The red in her eyes even faded to a light pink. "And that was your one free pass at bullshit. Good job wasting it."

Vee fished her joint out of the glass, rubbed it against her shirt, and shoved it back in her pocket. She jumped off of her stool, giving me the chance to sit back up. Sneering, she took one last look toward the bartender. His back was still to her, so she reached over and snatched a bottle of vodka off the shelves. The bartender still didn't notice a thing. She took a straight swig of the vodka, shuddered a bit, then headed right to the exit.

"Don't get yourself killed, kid," she called, "because next time I see you, I'm kicking your ass."

She slammed the door behind her, and the bar instantly became warmer. I didn't know whether to be angrier at the rudeness or the weird sexual undertones.

A door on the other side of the bar creaked. I craned my head, but I couldn't see anything. The bartender walked to the far end of his bar and muttered a few words to whoever was on the other side of the door. The bartender carefully walked from his perch behind the bar—only then noticing the broken glass— and walked onto the stage. He grabbed the microphone, which almost slipped out of his hands from his halfhearted grip.

"Ladies and gentlemen—wait, no, just gentlemen," he droned. "Tonight's entertainment has arrived. Please put your drinks up for McDuffie's favorite violinist, Yvonne Spears."

Yvonne came out of the backroom door and walked to the stage. She was absolutely gorgeous, with a sequined dress that showed off all of her Egyptian tattoos. *All* of them. But even with the flamboyance of her outfit, her demeanor marred it. With her height, the color of her skin, and the way her braids covered her face, she looked like a human weeping willow. Her gaze was to the floor as she walked. She walked flatfooted, and every footstep slapped on the old wood like a fish. The other people in the bar weren't watching her, with the exception of a man with a neck tattoo in the back. His eyes were planted on her.

When she stepped on stage, Yvonne put her violin on her collarbone and glided the bow across the strings. Her face was as somber as it was before she got on stage, but her hands were supersonic. Her music resonated through my body, and for a brief moment, I felt alive.

One day before, I was just fine, joking with Yvonne and talking about some weirdos across the street. Flash-forward twenty-four hours, and I was dead. I wanted to go up to the stage and hug her, just like how Vee could talk to the bartender, but I knew I couldn't. All I wanted was a proper goodbye.

In many ways, Yvonne was the closest thing I had to an aunt. She was always there for Thanksgiving, Christmas, and Faye's birthdays. She even went with us on vacation a few times. I always loved the contrast between her and Faye. My elegant grandmother would glide through the door with pearls and curled hair, and then a woman half her age would slump in with leather pants, colorful hair, and a fresh tattoo.

Faye and Yvonne never really explained how they became best friends, but I pieced a few stories together. Yvonne was kicked out of her house at seventeen because her family was in a cult. And no matter how many times Faye said it wasn't a cult, I knew it was a cult. Any religion that said God wants all of "those transgenders" dead was a cult, and Yvonne was lucky she escaped before they buried her in a suit and tie.

For a brief moment, Gabriel entered my mind again, but I

shook that thought away before it could develop. If he wanted my pity, he wouldn't've been in a cult.

Yvonne finished her set. She gave the audience a tiny bow. A few of the men quietly clapped, others were too drunk to do anything but drink more. Yvonne stepped off stage and headed to the back room. The man with the neck tattoo stood up and followed her. With her exit, I realized it was time to make mine. I didn't know when I would be back to McDuffie's, or if I'd ever let myself come back at all, so I let myself breathe in the atmosphere one last time. And looking around, I realized that McDuffie's really, really sucked. I headed to the door and left.

The streets were packed with cars, but the sidewalks were practically empty. I drummed my fingers against my elbows and looked in every direction. No sign of any other Geist. The only people around me were seemingly innocent pedestrians.

The door of McDuffie's opened again. Out stepped Yvonne and the man with the neck tattoo. The man was in a huff and stomped on the pavement with every step. Yvonne trailed behind, holding her violin case and a small clutch. The man stopped Yvonne and grabbed her wrist. Yvonne shuddered and opened her clutch. She fingered through it and pulled out five twenty-dollar bills. The tattooed man pocketed the money. He pulled her closer to him and gave her a giant, open-mouthed kiss. Five seconds later, he pulled away.

"Thanks, babe," he growled.

The man crossed the street without looking either way. Yvonne watched him leave, unmoving. My fingernails dug into my arms so hard I could almost feel my skin breaking. Yvonne closed her clutch. Using her slightly-purple wrist, she wiped the man's spit away from her lips. I sighed and stepped a little closer to her.

"Yvonne," I said. "Yvonne Spears! Yvonne, please look at me."

Yvonne didn't respond. I closed my eyes, took a deep breath, and tried one last time, hoping that maybe this time my eyes returned to normal. Still, she couldn't hear me. Yvonne went on her way, no doubt heading home for a sleepless night. I turned away and headed in the opposite direction. That was enough "real life" for one night.

I crossed a small, dark alleyway, barely wide enough for someone to fit through. A tiny red light flickered in the darkness. I looked closer and saw a boy in the alley, sitting on a rusty air conditioner unit. He was fairly large, making me wonder how he even fit back there. He rose an electronic cigarette to his lips.

The boy puffed a cloud of vapor toward me. Once the smoke cleared, I saw the sunglasses wrapped around his face. They looked almost like goggles, with an intense white tint to the lenses that I could make out even in the darkness. The second I saw his patchy beard and ratty hair, I recognized the boy instantly as James from the Brotherhood.

I edged away from the alleyway. He couldn't see me. I knew I was invisible. James put his e-cig away. He pushed himself away from the wall and walked toward the end of the alley, right in my direction. I turned back to the crosswalk and tried to book it. When I took my eyes off James, I saw someone else. Gabriel was tearing down the sidewalk toward me. He readjusted the white goggles around his eyes, then slipped on a long, metal glove over his right arm. He raised his arm, reached forward, and grabbed my face.

"Pray."

His glove sparked. Before I could make a sound, I felt a jolt of searing heat surge through my body. James broke out into a sprint. He shoved the alley's gate open and pulled me into the alleyway. Gabriel messed with his glove and the entire device glowed white.

My head was reeling. I felt like I was about to vomit, but nothing was coming up. My vision cleared and focused in on the two Brothers again. I tried to scamper away. James pressed his own glove against my stomach and shot a spark of plasma through me. A concussive force flowed through my stomach and slammed me against the wall again. I fell onto my side and coughed.

We were pressed body-to-body in the alley, and everything was moving so fast, everyone started to look like one big blur. I started kicking and scratching at anything vaguely human-shaped. My foot hit something. I heard a stomp, then a yelp, and then a crash. I clawed my way to my feet. In my panicked scuffle, I had kicked James in the face, making him crash into Gabriel and collide with the gate.

And then, I felt a tiny pull, as if gravity shifted but only slightly. As my vision cleared, I saw a small, barely visible line of blue light shooting out of my necklace. Just like the tiny gravitational pull, it was pointing to the other end of the alley. Something was telling me to go deeper. I looked back at Gabriel and James, and then I looked down the dark alley and decided I should take my chances with the darkness. I didn't know what the pulling or the light was, but I prayed it was something Geist-related.

I booked it. My footsteps clamored down the small alleyway. The alley seemed to get narrower as it went on. With each step, I felt the pull get harder. I gripped my necklace in my hand and used it as a compass, with the blue light still pointing me onward. The stomping behind me also got louder. I, stupidly, looked behind me. Gabriel was hot on my tail. James was a little ways behind him, struggling to slip through.

The other end of the alley was getting close. The alley led to a filthy backstreet with more dumpsters than I could count. I kept my pace. I was almost free. I dashed out of the alley. And then I tripped on someone's leg, screamed, and fell right onto my sternum.

I tried to jump to my feet again, but it was too late. Gabriel grabbed me by the scruff of my neck, pulled me upright, and shoved me against the wall. From the corner of my eye, I could see what I tripped over. The leg was attached to a withered old man who was wearing at least three layers of jackets and pants. His eyes were wide open, and his mouth was agape. He was dead. I tripped over a corpse. And the blue light was pointing right at him.

"What did you do to him?" Gabriel hissed.

"N—"

I couldn't get a word out. James stumbled out of the alley and stepped on the dead man's leg. He yelped in a voice much more nasally than I would have expected.

"We're too late," said Gabriel, keeping his grip tight on me. "He already got one."

"I—I didn't—" I gasped.

Gabriel glared at me. He nodded toward James, and he started walking closer to me. His glove glowed brighter and sparks of light flew out of it. I shut my eyes and braced myself for whatever was about to come.

I heard a loud cough and opened my eyes again. James grasped his neck and his stomach started to convulse. Gabriel let go of me as he struggled to breathe. They fell to their knees and gasped for air. I slipped away, not taking my eyes off the choking men.

A quiet tutting sound echoed through the alley. Clementine, holding two bags practically overflowing with fabrics, briskly strode into the backstreets. She looked down at the two boys, both still struggling for air. She knelt down next to them, let go of her bags of fabric, and pulled them to their feet by their ears. Clementine puffed out a tiny breath of air and, suddenly, both men gasped and could finally take another breath.

"You children come after my friend like that again, I might forget to let y'all breathe again. Y'all want that?"

James sneered at Clementine. Gabriel glanced over at me, still winded and struggling to regain his breath. Clementine let go of both of their ears. Without hesitation, both Brothers ran down the alley. Within seconds, they were invisible in the darkness.

Clementine picked her bags back off the ground. Her lady-like demeanor returned, but I could still see a flicker of fury in her step. Before she could say another word, I ran forward and hugged her so tightly I might have started choking her.

"Sorry, Ash," she coughed, "when my friend called me over to help out with something, I didn't expect it to take all goshdarn night!"

I let out a nervous chuckle. Clementine smiled, and for a moment the entire city quieted itself, and all I could hear was Clementine's breathing. And then we both heard a cough. I craned my neck to look toward the supposed corpse.

I stumbled back when I saw the thing huddled next to the homeless man's corpse. It was a ghost, but definitely not a Geist. The figure was translucent, with all of the color washed out of him. I could see the dirty street distorted through his bleached skin. He looked exactly like the dead man, except much younger and healthier. Instead of wearing layers upon layers of tattered clothes, the ghost was dressed in a simple robe. The exact same robe I wore when I died.

"Oh dear," sighed Clementine.

Clementine walked closer to the figure. She knelt down and rubbed the ghost's shoulder. I stepped forward, too. Seeing her fully-formed hand grasp a barely visible man's shoulder hurt my brain a bit. The ghost shuddered, unable to keep his cloudy eyes on one thing. They always managed to land back on, of course, his former body.

"Wh—" the ghost mumbled. "Whsgonon?"

Clementine lifted the ghost to his feet. She did her best to keep his eyes off of his former body, insofar as pulling him a little into the alley to keep some distance. I trailed behind Clementine, studying the minutiae of her body language. She didn't make any sudden movements. Everything she did was slow, with ample time to see exactly what she was doing.

"What's your name, sugar?" Clementine whispered. The ghost didn't answer. He just kept frantically looking around. "My name's Clementine. This is Ash." She gestured toward me. I gave him a weak wave. "It looks like you've had a bit of an accident, but don't you fret about nothin'. Ash and I are gonna help bring you up to Heaven. That sound good?"

The ghost blinked. He still seemed extremely out of it, but he was lucid enough to nod at the two of us. Clementine beckoned me closer, and she led me and the ghost back toward the street.

Clementine kept her arms around the ghost as we walked back to Zinda Mansion. I stayed a few steps behind her, staring at my feet and carrying her overflowing bags for her. I knew I was safe with her. I didn't have to worry about the Brotherhood, at least. All I had to worry about was looking my future straight in the eyes. Clementine picked up a dead guy from off the street and was going to "bring him to Heaven." I wondered if, maybe, she said the exact same thing to Zack.

After a few blocks of walking, the ghost was finally able to form a complete sentence.

"Miss Clementine," he asked. "What's Heaven like?"

"All I know is what my pastor taught me." Clementine paused. "But I have faith it's gonna be everythin' you hoped and more."

We kept walking until we finally made it to the clearing under the station with the glowing lily. The ghost looked just as confused as I was when I first saw it. Clementine nodded toward me, and it took me a second to register what to do. Mimicking what she did earlier, I took my necklace and tapped it against the lily. The lily glowed a vivid blue color. Just like the night before, the ground opened up and the dark stairs formed.

Clementine looked the ghost in the eye and flashed a smile. "Are you ready?"

He cautiously nodded. We all walked down the stairs to the mansion. Clementine opened the front doors and led us inside. On the other side of the foyer, between the two winding staircases, stood the wide set of doors. My eyes honed in on the marks by the doors. Asking Clementine about the marks was the last thing on my mind. As we headed toward the doors, all I could think about was that this is was what people saw before, well, whatever happened after death.

Clementine opened the basement doors. There was no light on the other side. All I could see was a few metal steps. I put Clementine's bags down next to the doors. We stepped in, and I saw a long, rickety set of stairs made of metal grate going around the perimeter of the massive room. I looked over the edge of the stairs and could not see the floor.

"We can't get power down here. Sorry, it'll be a little dark," said Clementine.

Clementine took the first step down the stairs. The ghost

followed close behind, as if moving on auto-pilot. I put my foot onto the first step down, and I shuddered. The rickety stairs were as wobbly as baby teeth. I kept my other hand against the wall to help with my balance. As my hand slid along the cold wall, I felt something strange in the stone. More claw-like cuts going all the way down the path.

Walking down the steps, in my head, took even longer than walking from McDuffie's to the mansion. I could only see a few feet in front of me. The light poured in from the open foyer door, but even with that, I still felt I was walking in place. The only thing that told me I was making progress was the thick sloshing sound coming from below us. Just when I was going to ask Clementine if we were almost at the bottom, she stopped us. At the very bottom of the stairs was a whirlpool of what looked like black and purple ink. Either that was a portal to the afterlife or the basement sprung a colorful leak.

Clementine gripped the ghost's arm. She smiled at him, making sure he was looking at her and not the portal.

"The first few steps are always the hardest, but once you step on though, everything's going to be so much easier. It's not as scary as it looks. I swear."

The ghost put his toes into the darkness and flinched. Clementine whispered a few more encouraging words into his ear, and he took a few more steps down. The ink went up to his waist, then his chest, and then his neck. Without another word, he took one last step, and his head was submerged in the portal. He was gone.

I had seen enough. My posture straightened. I rushed back up the stairs, keeping my eyes away from the portal. Even though it took what felt like years to get down the stairs, it only took a few seconds for me to get halfway back up. Clementine rushed up the stairs to keep up with my bounding. For every one step she took, I took four.

"Ash, wait!"

I stopped. Clementine ran up the rickety stairs and grabbed my arm. I looked back at her. My eyes were not watering. My breath was steady. I was not about to cry. Clementine and I continued up the stairs, only at a much slower pace. Clementine studied my face as if she was waiting for a tiny clue.

"I know this is a lot to take in. Please, don't be scared."

"Did you—" my voice started to falter. I paused, then tried again. "Three years ago, did you bring a guy named Zack Murphy down there?"

Clementine's expression fell. "Ash," she whispered.

"He was about six feet tall and he had curly brown hair and a real intense jawline and—" I clenched my jaw. A tear formed in my eye. "And there's no way you'd even remember him, if you spend every day wheeling bodies back here."

Clementine and I stared at each other for a while, uncomfortable and a little confused. But she moved her hand to my face and wiped away a tear I wanted her to ignore. We walked out of the basement, and she closed the doors behind us. I stood in the foyer of the grand Geist mansion. I felt uncomfortable. I felt scared. But for some incomprehensible reason, I felt like I was in the right place.

"So, is every day gonna be like this?" I asked.

"I'm gonna do everythin' I can to make every day a blessin' for you." She blinked a few times, then smiled. "I've got a proposal for you," Clementine whispered. "How'd you like to meet some of my friends tomorrow around lunchtime?"

I raised an eyebrow. "As long as they're nicer than Vee, I'm good to go."

Clementine slapped my shoulder and chuckled a bit.

Clementine leaned in for another hug. My spine stiffened, and it took me quite some time to relax. I returned the hug and wrapped my arms around her small frame. I started looking at the massive mansion around me, but I closed my eyes before I became distracted by my family, or my death, or the Brotherhood. All I needed to think about was Clementine.

Chapter 5
Obsessions

Morning came. The first thing on my mind when I woke up wasn't my own fiery death, but the obvious surprise party Clementine was planning. I wasn't going to waste any time. The second I woke up, I ran to the nearest bathroom. If I was going to meet Clementine's *actual* friends, I wasn't going to let myself look like a tired, unshaven mess. The bathroom was giant, like everything else in the mansion. A rainbow of shampoos, conditioners, and bubbles sat on the bathtub, and each one had a little picture of an orange on it. The perfume bottles by the sink also smelled like orange. Clementine had a brand going, and I was not about to fault her for that.

I slipped off my clothes, sunk into the bathtub, and went absolutely overboard. The bathtub overflowed with so much bubble bath that there was more soap than water. I had almost half a bottle of conditioner in my hair. I took a razor and shaved my whole body so that I was completely hairless from the nose down and smooth enough to ice skate on.

After an unreasonably long time, I got out of the bathtub. I went over to the sink and rummaged through the drawers until I found tweezers. I went to town on my eyebrows until my face was free from any stray hairs. Then I grabbed a can of hairspray and styled my hair. Finally, I was perfect. Faye's voice echoed in my head again. It's better to look good than feel good.

I snuck into Clementine's workshop once I was good and clean. Rummaging through dozens of outfits, it took me almost an hour to narrow my options down to two shirts. One was a button-down with a weird tentacle pattern on it and the other was a mint-and-pink short sleeved hoodie with a little frog on the chest. Despite the showstopping possibilities the tentacle one possessed, I didn't want people to assume I was some sort of pervert, so I went with the froggy shirt. I sat on the bottom step of the grand staircase, waiting for the Clem to take me to whatever surprise party she and her friends spent the entire day planning.

Footsteps clamored on the other side of the front doors. Vee shoved them open and walked in with a scared transparent man trailing her. His trembling little steps could barely keep up with her long strides, and at times it looked like an invisible force was dragging him along. Vee led the man over to the portal door and pointed.

"Walk down the steps and into the swirly thing." Her words were much crisper than earlier. She must have been halfway sober. "Then you'll be in Heaven or something."

"Will I finally see my wife again?" asked the man.

"No." The man did not react well. Vee laughed. "Oh my god, I'm kidding." She pushed the ghost through the door. "You might see her. I don't know."

Vee slammed the door on the terrified, recently deceased man. She saw my look of distaste and smirked.

"'Sup, Princess?"

"Shouldn't you have a little more finesse when reaping souls?"

"*Pfft.* Yeah, I better be careful or he might talk to my manager."

Vee sat next to me on the steps, imitating the exact way I was sitting. She took off her backpack and pulled out a beer, a footlong sub, one of the million brownies I made, and her erotic novel, *Utterly Destroyed by my Reverse-Mermaid Stepdad*. She leaned against her bag and rested her legs on my lap. I brushed them off and she put them right back on. I relented.

"I'm gonna take a long lunch break today. I deserve it since I'm doing a double this week," she said, unwrapping her sandwich. "Don't tell Clementine, though. She'll get all pissy again."

"What's she going to do, ground you?"

"That's what I like to hear!" She pointed at me for emphasis. "So, when're you going to get roped into the business of flushing ghosts down our basement?"

"Oh God," I moaned, looking over at the basement doors. "Hopefully never."

"Sounds like a good plan," she said, taking a giant bite of her sandwich. "Lucky for us, there's a hospital in our district, so we never have to look too hard for anyone." She kept talking, even with her mouth full. Specks of bread flew everywhere. It was agony. "So, why're you all dolled up, Princess? You getting ready for your surprise party?" She took another bite. "Oops."

"Surprise party?" I faked a shocked face, as if I didn't already know. "So, I take it you're not going?"

"I'm on the clock. Plus, I can't stand Clem's friends. Just a bunch of sorority girls and her hick boyfriend." A devilish smile crossed her face. She swallowed and put her sandwich down. "How much has she told you about him?"

"Absolutely nothing."

She pulled the tab on her beer.

"His name's Cooter."

"No, it's not."

"No, really, it is. He's a total hillbilly, so it fits. He and Clementine are a perfect match. Put them in a room together and it's just 'Y'all, y'all, y'all'," she laughed. "Seriously, he's borderline short bus. I once saw him try to eat decorative fruit."

I rolled my eyes so hard I noticed Clementine on the second floor. Clementine pattered down the steps, holding two tote bags filled to the brim with clothes. She took one look at Vee and stomped her foot.

"Vee, why ain't you on patrol?"

"I just got back with a dude. New kid saw me. He knows." She gestured toward me, expecting me to vouch for her. I did not. "I'm just taking a little breather before I get back to work, I swear."

"Y'know how many times I've heard that line in the past decade? How many more times do you think you can say that before I just start whappin' you with my purse?"

A thick knock echoed through the almost-empty foyer. Clementine's face turned a bit red and she quickly readjusted her skirt and ran her fingers through her hair. Vee moved aside, but gave no indication she was going to get up off her ass. I stood up, walked toward the doors, and pulled them open.

My stomach—along with other body parts—tingled when I saw one of the most attractive men I'd ever seen. A boyish face offset his massive height and a T-shirt tight enough that I could see every giant muscle on his torso. I was six feet tall and had a pretty solid two-pack going, but next to him I felt like an infant. Scraggly white hair poked out of his green-and-yellow baseball cap and he had the start of what was probably going to be an extremely goofy beard. Never in my life had I seen a man I would call "All-American," but there he was, standing right in front of me. I had to remind myself that he was Clementine's man to keep myself from pouncing on him right then and there. Of course, his eyes weren't on me. Clementine rushed down the stairs and flew into his arms.

"Sugar pie!" he screamed, his accent not too different from Clem's.

"Welcome home, hon!" she said into his chest.

The giant man tossed aside his luggage, picked Clementine up, and spun her around. Clementine giggled and kicked, demanding to be put down. Her man plopped her back to her feet and gave her another bear hug. I tiptoed away, glancing toward Vee. She was staring at me with another giant, shit-eating grin. Once the couple broke away, I worked up the courage to speak to the perfect ten. I held out my hand toward Clem's man.

"Hi, you must be Cooter!"

Vee's laughter shook the building's foundation. Clementine's face froze. Her man looked confused, then held out his hand and shook mine. I noticed the looks on their faces and went over what I did wrong. Then the obvious dawned on me. Clementine grunted and curled her lips into her mouth.

"Name's Jesse," said the man who I should have never assumed was named Cooter.

I smiled and nodded and pretended to let everything slide away like water off a duck's back. Jesse seemed unfazed. He just kept his giant, crooked-toothed smile on his face like it was tattooed on. Clementine's face turned pink and slumped her way over to Vee.

"Virginia Zhang!" she screamed.

Clementine pulled Vee to her feet by her ear. She shoved Vee's backpack into her hands and shooed her toward the doors. Vee rewrapped her sandwich and tossed it and her smut into the backpack, then headed back out.

"Jeez, hit me with a broom, why don't ya?"

"I might have to if you keep slackin' like a lazy bump on a log!" yelled Clementine.

Vee raspberried Clem and made her way down the sidewalk. I stared at her, my eyes bulging out of my head as I tried to think of ways to re-kill a Geist. I shook my head and looked toward not-Cooter-really-Jesse.

"Can I re-do everything that just happened?" I asked him. "Like, you leave, come back in, and I reintroduce myself, minus the whole calling you the wrong name part?"

"Hey, don't sweat anythin' like that." Jesse readjusted his hat. His shirt strained every time he moved his arms. "Little piece'a advice for you. You seem like a nice kid, but never listen to a word that Vee lady says. She's a troublemaker." His eyes widened, as if suddenly looking at me for the first time. "Wait a tick, what's your name?"

"Ash Murphy."

"Ash? The man of the hour?"

Jesse hollered at the ceiling. He grabbed my sides and pulled me into the air. I shrieked. He twirled me around like I weighed nothing, laughing and cheering as he did. Clementine's face turned back to its normal color, and she clasped her hands together. Everyone else was so happy. Meanwhile, I nearly vomited.

"Jesus Christ, put me down!" I gurgled.

"Sorry! Sorry!" Jesse laughed as he stopped twirling me. "Heeew, dog. We're gonna have such a dang good time at your surprise party!"

Clementine smacked her forehead. Jesse put me down and pulled down the brim of his hat to cover his eyes.

"Oops," he mumbled.

"You all *suck* at keeping secrets," I droned.

"Just pretend to be shocked when we get there. Nothin's more important to the girls at La Maison than spectacle." Clementine dipped down and rummaged through one of her tote bags. "That reminds me. Winona wanted me to make sure you both fit the 'dress code.'"

Clementine pulled out a kickass leather jacket. Jesse's eyes sparkled as Clementine held it up to him. Jesse looked at the back of a leather jacket, slowing the same green A logo that was on his hat.

"You made me a Birmingham A's jacket?"

"It's nothing, really. It just took a little bit of sewing and—"

Jesse leaned down and kissed her lips before she could finish. Clementine's face turned from brown to red to pink to some weird color that could only be described as twitterpated magenta. When Jesse started to move away, Clementine leaned her head forward to keep the kiss going for just a little longer.

Why was I watching that? I averted my eyes.

Jesse swung the jacket around and pulled it on, seventy-degree weather be damned. A sweet jacket to match his tight shirt and tight jeans, all no-doubt made by Clem herself. I wondered if Clementine made clothes for Jesse that specifically showed off his assets. That kind of manipulation appealed to me.

"Aw, sweet! Look at these pockets!" he said, swirling around like a dog chasing his tail. "These'll be great for Daisy!"

Jesse took off his hat. Something moved around in his shaggy white hair, and I gripped Clementine's shoulder with all the strength I had. A small albino rat wearing a brown bow scampered down Jesse's head and rested on his open palm. Jesse scratched her head and she made a little "peep" sound while I made a giant, unattractive "Guaahhh" sound. Jesse moved his hand toward his new pocket. Daisy jumped into her new home. I kept my hand on Clementine's shoulder, my eyes fixated on the little movements coming from Jesse's jacket.

"Hand," Clementine demanded, and I let go. "Anyway, let's get a move on. The girls at La Maison can't wait to see you."

"And don't worry." I smiled, readjusted the flannel around my waist, and pretended there wasn't a disgusting rodent a few feet from me. "I'm a wonderful actor. I'll pretend I'm surprised." And I wasn't killed in a fiery car crash, and there wasn't a cult out to kill me, and, and, and… I did my best to brush away those thoughts as we headed toward the train.

La Maison de Beaux Fantômes, as Clementine called it, was smack dab in the middle of Millennium Park. As tourists strolled on by to take pictures of the stupid, ugly, worthless Bean, they bypassed a glowing lily growing right out of the concrete. Jesse pressed his hat against the lily, turning it a weird shade of green. The passersby were completely oblivious as the stairway opened up and the three of us were able to walk on down without anyone even looking in its general direction.

Clementine opened the magical obsidian door into La Maison, and we walked in. The interior screamed "We have a competent decorator, unlike a certain other mansion in town." While everything in Zinda Mansion was white, La Maison seemed coated in gold and red velvet. Everywhere I looked, I saw huge chandeliers, mahogany furniture, and marble statues that were probably missing from the Louvre. The second Clementine shut the door behind her, all the lights went out and a spotlight shined directly into my face.

"Ladies and Gentlemen! Please welcome to the stage Ash Murphy!" shouted someone from one floor up.

A door swung open and a giant blast of symphonic music crashed out of a grand ballroom. Dozens of beautiful white-haired people ran out of the room and surrounded us. They all threw blue and silver confetti into the air. Everyone started clapping and yelling "Welcome." Then, tripping over her own feet, a freckled Geist ran out of a bathroom and said "Welcome" about ten seconds too late. I was so surprised, I forgot to fake a surprised face, and instead I just stared forward, blankly.

From the balcony above us, the announcer readjusted her peacock feather-clad cocktail dress that exposed a fair bit of cleavage. Her copper cheekbones looked like they could cut diamonds, her long white hair was snatched into a thick ponytail that went down to her waist, and she was wearing the longest heels I had ever seen on someone walking down a grand staircase. Which, admittedly, was a fairly niche category. The busty lady danced down the giant staircase, flamboyantly flailing her arms around as if she was performing Shakespeare. She reached into her cleavage and tossed a flurry miniature peacock feathers into the air. But within seconds, she shrieked and clicked her heels down the stairs so violently I hoped she didn't chip the marble. She danced around me like a small child needing to pee. Everyone stepped aside, giving her room to flail. Then she grabbed me with one hand, lifted me off my feet, and tossed me into the air like a baby doll.

"Not again!" I shrieked.

"Ash Murphy!" she screamed, still throwing me up and down as if it was a perfectly normal thing to do. "New Geist! New Geist! New Geist!" She stopped tossing me around and switched to pinching my cheeks. "He's such a cutie patootie, too!" She slapped her forehead and huffed at herself. "Where are my manners? I'm Winona Iron Cloud, the head of house over here at La Maison de Beaux Fantômes."

"Charmed," I said in between gurgles.

Winona wrapped her arm around mine and whisked me away into the ballroom, where the symphonic music was quickly replaced by more modern music, and I was almost positive every other song was something by Cher. Punch bowls lined the room, each with a different kind of cocktail in them. Gray, blue, and black balloons floated around the vaulted ceiling, and I tried to keep my eyes off of them. I so desperately wanted to ask somebody—*anybody*—what was up with the balloon room at Zinda Mansion, but I was honestly too afraid of the answer.

Winona pulled me to the center of the room and handed me some weird purple drink in a Red Solo martini glass. Clementine and Jesse were right behind us, and once Clementine saw my drink, she almost snatched it right out of my hand.

"Is that alcoholic, Winona?" Clem asked. "Ash's only eighteen."

"What are you, a cop?" laughed Winona. "We're Geist. Age doesn't matter anymore!" She turned to me. Every word that came out of her mouth sounded like a song. "We all look young and beautiful, but we've got people here in their twenties, and people here in their sixties, and people here as old as her!"

She pointed to Clem, and Clem let out a thick, annoyed grunt. Winona then twirled closer to me, not even thinking about giving me an inch of personal space.

"And let me just say! When Clementine told me that she found a poor boy on the highway the other day, I knew I needed to create a giant party in your name!" She waved her arms around, showing off the spectacle. "Anything less than this, and you might think I don't like you!" Winona wistfully sighed and put her wrist up to her forehead. "Such an intimidatingly attractive boy, wilted before his time."

I bit down on my cheek and tried to think of any response to that. Nothing came.

Two more Geist hurried over from a punch bowl, holding more glasses of the swirly purple drink that looked like our basement portal. One was the freckled Geist who missed her cue earlier. She was a cute, somewhat pear-shaped girl with frizzy hair who was barely tall enough to poke my chest with her nose.

The other was a dark-skinned woman dressed in far too many layers for mid-summer. She wore an ornate pair of cat eye glasses that made it look like she was going to either kick me out of a library or whip me. Judging from her intense eye makeup, I was leaning toward the later, but the sensible cardigan pointed toward the former.

"Winona, dear," said the conservatively dressed Geist, "you're scaring the child."

The freckled Geist handed a drink to Clementine and Jesse, then stared at me, wide-eyed. She stumbled closer to me, pulled the flower crown made of white and blue lilies off her head, and plopped it onto mine. She had to do a little hop to get it all the way up there. She then gave me a weak-armed hug and yawned.

"There. Now you're perfect."

"Oh, Ash," sang Winona. "This is Teresa Quinlan, the queen of horticulture. She grew those lilies herself in our greenhouse upstairs." She ran her hands across Teresa's head, and Teresa gave me a goofy smile.

The conservatively dressed Geist raised an eyebrow at me. She ran her hand through her short, swooping hair as stared me down. She handed Winona a glass, gave her a kiss on the cheeks, and rested her head on Winona's shoulder.

"And here is the most gorgeous, intelligent, angelic woman who I ever had the blessing to marry," she sang, flashing her wedding ring. Then Winona ran her hands across the woman's entire body. "Farrah Alam, the queen of my heart!"

My heart soared when I saw their matching rings. Gays! Finally! My people! Farrah's stern face turned into a smile for a second, then went back to normal, and she took a sip of her ice water. Winona raised her glass.

"To Ash," she said, and the others followed.

We all clinked our little plastic cups together. Everyone took a drink from their glasses. Jesse winced, Winona recoiled, and Teresa muttered "icky" under her breath and made a very sour face. I tried to keep my cool before discreetly dribbling everything in my mouth back into the glass. Winona took a second sip and pretended that her face wasn't collapsing in on itself.

"How much vodka did you add, love?" asked Farrah.

"Not enough," Clementine said into her empty glass.

Everyone put their drinks on whatever flat surface they could find. Except Jesse, who gave his to Clem. Then, jumping right back into hostess mode, Winona grabbed my arm and started to drag me around the room. In the span of two minutes, she presented me to each and every Geist in the room. Winona would shove me right next to someone, they'd introduce themself, I'd introduce myself, and we would get half a sentence into a conversation before Winona whisked me away to the next person. Clementine tried her best to keep up with us, but Winona was like ninety-percent leg so she was a lot faster than her.

I did my best to remember their names and faces, but when everyone at the party had the same hair color, people started blurring together. Everyone was beautiful and thrilled to be at such a lavish party, and not a single person looked older than thirty—it was honestly disconcerting seeing women named Agnes, Mildred, and Enid look just as youthful as Addison, Kayden, and the fifteen Avas. Of course, the weirdest thing about the party was that people seemed genuinely excited to see me.

Once she finished introducing me to everyone in the ballroom, Winona pulled me toward the corner of the room. We had completely lost Clementine and the others in the crowd, which meant that I lost my only lifeline in this party full of strangers. Winona, however, didn't seem to see me as a stranger, because she snuggled up real close to me and smiled.

"Okay, real talk, perfect-ten-to-perfect-ten." She was

absolutely beaming. "I know we just met, but you are probably the most beautiful man I've ever met and Clementine really seems to like you, and since Clem's my best friend and my personal Bob Mackie, that means I like you, too."

Winona then pulled me in for another hug. I bit down on my cheek. It took an embarrassingly long time to reciprocate the hug. She seemed too genuine. Everyone seemed too genuine. The sincerity of the entire party was so unreal to me. I couldn't process anything. It was already weird enough that Clementine took a liking to me, let alone an entire mansion full of people. I was still expecting a bucket of pigs' blood to drop onto me.

"But," she whispered, "it's time we talked about love." She poked my nose with her long finger. "Tell me, what's your ideal soulmate?"

My eyes darted toward the mass of partygoers. I could actually see Jesse tower over some others in the crowd, stumbling around and probably still on the hunt for me. My eyes lingered on him a bit too long, and Winona flicked my temple.

"No! Bad! He's straight!" she scolded. "Never crush on anyone who can't love you back! And especially not Jesse. He's got Clementine on such a high pedestal that the only thing that even comes close to her is Daisy."

My whole body seized at the thought of the rat again. But I shook my head and tried to regain composure. And also act as if I had any experience in the dating field. I readjusted my flower crown and made sure to flex a bit as I did it.

"Lemme think," I mused. "I guess I like fit guys. The tall, dark, and handsome type. Kinda scruffy—" Maybe a scorpion tattoo?

I stopped myself once I realized I was describing Gabriel. I took in a deep breath and tried to evict him from my mind. Instead, I evicted every ounce of composure I had. My hands started to shake. I shoved them into my pockets before Winona could notice.

"Alright, I'm gonna hit the pause button right now." I tried to think of a nice way to say what I was about to say, but there wasn't any. I decided to be blunt. "I just died. Last time I went on a date, the guy was a no-show and then I got killed on the way back home. I'm not in a place right now for dating."

Winona didn't seem hurt. I tried to read any facial queues, but she seemed perfectly content with my answer. Somehow. She just started pulling me back toward the crowd.

"Well then, maybe instead of looking at boys, we have fun dancing."

She smiled again. Her smile was so wide it completely changed the shape of her face. I smiled, too. At first, I just gave a little Mona Lisa smile. No teeth, just a simple tilt upward. But then I looked around at the party again. I saw Clementine and the others emerge from the crowd and walk toward us. When I realized that no one was going to dump pigs' blood on me, I allowed myself to be sincere. For probably the first time in years, I smiled for real.

"I'd like that."

Winona whistled. Someone ran up to the sound system and turned a few knobs. The lights dimmed around us and the music's volume skyrocketed. An upbeat Kylie Minogue song blasted from the speakers. Winona shimmied back toward Clementine, Jesse, Farrah, and Teresa, and I followed her lead. It took no time at all for Winona to start whipping her ponytail around. Teresa joined in on Winona's flailing, but her flailing was nowhere near as graceful. One of her shoes flew off her foot and just barely missed Addison's face. Instead of going after it, she just kicked off her other one. Farrah only swayed back and forth, but Winona pulled her closer, and the two started to dance together. At first she looked uncomfortable, but she started to enjoy herself once Winona kissed her on the neck. Clementine and Jesse grooved a little closer to me and started doing some kinda grandparent dance.

And so, I started to dance, too. I started slow. I knew that if I danced too carelessly, I'd look like a stork having a seizure. But the second I started moving my body, Winona spun closer to me and I was in the exact center of my circle. For a brief moment, I stopped. But then I remembered: sincerity. There wasn't any pigs' blood above me. I was at a party specifically made for me. So I let myself get a little wacky. I moved my hips and raised my arms. I shook my head so hard my flower crown covered my eyes. I didn't care. I was having fun. People liked me. It was weird.

A few of the other partygoers joined in on our little circle, too. Agnes and one of the Avas ran over and started to dance right next to me, spilling their drinks all over themselves. Mildred was giving me bedroom eyes and frequently readjusted her strapless leather dress. She was in for massive disappointment. Ignoring them, I grabbed Clementine's arms and started to twirl her around. She laughed, then hiked up her sundress a bit to show off some fancy footwork she pulled out of nowhere. I tried to mimic it, but I ended up just getting my legs tangled up. I landed right on my ass, but I was perfectly fine. I even started to chuckle. Jesse leaned down to pick me back up. I got to my feet and saw dozens of people encircling me. And for a brief moment, I forgot I was dead. I felt more alive than I had in a long time.

Exhausted from dancing, Clementine, Jesse, Winona, Farrah, Teresa, and I found a nice area in the ballroom to sit and talk. Winona told me several stories about her escapades backstage at concerts, and I was glued to every word. She caught me off-guard when she mentioned sneaking onstage with Whitney Houston, and I had to remind myself that we were all immortal ghost-things.

Winona kept pawing at her wife. If she were any closer to Farrah, she'd have been on the other side of her. Clementine and Jesse kept a more modest distance from each other, but still stayed attached. I assumed that Teresa and I could be third wheels together, but it turned out that Teresa had a long-term boyfriend. So, Daisy and I were third-wheels together. Daisy scampered out of Jesse's pocket once in a while to grab a cracker from Jesse's hors d'oeuvres plate, then retreat back into her hidey-hole. And each time, I cringed.

"Any of y'all seen Olive?" asked Clementine.

"Oh, she's probably being a party pooper upstairs or something," said Winona.

"I'll be back in a second. I need to drop some dresses off with her."

Clementine headed toward the door and grabbed the tote bags full of clothing she dropped on the way in. Before she got too far, I got up and started walking with her.

"I'll head up with you," I said. "I'll protect you in case we see the Brotherhood again."

If Clementine ever rolled her eyes, she would have right there. We headed upstairs, and the party kept on going as if I never left. Upstairs was, of course, gorgeous and filled—ironically—with life. The walls were lined with possibly hundreds of photos of Winona posing with various celebrities. Cher, Madonna, Cher, Cher, RuPaul, Cher, Eartha Kitt, professional Cher impersonator. The meet-and-greet photos went on for miles, and each one had Winona dressing much more extravagantly than the celebrity.

"You didn't have to come up with me, y'know," Clementine

said, ruining my train of thought. "Winona'd be more than happy to get to know you better."

"Just need a little time to breathe. Parties like this always get me a little antsy." My eyes traveled down the celebrity wall. Cher. Cher. Infinite Cher. "My parents had to go to a lot of big parties, but they never took us, since it was business. And I never went to many parties in high school, mostly 'cuz I wasn't invited."

"Really?" Clementine asked. "Cute boy like you?"

"My looks weren't the problem, it was because I was…" I stopped myself. I made sure to flip my hair and kill any insecurity I had in my voice. "I didn't care, though. I had other stuff to do."

Clementine slowed to a stop. "Because why, sweetie?"

I didn't respond. I just looked away. Clementine craned her head around so I had to look her in the eyes.

"Downstairs, we got people that are gay, bisexual, transgender, genderqueer, you name it. You ain't gotta worry about people ignorin' you because of who you are anymore."

I blushed. My face felt inhumanly hot. I bit my tongue and thought of disgusting things. Ska music. Armpit hair. Slow walkers. Animals that are way too friendly. Did I mention ska yet? I corrected my posture and, through sheer willpower, turned my face back to its normal pasty white.

"Alright, new topic: we've become fairly close in a short amount of time. We've had some long, deep conversations. You couldn't even casually slip 'Oh, I have a boyfriend. His name is Jesse, not Vagina?'"

Clementine chuckled uncomfortably. "It ain't that big a deal, hon."

"It is a big deal, Clementine!" I said, clenching my fists. "You know why? Because now every time I look at him, I'm going to remember when I called him Cooter. And when I look at Vee, I'll remember when she tricked me into calling him Cooter—"

"Please stop usin' that word."

"And in five years, I'll be walking down the street, minding my own business, when all of a sudden my brain will betray me and say 'Hey, remember when you stupidly listened to Vee and called Clementine's boyfriend Cooter? Good times.' And I'll never be able to make a second first impression, and I'll never be able to stop thinking about Coooooooooteeeeeer!"

A door opened next to us and a goddamn demon stared back at me.

"Jesus Christ!" I screamed.

I jumped toward Clementine's arms. Of course, she didn't bother catching me, so I just awkwardly slammed into her chest and huddled behind her. Clementine paid it no mind and waved toward the demented thing on the other side.

"Afternoon, Olive," she said. "You know there's a whole party goin' on downstairs, and I'm sure they'd love you to come down."

"I am aware, and they would not."

Olive opened the door wider. She looked like a stretched-out five-year-old, with long, thick pigtails and giant eyes that seemed way too big for her tiny pupils. An oversized patchwork rabbit was strapped to her like a backpack. She stared me up and down like a prized pig at a county fair, her pupils becoming even smaller.

"And you must be Ash. It's nice to finally see you around. Winona just couldn't stop talking about you when she heard Clementine adopted you. Everyone seemed to spend hours and hours just preparing this little Deathday party." She drummed her chewed-up fingernails against the doorframe. "We all have our obsessions."

Clementine, somehow not freaked-the-Hell-out, handed the two bags of clothes to Olive. Olive disappeared into the shadows of her room for a second, then came back into the light holding two empty bags and an envelope overflowing with bills. She handed everything to Clem, and I was almost positive she didn't even blink once.

"It's a little more than I promised," she said. "One guy thought he was good at haggling. Turns out I'm better."

"Olive, if that's code for 'you hurt him,' I'm not happy," Clementine stomped her foot.

Olive gave her a little kitty smile. "It is."

Clementine grumbled, but slipped the envelope into a bag. She gave Olive another hollow smile, said it was always nice doing business with her, and started heading toward the party again. I turned my back to the terrifying girl, but her clammy hands grabbed my shoulder, and I felt my entire soul get sucked out of my pores.

"I heard all about what happened, Ash." Her high-pitched voice rattled my bones. "Such a terrible accident. Everything must still be fresh on your mind. It's a miracle that a Geist got to you before you expired." Olive leaned in closer to me. "But, I think there's something you should care about more." She was so close, I could feel her breath on my face. "Ask Clementine about Revenants."

Olive shut the door, and the hallway became silent. I ran back downstairs before she decided to talk to me again.

The party wound down a few hours later, with all the other Geist either heading back home or retreating in pairs to the bedrooms upstairs. As the sunlight faded outside, only six people remained in the ballroom: me, Clementine, Jesse, Winona, Farrah, and Teresa. Seven, counting the rat. After a while, Teresa tilted her head to the side and loudly mentioned how hungry she was, and Clementine said that she'd love to have them all over for dinner.

"After-party!" Winona shouted in glee.

The Maison ladies quickly changed into something more casual, and then we all walked out of La Maison de Beaux Fantômes. The sun drooped over the horizon, slowly bringing Chicago into twilight. Millennium Park's lights, one-by-one, turned on and all of the tourists made their way out of the park.

We headed onto the Green Line and hopped off a few stops away from the mansion to pick up some food from Winona's favorite restaurant, which she described as "Pan-Asian cuisine with a Latin twist that's completely halal and vegan." As we walked back toward my new home, weird fusion food in-hand, a light breeze pushed us onward. The momentum cleared my head of anything bad. I didn't need to think about the past week, I just needed to think about the present. I did my best not to think about Zack or the Brotherhood. I was with people who wanted to be with me, and that was so foreign and so wonderful.

Clementine and Jesse walked hand-in-hand, and Farrah walked with Winona, her face nuzzled into Winona's arm. Looking at their intermingled hands, it made me wonder if it was still considered necrophilia if both parties were dead.

Despite telling Winona I wasn't in a dating mood, I had to admit to myself that was only mostly true. When I was alive, I never had a boyfriend. I was hot, sure, but my social skills were absolute trash, and it wasn't easy finding another out gay kid in a Catholic school. I did have a girlfriend, briefly, but I did my best to forget that ever happened. And it would've been a lie to say I was a virgin, and it would've been a lie to say I didn't lose my virginity to an alleged heterosexual teammate on my cross-country team, but he did his best to forget that ever happened. As did the other three.

Being a lonely, bitter homosexual sucked.

"How long have you all been together?" I called ahead.

"We've been together for about eighteen years, but we've only been married for ten," said Farrah, and I once again had a horrible everyone-is-immortal-and-ancient revelation.

"Oh dear, when did we start dating?" asked Clementine. "It was a while after we both moved to Chicago, wasn't it?"

"Nah, Clem, I was your boy the second you gave that Spark to me and you know it."

The two of them blushed. Repulsive. Jesse pulled Clementine's hand up to his lips and kissed the back of it. Clementine giggled. Revolting. My teeth rotted from the sweetness. Can Geist get cavities? I added that to my list of five million questions that would no-doubt remain unanswered.

"About sixty years? Give or take?" Clementine finally answered.

"Sixty years?" I knew I shouldn't ask why they weren't married. But still, I let my confusion get the better of me. "And you're still just boyfriend and girlfriend?"

Farrah looked back at me and widened her eyes, as if to say "Too many questions."

"It's what we've grown accustomed to," said Clementine, completely monotone.

Winona kept the conversation going, but Clementine and Jesse seemed less openly affectionate after my question. My head ached in aggravation. I wondered if I should really have expected anything more than a quick response, after her neglecting to mention that Geist can turn visible, or how her boyfriend's name wasn't Genitals.

We quickened our pace a bit as the night grew darker. I grew more paranoid with every step. My eyes darted from person to person on the street. None of them could see me, but I knew, somewhere out there, there was a whole organization that could. No one else in the group seemed to really be on the lookout for danger. Winona was still basically shouting everything she said. But I knew every person who passed me on the street was a possible member of the Brotherhood. Even if I didn't see any goggles or gauntlets, anyone could be trying to kill me. Even the tiny kindergartener holding his grandpa's hand could have been hiding a gauntlet in his backpack.

"Oh, I just wish we could have met a little sooner, Ash!" exclaimed Winona. "Then we could have spent more time with you before we left! But, alas, you'll see us when we get back."

"Where're you going?" I asked, barely able to pay attention.

"Nowhere too special, just Aruba."

"Just Aruba," laughed Clementine. A raggedy man looked her way, and my heart jumped, but he kept walking.

"Opulence," whispered Winona, giving us spirit fingers. "We're going to hop a red-eye, and by tomorrow night, we'll be all ready for our fourteenth honeymoon."

I tried to do the math in my head. Was Clementine the only Geist in the city that actually did her job?

"This'll be your third vacation this year! Ain't that a bit much for June?" said Jesse. A man on the other side of the street reached into his pocket. He turned the corner before I got to see what he pulled out.

"No, we had one vacation and one pilgrimage to Mecca." Winona gestured to Farrah. "Religious obligations don't count as 'vacations,' Jessebear."

I had never walked through the neighborhoods we journeyed through. The streets grew less populated as we walked through the city, and it was shocking to see the sudden change from "metropolis" to "squalor." Half of the buildings looked abandoned, probably not having anything in them since the

1920s. We walked by an old factory with poorly drawn graffiti covering it. Most people stayed off the sidewalk, leaving only the occasional pedestrian walking out of a building or junkie shooting up in an alley. Even if we only went by a few people, my eyes kept locking in on everyone in front of me. No one escaped my sight.

Someone grabbed my wrist. "Don't turn around."

I turned around. A brunette woman with a gaunt, foxlike face in a huge army jacket stared back at me. It was Dinah, the Brotherhood preacher. I couldn't see her eyes, since they were covered by Brotherhood goggles. She also wore a gauntlet on her right hand. A number of emotions flowed through me, and they all fought and contradicted each other until a loud, exasperated groan left my mouth.

"What the fu—"

Everyone looked back at me. Before I could finish my sentence, Dinah pulled me into the parking lot next to her. Tiny jolts coursed through me as she held on. Dinah threw me to the ground and clasped my neck with her gauntlet.

Clementine, Winona, and Jesse ran to me, Teresa and Farrah not far behind. Jesse grabbed Dinah by her waist and pulled her away from me. I stumbled to my feet, trying to shake off the voltage that flew through me. Farrah and Teresa gripped my sides and held me up. I told them I was fine, despite my deep breaths and buckled knees saying otherwise. Dinah ran at Jesse, Winona, and Clementine, her hand sparkling. Jesse and Winona pushed Clementine back, but she stood strong and walked toward the oncoming lunatic. Dinah leaped at Clementine, and just as she was about to make contact, Clementine took in a deep breath. Dinah's throat lurched. She tumbled to the ground, completely breathless. Clementine knelt down beside her.

"Listen here, now. I told you children never to—"

Dinah shoved her fist into Clementine's stomach. A giant

light exploded from her gauntlet. Clementine screamed and shot into the air, collapsing onto her back. Jesse cried out and ran to her, prying her off the ground. Dinah pulled a whistle out of her pocket and blew into it.

The door of the factory flew open, and fourteen Brothers ran out, all of them with gauntlets and goggles. Leading the charge were Gabriel and James. My head shook, looking from my fellow Geist to the impending Brotherhood. I stumbled to Clementine and Jesse, not turning my back to the men running toward us. Jesse cradled Clementine in his chest and grabbed my arm. Farrah and Teresa pulled me closer to the others, both of them keeping a tight grip on me. Clementine wheezed, unable to take in a full breath of air.

"Circle up!" screamed Dinah. She finally got back to her feet, wiping gravel off her jaw. "If any of you let these assholes escape again, I'm going to make sure Father Abram excommunicates you so hard you'll all have to sell your testicles just so you can afford a cardboard box to sleep in!"

Father Abram. The name echoed in my head. My heart stopped beating. I huddled closer to Jesse, feeling just as terrified as I did during the crash. All the men and women surrounded us. The Brothers stood straight, in a perfect circle, leaving us no room to slip out. Their faces were completely blank, except for Gabriel. He looked furious. Clementine forced her eyes open.

"Dinah," wheezed Clementine. "Don't do this."

"Shut your mouth and don't you dare try to get friendly with me," Dinah spat. "You say my name again, and you'll be the first to get exorcized."

Jesse put his head by my ear. He pushed Clementine closer to me and wrapped one of her arms around my shoulders.

"When I say go, I'm gonna need you to carry Clementine

and run like mad outta here with the girls. It doesn't matter where, just get anywhere but here."

"Oh, yeah, you think you can distract all fifteen of them?" I sneered.

"Don't you dare try and be a hero, you big lummox." Clementine pulled her arm away from me and got to her feet. I saw a large burn on her dress, and for a second, I worried about all the wasted effort she put into it. "I ain't about to run away and leave my sugar behind."

Dinah took another step forward. She brandished her gauntlet, pressing a few buttons on her wrist. Two thick blades popped out of the gauntlet's knuckles, and a current of light flowed between them. I clutched Clementine's arm and trembled. Clementine stepped closer to Dinah, her head held high. Even if she was the shortest one in the circle, Clementine stood the tallest.

"Clementine, do the breath thing again," I stuttered.

"Oh, hon. I can do more than just 'the breath thing.'"

Winona snickered, then pulled Farrah and Teresa to her chest. Clementine took in a deep breath. Dinah pulled her hand back. Clementine grabbed Jesse's arm and wrapped her other arm around me. Jesse's long arms wrapped around all of us. Before I could react, Clementine aimed her head to the ground and blew. All six of us shot off the ground and into the air. I wrapped my arms around Clementine and shrieked. The power of the wind knocked the Brothers off their feet and onto the ground.

"What?" I shrieked, kicking the air. "Whatwhatwhatwhat-whatwhatwhat?"

We flew through across the parking lot in an arc. Jesse pulled all of us close to his chest, as if cradling five babies at once. All of the food we had been carrying flew everywhere, coating the parking lot in fake beef and soy sauce. We came crashing to the ground not too long after we lifted off, with Jesse landing flat on his feet. A huge crack echoed through the parking lot, and Jesse grunted and stumbled, but within a second, he was fine. Clementine jumped out of Jesse's arms and helped me down. My brain stopped functioning after two seconds in the air. I looked over at all of the confused and angry Brothers. Some were stumbling to their feet. Others were already running after us. Gabriel was sprinting at full speed.

"Teresa. Farrah. Get Ash to a safe place." Winona's voice instantly changed from pop princess to chain-smoking rocker. "We'll make sure these queens learn their lesson this time."

"There's fifteen of 'em. So we got five each?" Jesse asked, a sly smile forming. He handed Clementine's bags to Teresa, his arms now free to pose like a fighting game character.

"Oh, you know how I don't like to make this into a game," Clementine said.

Clementine, Winona, and Jesse ran toward the impending cultists. Farrah and Teresa pushed me toward the street, and we started running. Adrenaline replaced all brain functions, and I dashed so quickly I was already back on the sidewalk before they left the parking lot. I heard Jesse cackle from all the way across the lot.

"You part horse, boy?" he laughed.

I turned around, just in time to see the action start. An inhuman glow illuminated the parking lot when plasma sparked out of fifteen gauntlets at once. The fifteen Brothers clashed with the three Geist, and I felt sorry for the Brotherhood. Jesse grabbed two Brothers by their shirts, pulled them up from the ground, slammed their chests together, and unceremoniously dropped them to the ground. Winona kept her movements a little more fluid. As if to the beat of a song—probably something by Cher—she punched, posed, punched, posed, punched, kicked,

kicked, posed, and slammed her high-heeled foot into the crotch of a poor, unfortunate Brother. Clementine danced around the Brothers, swirling in the wind like a ballerina. Whenever a Brother tried to touch her with their gauntlet, she would already be behind them, ready to blow them off their feet. It was terrifying, badass, and absolutely beautiful.

Out of the corner of my eye, I saw a little streak of brown and white skitter around our spilled takeout. I grimaced. That wasn't Daisy, I lied. It was just a different rat with a brown ribbon. The real Daisy was surely safe in Jesse's pocket. The little streak scampered back into the thrall of battle, and I realized there was a zero percent chance Daisy stayed in Jesse's pocket during our blast off. Jesse threw one of the Brothers toward the rat, and the Brother fell within three inches of her, almost crushing her tiny bones.

"Crap," I mumbled.

Just as Farrah and Teresa made it to the sidewalk, I dashed past them and ran for Daisy. Farrah tried to grab me, but missed.

"Ash, stop!" Farrah cried.

"Safety is this way!" screamed Teresa, flailing her arms. "That way is the opposite of safety! Anti-safety!"

Daisy slid and skidded along the pavement as she tried to avoid the giant feet about to crush her. I strained my eyes, trying to keep a tight grip on her location, even in the chaos. The second I stepped foot into the light, all of the still-standing Brothers stopped attacking Jesse, Clementine, and Winona and ran straight for me. I yelped, but I kept up my mad dash, flailing my arms around as I leaped across the pavement looking for the rat. Daisy ran toward the building the Brotherhood flooded out of. I chased her, hot on her tail, and the Brotherhood chased me, hot on mine. Clementine, Winona, and Jesse ran after me, all extremely panicked and extremely aggravated.

Daisy ran toward the front steps of the abandoned factory. Before she could even attempt to climb the steps, I leaped forward and stumbled to the ground. If rats could scream, Daisy probably would have when I clamped my hands around her little body. I jumped up, victorious.

"Gotcha, bitch!" I cackled.

I shoved the gross-but-kinda-cute rodent into my pocket. Then I heard the cacophony of footsteps racing toward me, and a cold sweat drenched my entire body. I started to think that, just maybe, it was a stupid idea to go back for Daisy. Why was I risking my life for a rat that probably wouldn't live past Christmas?

So I stood there, realizing my stupidity, just as Clementine, Winona, Jesse, and six Brothers ran up to me. James jumped toward me. He yanked my head down and raised his gauntlet. Clementine, angrier than I had ever seen her, slammed her foot into his stomach. A giant gust of wind threw him backward, right onto the chest of another, even larger Brother. Both of them fell onto the pavement with a hard thunk. Jesse punched a member square in the jaw. I heard a pop. I hoped it wasn't a bone. Winona grabbed another member by the waist and, like a damn gorilla, picked him up and threw him at the one Jesse just punched in the jaw.

Dinah aimed her gauntlet right at Clementine's face. She lunged forward. Before she could get anywhere, I yanked her leg with both hands. Dinah made a guttural throat noise and slipped to the ground, face first. She tried to pick herself back up, I slammed my heel into Dinah's back as hard as I could. Then I knelt down, pulled her arm up, and grabbed her gauntlet. The gauntlet slid right off, and suddenly, I had a new souvenir.

Gabriel noticed my new toy. While Clementine, Jesse, and Winona were taking care of all the other members, Gabriel decided to go after me. He kicked my foot off Dinah's back. I tumbled back and fell onto the steps, dropping the gauntlet next to me. A squeak peeped out of my pocket, but I knew better than to take my eyes off my attacker. Gabriel grabbed my neck and dragged me off the steps. I tried to pry his fingers off my neck, but his hand stayed clamped around me. His gauntlet started sparking. As he raised his gauntleted hand toward my face, for a brief second, I saw the fire that killed me. I gritted my teeth, and the world around me grew even hotter.

"Don't touch me, goddammit!" I shouted.

I careened my body around and kicked him right in the stomach. Right as my shoe made contact, my entire foot became engulfed in a blue flame. We both screamed, and he let go of me. His shirt caught on fire. The fight stopped and everyone gasped as Gabriel's shirt spontaneously combusted. I stumbled back to the ground and gazed at the flames. The blue fire disappeared from my foot, but the fire on Gabriel's shirt spread, and his scream could be heard across town.

Clementine rushed forward. She grabbed onto Gabriel's shoulders, trying to calm his panic. She blew on the flames, instantly extinguishing them. Gabriel was still in a frenzy. He peeled his shirt off of his body. My eyes went right for his stomach. I saw the reddened area of his burn. It only looked like a bad sunburn. Gabriel stood still, stunned, staring down at me.

His burn turned into my burn, and my heart stopped again. His reddened skin disappeared, and my charred flesh replaced it. I closed my eyes, but in the darkness, I could still see paramedics pull a limp, scorched arm from the wreckage. I opened my eyes again and saw Gabriel's tiny burn.

I got up from the ground. I took one look back at Gabriel, grabbed Dinah's gauntlet from the steps, and then ran. I rushed back to the street as quickly as I could, stampeding past Farrah and Teresa and making a bee-line for home. My vision grew wet. I did not turn back around to see if anyone was following me.

It took a lot of effort to stop running. I must have been several blocks away from the old factory before I slowed down even slightly. I came to a stop when I saw a well-lit gas station. I huddled down on the sidewalk, squeezing the stolen gauntlet against my chest. Everyone else caught up a few minutes later, all out of breath. All five of them sat down beside me. Clementine put her hand on my knee and rubbed it. I pulled a terrified Daisy out of my pocket and handed her to Jesse.

"Saved your rat."

"Daisy!" Jesse cried. He kissed the rat on the top of her head. Daisy skittered back into her rightful home under his hat. "Bless you, Ash."

"Thanks. Hope I didn't cause too much trouble back there." I tried to add a bit of humor in my voice. There was no chance it came through.

"Ash, we weren't in grave danger." Clementine shifted closer to me.

"Then how come Vee kept saying they were gonna exorcize me?"

It took them way too long to answer my question. Winona patted me on the back a little too hard.

"Don't worry about those guys," said Winona. There was no confidence in her voice. "This isn't the first time we got in a tussle with those dudes, and it isn't even the worst. There's no way they could 'exorcize' us or whatever Vee told you."

A car sped past us, going way over the speed limit. I jolted upright, knocking both Farrah and Teresa back. I sat back down, still shaking.

"You're still hurtin'." Clementine wiped her finger across my face. *Dammit.* I must have let a tear escape. "What else is on your mind, hon?"

I shook my head. "Let's just get home."

The walk home remained calm. Everyone kept a steady pace while Jesse carried me, piggyback style. I burrowed my face into Jesse's back, keeping everything else out of my mind. Every few steps, Gabriel's burn came back, and I tried to push it away with happier thoughts. Vee playing pranks, Winona fluttering, Clementine and Jesse acting cute together, anything that could get me to laugh instead of panic.

Twenty minutes later, we made it to Zinda Mansion. I hopped down from Jesse's back, and we all walked in. The second our feet hit the tile, Vee's door swung open, and she burst out, holding her smut novel and a self-rolled cigarette.

"Clementine!" she called down the stairs. "Hey, did you eat dinner already? I didn't eat yet 'cuz I figured you'd make something when you got home."

"Vee, your shift ain't over till—" Clementine sighed, completely defeated. "Never mind. I'm puttin' dinner on now." Clementine looked over to me. "How about we make something nice? Maybe show off your cookin' skills to your new friends?"

It took me almost a minute before I realized she was talking to me. I blinked a few times, then nodded. I forced a giant, toothy smile. No sincerity, but I hoped I could at least fake it. Clementine gave me a little smile, then headed into the kitchen. I tried to compose myself a little better before I headed on in with her. Vee slid down the stairs and hopped over to me. Before she went into the dining room, she poked my forehead and snickered.

"Have fun with Cooter?" she whispered, making an obscene hand gesture.

I slapped her hand away and walked toward the kitchen. I didn't make eye contact with anyone in the dining room when I walked by. I started going through the motions as I helped make a simple dinner for my new friends. All I could think about was the cult that wanted to kill us. The cult that thought that Clementine and Winona and Jesse were demons. Good people who that, almost instantly, decided to call themselves my friends. And I grimaced.

Olive said "We all have our obsessions." Clementine loved to sew. Winona loved celebrities. And I decided, right then and there, that my obsession was going to be tearing down the Brotherhood with my bare hands.

Chapter 6
Eternity

I knew better than to run into a mass of Brothers, guns akimbo. I needed to be calculating, like the Count of Monte Cristo or Beyoncé. More importantly, I needed time to cool down. If I wanted to destroy a crazy lightning cult, I needed to keep my emotions in check.

The morning after the fight, I went straight to the library and spent all day reading to calm me down. I was initially against going near flammable books, since I lit a boy on fire not a day before, but I convinced myself that was a fluke. It was totally because his gauntlet malfunctioned or something. I stayed in Clementine and Jesse's section, since Vee's section was mostly porn and Johanna's was nonfiction philosophical trash. It was filled with a few popular books I never got around to reading in addition to something I never heard of: *Sweet Clementine, Vol. 3*, by Jesse Darwin. I snickered and brought that one to my room for later.

The day after that, Clementine and I decorated my room with some random stuff we found in the storage rooms upstairs. My room became more livable, but I still had trouble thinking of it as "my room," just like I still had trouble calling Zinda "my house." The spooky, sterile mansion never gave the feeling of welcoming, and that made me think that if Winona had found me instead of Clementine, I could have lived in the fancy chateau in the park. I liked Clementine enough to deal with the spookiness. Also, I'd rather live in a cold mansion with slightly weird people than live in a luxurious mansion with the possibility of waking up and seeing Olive smiling down at me with her tiny pupils. In a contest between Olive and Daisy, I would much rather wake up to find Jesse's pet rat in my bed.

Even if I wasn't about to start reaping, I still helped out around the mansion. Johanna took care of laundry, Vee did absolutely nothing useful, and Jesse did a lot of the electrical work. This included making sure the generator was always running—which explained how we had electricity—and all the lightbulbs behind the windows were lit—which explained the weird, divine glow coming through stained glass. Still didn't have any idea how we got water, but I had enough answers to keep me satisfied for a while. Naturally, I made myself at home in the kitchen. I started helping Clementine out with meals, and cooking with her was wonderful. Except when we made lemon bars and Vee cussed me out for making something so sour.

At one point, Clementine asked if I wanted to go with her to church. I *desperately* wanted to say no, but I went anyway. Partially because I wanted to be a good friend, partially because I had to go shopping. Every time I asked Clementine if there was an iPod charger in the mansion, she came back with something unimaginably wrong—first time, a box of batteries; second time, a universal remote. So one Sunday, Clementine, Jesse, and I went to a large Baptist service. We sat in a pew in the very back with a few other religious Geist that were all too eager to jump up and scream "Praise Him!" whenever possible. It knew it was gonna be a lot different than the Catholic masses I was used to but I thought, hey, Christ is Christ. Turned out I was horrifyingly wrong because the service was almost three hours long. On the way home, we stopped by a used electronic shop and picked up an actual iPod charger. Hallelujah.

Occasionally, I ran into Johanna. She never said much and only said some polite hellos before going about her own business. If I wanted to, I could have been a perky go-getter who sat down with her and had emotional bonding time, but I was neither perky nor a go-getter and I enjoyed the distance Johanna kept. She freaked me out. Not to the level of Olive, but still, she gave major creep vibes, mostly because she carried a Bible with her all the time, no matter where she went. I asked Clementine about the Bible, and she said it was Johanna's Memento. I was not surprised in the slightest and hated myself for not realizing that right away.

After about a week, I got into a nice cycle. I'd wake up, make breakfast for whichever three Geist weren't on patrol, then read a book until I had to make lunch. If Clementine didn't have any bright ideas for our afternoon, I'd spend the day in the workout room, trying to get in my cardio. Afterward, I'd start work on dinner and dessert, then spend a little time with Clementine before bed.

Clementine strolled into the gym one day as I was running on the treadmill. She just stood by the doorway, watching me run in place. After a few minutes, she sat sidesaddle on the weight bench, still watching me run. Her lower lip jutted out and her posture like a cooked noodle.

"You run a lot?" she asked.

"Yeah." I slid my headphones down to my neck. "I ran cross country in high school."

"Oh right, yeah, I think you mentioned that." Clementine looked me in the eyes, her posture shooting back up to its usual ninety-degree angle. "It's been three weeks."

"No, it hasn't," I said, slowing my jog.

"You came to the mansion on June 12. It's now July 1. So a little less than three weeks."

I ran the numbers through my head. Move in day, followed

by the surprise party, then a bunch of days where I did random crap around the mansion. Everything blurred together and felt like one big day. I counted the number of times I went to bed, and that's when I really realized that June had essentially disappeared.

"Oh my God, how has my sense of time become so shot?" I palmed my forehead. "Is this what death is? You blink and suddenly it's been ten years?"

"You'll start wishin' it was just ten years." She got up from the bench. "But Johanna says you gotta go out with Vee today on duty."

"What?" I stopped the treadmill and kept my eyes on her while I slid off. "Already?"

"Johanna's been pesterin' me for a few days. Normally we'd let you wait a bit longer, but we're trying to fix up the schedule issues we've been having and, uh, Fourth of July's comin' up and—"

"And you think there's gonna be a killing surge?" I panicked. "Because I know we live on the South Side, but it's not like we're in Englewood."

She squinted at me. "Okay, Ash, for starters, we live in a very nice neighborhood with very friendly people. Just because we got Brotherhoodlums here doesn't mean there ain't any in your little suburb." She coughed. "Thing is, holidays generally have a higher mortality rate, and it's real—" she paused, "uncouth to keep spirits in the livin' world. That goes triple when there's homicide involved." She then kept talking, as if I was just supposed to ignore that strange bombshell. "So, Johanna wants Vee to train you today while she's out on her route."

"Hold up, pause. What exactly happens when a spirit isn't put through the portal?" I lowered my voice. "Does this have anything to do with the claw marks by the portal door?"

Clementine rested her head in her hand. Then she put her hands on mine.

"We don't want to leave the spirits alone for too long because it's terrifying for them. And sometimes, they get violent." She said violent so quietly, I wondered if she actually said it or I just imagined it. "We know what it feels like to die, but we were blessed with the chance to continue on. They don't have that chance, so we need to help them move on to the next life. You understand?"

I flat out didn't believe in anything God-related, weird basement-portal be damned, but I nodded. It was second nature for me to tread religious topics lightly with people I didn't hate. Faye loved to talk to me about Heaven, especially during her cancer scares. She said that the first thing she was going to do was meet up with her old Jewish friend Kurt Kramer, and she could finally prove to Kurt that Christians were right about the Jesus thing. She told that story about three times a year and each time I cringed, smiled, and forced a laugh.

Of course, I was dealing with the real afterlife and not Faye's idealized version of it. And I wasn't exactly happy about that.

"Uuuuuuugh." I slid onto the floor. "How am I supposed to help calm people down when they die, Clementine? I'm not built for that motherly stuff."

"Well, y'ain't wrong, but it's your duty, darlin'. It hurts, seeing people in those situations. But we gotta be the strong ones. It's the price you pay for immortality."

"So, the fact that I can never see my family again isn't the price? Was that just the sales tax?"

Clementine frowned, giving I'm-not-mad-just-disappointed mother vibes. I groaned again, and I jumped back to my feet. Standing in a triumphant superhero pose, I faced the door, ready to head out into the world.

"Fine, I'm going. I'll make you proud, ghost mom."

Clementine told Vee that I would be joining her on the route. Even though it was well after when she needed to start her day, she took an extra-long breakfast break that coincidentally lasted until her lunch break. Vee had the same reaction I had when Clementine told her that she needed to give me some on-the-job training, except she used more obscenities.

Clementine went into her big sewing room and came back with a cute blue messenger bag with my name emblazoned on it. It looked almost exactly like Vee's backpack, except hers was teal. I asked Clementine who assigned us these theme colors, and she just told me that she follows the colors of the skulls on the magic skull board, which was not a sentence I ever thought I'd hear in my life, ever. Clementine already packed a few granola bars and a water bottle. Sweet, sweet ghost mom. She then told me to go around the mansion and quickly gather anything I'd need for a day-long trip around the city.

I went into my room and threw in my iPod. On my dresser, I noticed Jesse's book of poems, which I hadn't moved in so long it was basically fossilizing. I shoved it inside in case I got bored. My trophy from the big Brotherhood fight, Dinah's gauntlet, was stashed under my bed. I shoved the gauntlet into the messenger bag, too. Just in case.

I walked back downstairs and saw Vee, Johanna, Jesse, and Clementine all waiting by the door. Vee tapped her foot on the tile, glaring up at me. Clementine held a pile of random supplies I'd need. I was surprised she didn't have a camera so she could take pictures for a big "Ash's First Day of Geist School" album on whatever social media site dead people used. FaceBoo, maybe. I laughed at my pun. Everyone looked confused. I shut up.

Johanna cleared her throat, coughing loud enough that every Geist in the city must have heard it. She shoved her chest forward, held her head high, and opened her mouth wider than I had ever seen it, almost as if she actually wanted people to hear her when she spoke. For once.

"Ashton Murphy, I am glad you finally agreed to accept your duty and ferry the souls into the afterlife. I am aware this task can be daunting, but it is our responsibility as Geist to guide these lost souls to their rightful place with God." She turned her attention to Vee. "Virginia, you are to take Ashton along your route and explain to him the daily routine. If and when you find a soul that has been released, you are to let Ashton take the soul back to the portal. Since he has already done it once, he should know how to take it from there."

Johanna said more words to me in her micro speech then she had my entire time at the mansion. I had no idea if she didn't speak to me because she only spoke about business-business-business or if she was icing me out for not picking up dead dudes the second Clementine met me. Perhaps it was both. Either way, I really regretted letting my full name slip to her.

"Ashton, do you have any final questions before you and Virginia leave the mansion?" asked Johanna.

"Yeah. So, what do we call dead people?" I asked. "Like, are they ghosts, or souls, or spirits, or what?"

Simultaneously, Johanna said souls, Clementine said spirits, Jesse said ghosts, and Vee belched. They all looked at each other, annoyed. Clementine walked closer to me and shoved a stack of five-dollar bills into my hands. She gave me a quick hug and gripped my shoulders.

"Just in case you need to buy anything while you're out. Vee's gonna try to make you shoplift. Don't you dare listen to her." Clementine unzipped my bag. I shoved the money in and rezipped it before she could see the gauntlet. "And if you see any of those Brotherhoodlums, remember to run right home. You don't need to deal with them, you just gotta let them live their lives the way they choose. Oh! And I almost forgot!"

She pulled a flip phone out of her pocket and handed it to me. I flipped it open, looking at the archaic buttons. Never in my life did I need to press a button four times to text an S.

"It's your very own phone!" Clementine exclaimed. "I put in my number already, along with all your other friends'. So, if anything goes wrong, call one of us and we'll run right over."

"Thanks, ghost mom."

"I ain't your mom, and I ain't your ghost mom. Call me that again and you'll get these hands."

Everyone waved goodbye, and Vee and I exited the mansion. Once the door closed and stairs disappeared back into the Earth, we said the exact same expletive. I did not know what I expected the first day on the job to be like, but I expected to at least not have a looming threat of a cult chasing after me. Vee glared at me, again, and beckoned me to follow her down the sidewalk.

"I've been a Geist for almost a month, and I feel like I know even less than I did day one," I mumbled. "Geist are crap."

"If you actually make me do work today, I'll throw you down the basement with all the other dead saps we find today."

"Don't get it twisted, Virginia." I rolled my eyes.

"If you call me Virginia one more time, Ashton, I will smack you upside the head." She brandished her pimp hand. "Upside. The. Head."

"Ha, yeah, I'll get the hands or whatever. But I want to be out here just as much as you do, possibly even less. So, let's get through the day and collect as few dead people as we can. Then I can come home, lie about how productive I was, and start drawing out a plan on how to overthrow a doomsday cult."

Vee smiled. She wrapped her arm around my shoulders as we walked. I had neither the energy nor the gusto to brush her off. Instead, I just stared at her, dead-eyed. She did not take the hint and instead pulled me closer to her hard, freezing body. Zinda Mansion was always way too cold so I completely forgot how Vee could make June feel like December. If someone tried to lick her, would their tongue stick? I shook the image out of my head, for multiple reasons.

"Overthrowing a doomsday cult! That's something I can get behind," she exclaimed. "Let's head over to my office, and we can get this day over with. Honestly, this crap isn't as soul-crushing as working fast food or whatever part-time job you had, but it's still awful. Just terrible."

"Never had a job," I droned.

"How old were you when you died?"

"Eighteen."

"Eighteen-years-old and you never had to get a job? You rich little brat."

Vee's "office" turned out to be a hospital. Appropriate, since it was the easiest place to find dying people. We entered the hospital after a rather uneventful and Brotherhood-free jog, and Vee instantly plopped down on one of the couches in the lounge. She patted the seat next to her, as if to say "pop a squat" or some other gross and vaguely sexual cliché. I sat down, close enough to still be within a friendly range but far enough away so I wouldn't have to interact with her. She moved closer to me, making all my efforts for naught. The entire lounge dropped a few degrees. A man winced at the sudden temperature drop and rolled down his sleeves.

"So, is this your definition of patrol?" I asked. "Sitting in a hospital and waiting for people to die?"

"Listen here, Princess." Vee slammed her boots onto the end table next to the couch. "I am dead. You are dead. For some horrible reason, before I died, some bitch 'blessed' me so I got stuck in this quasi-purgatory, and now I have to spend the rest of eternity going on long hikes around the city just so I can chaperone actual dead people into a whirlpool in our basement. Honestly, this isn't even purgatory, it's straight-up Hell. So, while the religious freaks back at Zinda get their rocks off acting like shepherds all day, I'm going to spend my well-deserved immortality as far away from dead people as I can."

I imagined a future, around 2155, where I was still carting around dead people, except they were all cyborgs speaking in binary and memes. An eternity of that sounded absolutely miserable.

Vee opened her book. I took a peek at the cover, which showed a well-oiled man and a triceratops embracing under the title *Alien Dinosaurs Can Get It*. I raised my eyebrow. Did I even want to ask about those books? What if they had something to do with the balloon room? I kept my mouth shut. There were more important questions to ask.

"So, before you get too far into that novel of yours, you probably should explain some basics."

"I was hoping you forgot." Vee shut her book and dramatically rolled her face in my direction. "Ghosts go into portals. Geist build houses around portals. Geist gerrymander a territory for each house and then grab ghosts so they can shove them into the portals. It's pretty simple, so don't ask me again."

"What happens if we don't bring the ghosts to the portal?"

"I don't know. Apocalypse, maybe. I was just told that bad things happen. Don't bother trying to ask anyone else, either.

You won't get a straight answer." Vee reopened her novel. "Any other questions before I get back to my book? Because Captain Brockway is about to do very naughty things to By'Lungar's alien tricera-anus and I really want to have my full attention on the scene."

"How old is everyone? I've got a pretty good idea about when Clementine was born, but I haven't talked to Johanna enough to know much about her. I've been trying to get a rough estimate by what ethnic slurs they use, but they both seem pretty PC."

"And thank their god, because you don't want to know how many Geist in this stupid town still call me Oriental." A dry laugh escaped her throat. "Johanna's super old. That Puritan Bible of hers is a pretty good clue. The other two are younger, but still old as balls. Probably around eighty or ninety."

"What about you?"

"Nice try, Princess, but you're not getting anything outta me."

Vee shoved her face into her book, no doubt eager to continue reading about the budding romance of Captain Brockway and By'Lungar. She leaned back into the couch and shoved her face closer to the novel. I had a billion other questions, but Vee would, no doubt, answer none of them. Johanna and Clementine would also, no doubt, keep their mouths shut. It was entirely possible Jesse knew even less than I did, if that was possible. An eternity of unanswered questions and vaguely defined duties laid ahead of me. Geist were crap.

With Vee done "training" me, it was time to occupy myself. I slapped my headphones on and rummaged through my messenger bag to find something distract me until someone died. I reached for *Sweet Clementine, Vol. 3*. Before my fingers even touched the cover, though, my new phone buzzed. I pulled the little brick out of my pocket. I received a text from an unknown number.

Heeeeey. I heard you're on patrol. See any dead bodies yet?

Ominous. I quickly texted back asking who it was. And by quickly, I meant it took five tries to spell one word because the buttons were tiny and I had no idea how to use technology from when I was a toddler—not counting the iPod. Eventually, though, I finished the complete text.

It's Olive. I hope you're having fun. Anyway, ask Vee what a Revenant is.

My eyes bulged almost out of my head. I looked in every direction. Not a sign of Olive. I grumbled and shoved my phone back into my pocket. I tapped my foot on the ground. I grumbled some more. Vee was still reading her book about a triceratops becoming a tricerabottoms. Against my better judgment, I tapped Vee on the shoulder.

"Vee, what's a Revenant?"

"Like some kinda priest."

"No, that's a rever…" I stopped myself and sighed.

I should have known better than to ask. I shoved Olive and Revenants to the back of my brain as I pulled out Jesse's book. The book looked old enough to rent a car, so I opened it carefully so the front cover didn't turn to dust. I almost shrieked when I saw what was inside. There was page-after-page of poetry, and something inside of me, something messy and a little evil, wanted me to read each one.

<u>*Spiral*</u>
Eighteen million stars dim in your presence.
Cracks in your skin reveal the sun you hide
And you illuminate space with such brightness
It blinds me, and all I can do now
Is feel the burning heat from your radiant body.

Two swirling bodies pull each other
Into a force of gravity nothing can break.
Every night our bodies create a galaxy
In which two black holes collide
And create a force so great,
Space around us wrinkles.
I burst into you and explode
And turn you into a universe of our own.
I claw your back and peel away the skin
Keeping your sun veiled from me.
Your scream is lost in the vacuum,
But I can still hear your breath.
With a mighty scream, the last piece floats away
And I am a satellite to a woman glowing.

My entire body turned pink. Even with Vee's icy aura, the room became hotter, at least by fifteen degrees. One of the women sitting across the lounge shifted uncomfortably and fanned her chest. Vee remained unperturbed.

My head was filled with visions of Clementine and Jesse's sex life. Jesse throwing Clementine onto a bed. Clementine licking her lips. Jesse ripping his shirt off and tossing the shreds onto the floor. Clementine's granny panties flying across the room. Both of them slowly crawling toward each other, ready to go at it for the six billionth time.

The temperature rose again. Something felt extremely hot. My breathing stopped, and I jumped off the couch. A tiny blue fire burned right in my butt-groove. I recoiled and tripped over the end-table, falling flat on my ass. Vee pulled her face out of her book and looked at me, then the tiny fire, then me again, then the tiny fire.

"Princess, the couch is on fire."

"Yes, I am aware!" I screamed.

No one in the room noticed the fire. Even the smoke detector remained silent. The fire, though, still danced flamboyantly around my seat. Vee tossed her book onto the end table and stood up. She flicked her hand, like she was swatting away a fly. A flurry of diamond dust flew from her palm and twirled around the fire. Before the fire could spread any further, it drowned, leaving only a chilly puddle of water.

Vee had ice powers. Clementine had wind powers. And to my terrible, terrible horror, the incident with Gabriel wasn't a fluke. I, Ashton Matthew Murphy, gained control of fire.

My eyes strained to stay open. I wanted to say something to Vee, something sarcastic and sassy, but the only word running through my head was "Fire!" Vee stepped over the end table and stood over my prone body. She kneeled down and grabbed Jesse's book. I finally blinked and reached for the book. Vee swatted my hand away and looked through it.

Vee stopped on one page and slid her eyes around the words. I stood up just in time for her to laugh so uncontrollably that her eyes started to flash between Geist-mode and human-mode. A few people in the room actually turned to look at her. Everyone went back to ignoring us once Vee shut up and her eyes turned black again.

"Oh, you found Cooter's poetry collection!" she laughed. She flipped through the pages. "Which book is this? God, I hope it's the one with the poem where he calls Clementine an 'iced tea drinkin' angel of love.' Lemme tell ya, thinking about Clementine doing anything sexy at all makes me wheeze. She probably doesn't even understand half these innuendos." Vee moved her head closer to me, smirking. "Is that how you set the couch aflame? Are his poems stirring a fire in your loins? Maybe you and Coots should go at it. That way, he'll finally pop his man-cherry, because you know Clem's not gonna do it."

I pulled the book out of her hands and sat back down on the couch, avoiding the puddle. My bag fell over when I collapsed onto the seat. A few fingers of the gauntlet emerged from the opening. Before I could tuck them back in, Vee pulled the entire gauntlet out of my bag.

"Oh. Oh look. Here's another thing you gotta tell me about."

Even though I didn't want to, I explained to Vee how I snatched the glove from Dinah. I put a lot of emphasis on how I totally beat her in a fight, one-on-one, without using any dirty tricks. She looked bemused. At no point did Vee seem engaged in my story. She was more interested in pressing random buttons on the gauntlet.

"And then I kicked one of the boys and his shirt spontaneously combusted."

"Uh-huh."

"How much of the story do you actually care about?"

"Basically none, but I do like how you clearly cheated your way to stealing this." Vee slid her hand into the gauntlet and wiggled her fingers. Her eyes lit up. "Never seen one of these before."

"Seriously? They all have them."

"They actually don't. Clementine said they only started using these things two months ago." Her eyes were still fixated on the gauntlet. "Plus, I don't mess with the Brotherhood. You wanna know why? Because I'm smart. I have dealt with the Brotherhood a grand total of three times in all my years doing this. That's because I have a few rules. One, don't take any backstreets. Duh. And two, stay in populated areas." Vee gestured to the many people sitting around us. "So, if anyone ever finds out that I'm just lazing about here—" she leaned extra close to me. "—and they won't, I can just say I'm hiding out from the Brotherhood. Why'd you bring this thing along, Princess? Thinking about signing up for the Brotherhood yourself?"

"No, I'm going to dismantle them."

That sounded less ridiculous in my head, and I regretted saying it the second it came out of my mouth. Vee cackled again, pulled the gauntlet off, and tossed it into my bag. She stood up and stretched her arms. Grabbing me by my shoulder, Vee pulled me off of the couch. The two of us stood face-to-face, the first time either of us had ever made direct eye contact.

"You think you can take down the Brotherhood? Do you even know how to fight?" she asked. "Punch me."

"Excuse me?"

"Should I spell it? P-U-N—"

"No, shut up, I know what you said."

Gift horse. Mouth. I curled my hand into a fist. As hard as I could, I slammed it into Vee's chest. I definitely hurt my hand more than I hurt Vee. She looked down at my fist and grabbed it. She uncurled my fingers and readjusted them into a better fist.

"Well, first off, your thumb needs to be against your index finger, not under it. Otherwise, you'll break it. You know, if you weren't dead."

I punched her again, trying to give one-hundred and eighty percent of my strength into it. Once again, Vee didn't budge, and my hand felt like it just punched a statue. Every inch of Vee was covered in a thick, un-punchable layer of muscle and ice.

"What's wrong, kid? Are your limp wrists throwing you off?"

Two hundred percent! I punched her a little lower, right in the kidney. My knuckles were freezing with each punch, but I wanted her to at least feel a little pain. Sadly, the only punishment

I could give her were tiny bug bites. My fist ricocheted off of Vee's abdomen like a pinball. She laughed.

"Do yourself a favor. Next time you see a Brother, just kick 'em in the 'nads and run."

Before I could say anything snippy, my necklace began to glow. A beam of blue line shot right toward the ceiling. A horrible little sensation like an animalistic instinct told me that I needed to go upstairs. Vee grumbled and looked up at the ceiling as well. A trickle of teal light was shooting upward from her cleavage as well.

"Some asshole died, and now we gotta get his ass out of bed."

Vee and I grabbed our things and left the lounge. Vee pulled me into an elevator and slid her hand across every single button. We stopped at each floor, checking to see where exactly our Mementos were pointing us. When we reached the fourth floor, we were greeted by horrible screaming.

"I'm not dead!" yelped a shrill, young voice.

Vee glanced over at me, and we both walked to where the lights were leading us, which was unsurprisingly also where the yelping was coming from. As we walked by rooms in the hallway, no one else noticed the man's shrieks. Either the screams were coming from a ghost or doctors had grown really apathetic.

Vee stopped me in front of the door where all the screaming was coming from. We peeked through the open door. A doctor and a few nurses hovered over a fresh cadaver. Next to them, a short translucent man screamed into their ears things like "Look at me!" and "I can't be dead!" along with a number of cuss words. Every time the man said "Look at me!" a little flashback went off in my head. I did my best to stay in the present.

Vee and I walked into the room. My steps were calculated and quiet, making sure not to startle the recently-deceased boy. Vee barged in, flat-footed and slouching, not caring of such formalities. The ghost's head twisted so quickly toward Vee I almost heard a snap.

"Normally, they aren't this frantic," droned Vee, "but once in a while, some turd—"

"You!"

The ghost stumbled onto the bed and huddled against his former body. Vee took another step closer, and he sprinted to the wall. He grabbed a lamp from the bedside table, ripping its cord out of the socket. The ghost flung the lamp over the bed, narrowly missing a nurse's head. I ducked, but Vee stood still. Right before the lamp hit her square in the jaw, she grabbed it and threw it right back. The lamp smashed into the ghost's head and shattered. The nurse walked around the scattered porcelain, but continued to ignore any supernatural presence. The ghost, rubbing his translucent head, skulked around the other side of the bed, searching for anything to pick up and, I assumed, throw at Vee.

"You did this!" he yelped. "You hideous demons couldn't stick with murdering the unenlightened, could you? You had to kill me, too!"

"Hideous?" I spat. "Oh. Wait. Hideous demons. You're with the Brotherhood, aren't you?"

"Do not speak of the Brotherhood of Eternity with such contempt!"

Eternity? Vee and I looked at each other, no doubt thinking of the same insults for him. The boy clawed at us, making somewhat intimidating gestures and threats while staying behind the bed and unaware hospital staff. He was like a drunk frat boy who kept asking for his buds to "hold him back" from a fight, but no one was holding him back, so he had to improvise. I would have laughed if my stomach was not so heavy.

The Brother looked unfamiliar to me. He was not at the big

Brotherhood fight. From the look of his emaciated body on the bed, he had been in that room much longer than a few weeks. The fury in the Brother's face was missing from his corpse. In its stead was a weak frown on a cold, weathered face. Whatever killed the Brother, it destroyed him from the inside.

"But I'm not dead yet!" the ghost said, puffing out his chest.

"You clearly are!" said Vee, gesturing toward his corpse.

"If you think you can murder me, you'll have to catch me first!"

The Brother jumped over the bed. Vee reached forward to grab him. He pushed her hands away and slid right by her. He headed for the door. I realized right there that it was my chance to show up Vee. Even if I couldn't punch her, I knew I could outrun her. The Brother ran right out the door and, while Vee stood still, tapping her foot, I sprinted out the door.

"Stop running, you moron!" Vee called.

He skittered down the hospital hallway like a cockroach. He was running so quickly, I barely saw his legs hit the ground. I kept sprinting, keeping my pace with the bug-boy. Vee chased after us, showing more energy than I had ever seen her exert.

Our clanking footsteps filled the barren halls of the hospital. Right before the running man was about to collide head-on with a nurse, she stepped aside to read a random plaque next to a random door. We continued to run, uninterrupted.

Vee kept screaming "Stop!" The ghost grabbed a gurney from against the wall and rolled it to block our path. He thought a hurdle was gonna stop me? I increased my speed and leaped. Like a graceful gazelle, I flew through the air. Before I cleared it, my foot collided with its handles, making the whole thing slide under me. I let out a loud squeak and plummeted to the floor. I got back up and kept running, knowing Vee wasn't going to let me live that down.

The ghost headed straight for a window. He looked back at me, then kept running forward. He wanted to make an epic, melodramatic escape by crashing through the glass. Typical. Vee's cries became louder, but I ignored them. I was going to get the ghost before Vee, and that motivation helped block out her screams.

"I said freeze!" she said.

The pun made me look back at Vee. Her entire fist was covered in a thick sheet of ice. Vee punched the tile, causing the frost to pulse toward the ghost and me. Spear-like icicles shot out of the floor. The frost slid past me and reached the ghost. As the icicles shot out of the frost, I tried to avoid the oncoming onslaught. Before I could slip past, an icicle shot out of the tile I was standing on and pierced through my foot. I tried to scream, but only a confused wheeze came out.

The Brother was only a few feet away from the window. He reached out to the window, ready to jump. Vee had other ideas. At the end of the streak of frost, at least a dozen icicle spears shot out and impaled him through the chest. His whole body went limp.

As I continued to wheeze, Vee skidded her way over to the two of us. She danced her fingers along the icicles on her way over to me. Vee took a look at my speared foot, grabbed my leg, and yanked my foot out of the icicle. I wheezed a bit more, then I realized the icicle left no mark. One second there was a hole in my foot, the next second, nothing.

"Don't be such a pussy," she hissed. "We're dead. Nothing hurts."

Vee pressed her palm onto one of the icicles. The point pierced her skin, and she slid her palm down further. I inhaled. The icicle went through her whole hand, and the gash got larger as she kept going down the icicle. She pulled her hand out of the ice, showing that no mark was left, as if nothing had cut her.

"I told you to stop! Don't you know anything about ghosts?"

"You're supposed to be teaching me, not trying to kill me!" I booed.

"Again?" She smirked. I glowered. "Ghosts can only move around things with spiritual energy. You know, their corpses, the portal, and Geist Mementos. Just like how you can't go anywhere without your Memento." Vee reached into her shirt. She pulled out a dog tag attached to a ball chain around her neck. Before I could read anything on the tag, she shoved it back into her cleavage. "It's first-grade stuff. Got it memorized?"

I checked back over with the Brother. Vee and I crept closer to him. While the ice behind us started to melt, the spears in his chest stayed frozen. The Brother remained perfectly limp except for his eyes. He stared right at us, unable to speak but probably cursing us in his head. I huddled with Vee, whispering so the ghost couldn't hear us.

"What should we do about him?" I asked.

"Flush him down the basement like the rest of them, obviously."

"No, we could use him."

"Are you saying you want to interrogate him?" Vee scoffed. "God, *please* play with matches."

"He just told us the Brotherhood's full name. What else do you think he'll tell us?" I looked back at the ghost. "And, honestly, he seems like the monologue-ing type."

Vee walked closer to the Brotherhood ghost. Keeping a lazy, half-interested look on her face, Vee jerked the Brother out of the icicles, not even trying to remove him with any elegance. The icicles snapped, and Vee slung the ghost over her shoulder.

"Alright, we'll play your game." Vee stretched her back. She leaned in really close to me and poked my chest. I could feel her icy breath fill my lungs as she snarled right into my face. "But on one condition."

A half-hour later, Vee and I reentered Zinda Mansion with Vee carrying the ghost and me carrying five bags of fast food. Clementine, Jesse, and Johanna emerged from the living room when we got back. As I dropped the food off in the dining room, Vee dropped the ghost onto the floor of the foyer.

"Hey, everyone, we're back, and we brought Mexican! Who's ready to rock out with their guac out?" Vee smirked. "Also, we brought back some douche from the Brotherhood."

Everyone else hurried closer. Clementine looked down at the beaten ghost and clutched her metaphorical pearls. The ghost, shaking, got to his feet. Vee held the back of his neck like a vice grip.

"We are called the Brotherhood of Eternity!" he spat, still winded from the beating Vee gave him in the hospital. And the two other beatings she gave him on the way home. "Do you understand the mistake you wretches made?"

"Oof. Cringe. How old are you? Sixteen?" Vee chuckled.

The ghost's fist twitched. Vee tightened her grip. Clementine walked forward, her dress flapping with her rushed steps, and batted Vee's hand away from the spirit's neck. Clementine stared at the ghost in his pale eyes, but he turned away. She craned her head to try to match the gaze again.

"You look familiar, hon. Your name's Paul, ain't it?" Clementine sighed. "I knew it had been a while since I'd seen your face around town. I'm so sorry."

Paul glared at Clementine. Johanna glided forward, staring down at him. It wasn't until I saw him standing still next to

Johanna that I realized how small he was. He looked so delicate, like I could snap him in half with a nutcracker. How a boy like that ended up in the Brotherhood was unknown to me.

"Paul, were you in the Brotherhood?" asked Jesse.

"Brotherhood of Eternity," corrected Vee. "Gotta keep the pretention."

"I've been a member of the Brotherhood of Eternity for ten years." Paul tried to arch his back to look taller, even if he was barely bigger than Clementine. "It took you this long to kill me, but if you think you can keep this up, you're wrong. Father Abram's working on something that can finally send you demons back to Hell where you belong!"

Abram. I clenched my jaw and reached into my messenger bag. Everyone else stared at me when I pulled out the gauntlet. Paul stomped his foot. Vee grabbed his neck again to keep him from charging at me.

"This the something you're talking about?" I asked.

"How'd you get a gauntlet?" he growled.

"Stole it off Dinah."

"If Dinah had a gauntlet when she saw you, there's no way you'd still be alive." Paul jutted his jaw out. "Dinah Jonas was personally trained by Father Abram to lead the charge against Geist in this city."

"Who the hell is Father Abram?" I shouted, much louder than I intended.

I took a few steps forward, sandwiching Paul between the five Geist. Paul's eyes lit up, as if he was staring into the sun. He smiled, looking around at all of us, basking in our confused expressions. I'd found the secret word, and the monologue I was looking for was about to come. A chill shot down my spine.

"Father Abram's the only man on Earth who's brave enough to kill Death. He is the Second Advent. He is the savior who gave us the power to see you demons, and now he's given us the power to kill you." Paul's whole body shook. I felt like it was only a matter of time before he started speaking in tongues. "Because we know how to do it now! We've figured it out! All we need to do is destroy your source of Orgone Energy and then you'll be banished to Hell where you belong! When the Brotherhood of Eternity grows strong enough, Father Abram will come down like the fire of God."

None of us had a response to that. Even Vee was speechless. Clementine's breath was so heavy, it rattled my bones. I gripped my necklace, trying to use the warmth of the metal to calm me. It took me a grand total of half a second to realize what he meant by "source of Orgone Energy." The Brotherhood of Eternity became more than just a crazy lightning cult. Right then, they became something scary.

Johanna remained poised. She gripped Paul's shoulder and pulled him toward the doors to the basement. Vee, Clementine, Jesse, and I backed away from Johanna. Paul shook Johanna off and ran off toward the front door. When he got a few feet away from her, he was stopped in his tracks by an invisible wall. As Johanna walked closer to the basement, Paul was dragged by the wall, and he came closer and closer to the portal.

"We apologize for the grief we brought you during your life," Johanna said. "The fear we have caused you was toxic to your existence. I hope that, in the next life, you will be able to find it in your heart to forgive us."

"Shut up!" he yelled. Paul lost his footing and fell to the floor, still being dragged along to the door to the basement. "You all have your hands in the deaths of everyone on Earth. I'll forgive you when every one of you is boiling in the deepest layer of Hell!"

Johanna grabbed the doorknob to the basement. She kept her hand on it for a while, not looking back at anyone else. Paul stood back up and tried to escape his invisible prison to no avail. Johanna turned her head slightly, still not looking at anyone.

"I truly am sorry," she said.

Johanna swung the door open. She flew through the doors and disappeared into the darkness. With her every step, Paul slid closer to the door. He pounded against the invisible wall. Paul was knocked off his feet again, tumbling along the floor. He clawed at the floor, his barely visible nails scraping along the tile and creating an echo of pain through the foyer. Even from across the room, I saw terror in his eyes.

"Stop! Don't!" Paul screamed. His voice cracked, turning his voice from a thunderclap to a tiny drizzle. "I don't want to die."

The wall dragged Paul into the darkness of the basement. Clementine, Jesse, Vee, and I were left in the foyer, listening to the slowly quieting sobs coming from the basement. The three of us remained frozen until the sobs stopped. Vee was the first to leave, heading into the dining room to eat her dinner. Jesse gave Clementine a quick hug and said he was going head up to their room. Clementine squeezed my hand a few times and told me that I did a good job on my first day, then headed upstairs.

I stayed in the foyer for a little longer. I simply sat down on the stairs, eyes locked on the basement door. The claw marks by the doors were much larger than any damage Paul's small hands could have done. Paul's sobs still echoed in my head, even when I knew he was gone. Still, I waited for Johanna to emerge. And as I sat there, shaking, I decided that I hated my job.

Chapter 7
Give Us Faith

Clementine had been knocking on my bedroom door for two minutes before I heard her. I apologized to her, saying something about the music or how I was napping. I forgot my excuse the second I said it. Clementine was dressed in a nightgown, with her hair all wrapped up for bedtime. It took me a bit to realize just how late it was and how long I had locked myself in my room.

"I'm sorry your first day was a mess. I know that the Brotherhood can get a little persnickety sometimes, but they ain't nothin' to fret over," Clementine said. Something weird I picked up on pretty quickly was that Clem's accent went completely off the rails whenever she was nervous. Most people stuttered, but she just went full Dolly Parton. "Guess I should'a known you and Vee'd have a big ol' adventure."

"Yeah, guess I'm a whimsy magnet." I rubbed my eyes. "What time is it?"

"It's almost ten, hon. You didn't come down to eat dinner."

Truth was, I didn't really want to talk to Clementine that much. I was not angry at her. It was impossible to be angry at that dimpled face. But I had a tiny bit of resentment in my heart that I didn't like. Paul's speech about the Brotherhood reminded me of how scary they were, even if Clem pretended we were peachy keen and perfect. If they only had access to the gauntlets for two months, Clementine seemed a little too confident that they were just a light nuisance. But considering how she left out the "you can turn off your invisibility" thing, too, I knew I needed to get used to her little lies of omission. I would not have been shocked if, one day, I morphed into a station wagon and Clementine was all "Oh, y'all didn't know we could do that? Thought I explained that to y'all, honey pie."

After I convinced her everything was fine, Clementine gave me a hug goodnight and went on her way. I leaned on my doorframe, thinking about what to do. Baking cakes and half-finishing books was not my ideal afterlife. I expected more flying and harp playing and fewer evil cults trying to evaporate me.

Before I put my headphones back on, I heard a different kind of music. It rang from across the hall, almost silently. I poked my head out my door and honestly should not have been surprised that the sound was coming from inside the music room. I walked along the hallway, with the gentle ting of piano keys growing louder with every step I took.

The music abruptly halted. I stopped moving when I heard voices from inside the room. I almost heard a whimper. I closed my eyes, took a deep breath, and pressed my ear up against the door.

"He did a fine job with the member of the Brotherhood today," one of the voices said. It was obviously Johanna's. "I hope that Paul's final words did not scare him."

"Sure scared me." I'd have to have been an idiot if I didn't know whose Southern twang that was. "What if he's right, Jo? What if this exorcism stuff ain't just big talk?"

"You have every right to be afraid," Johanna said. Her voice was much louder than it had been every other time she spoke to me. "They may very well have the ability to forcibly exorcize us. How long have they had access to the gauntlet exactly?"

"I only started seein' 'em around May," Clementine whispered. "Jo, we don't even know how those goggles work, let alone the gloves. He even mentioned Orgone Energy today, and I've never even heard that word. I don't—" she paused. I almost felt like I heard a whimper, but it might have been a chair scooting. "I'm scared."

I gritted my teeth. The last thing I needed was someone telling me I needed to panic. Clementine's lies of omission at least helped keep my heart rate in check. Hearing her actually mention being scared was going to put me into cardiac arrest.

A gust of air blew against the back of my neck, and all of my neck hairs froze. I almost screamed but covered my mouth so all that came out was a muffled wheeze. I turned around and saw, of course, Vee ready to mess with me.

She smirked at me, smiling wide enough to flash her prominent canines. I kept my mouth shut. I was in no mood to have a snappy chat with Vee after the day we had together. I headed the stairs, but Vee decided it was time to talk.

"Is Goody Proctor scaring you?" she called. I looked back at her. "Don't worry, she's just having her weekly meeting with Clem." I couldn't tell if she was smiling or sneering or about to sneeze. Either way, it wasn't a pretty sight. "Don't expect an invite, by the way. Apparently, they consider anyone under ninety too young to enter their secret club."

I grimaced. "How do you put up with this crap?"

"Drugs," she shrugged.

Vee left me and walked into the workout room. I tossed my hair out of my eyes and walked down the stairs. Nothing in the mansion could really take my mind off of anything that happened that day. I skipped past the second floor and stood in the foyer. The door to the outside was right in front of me.

Outside that door, I was free range for the Brotherhood of Eternity. They could ambush me the second I left the mansion and exorcize me. More importantly, outside that door was reality. Away from the undead and the magic basement and the special powers, I would be standing with living people who had no idea what waited after death. People who lived their lives without having to think about death every second of the day.

I pulled open the door and left Zinda Mansion. The intense wind almost pushed me back down the dark, marble stairs as they slowly disappeared behind me. I kept my balance and continued on. With no idea where to go, I picked a random direction and started walking down the street.

My hand grazed my pocket. My new-old cell phone was still lodged in there. I pulled it out, flipped it open, and did something really stupid. I dialed my dad's phone number, bit my thumb, and listened to the dial tone. It kept ringing, and each second he didn't answer felt like a sign to hang up. Instead, it went to voicemail.

My hands shook, and I decided to call my mom. After a few rings, there was silence. And suddenly, she spoke.

"Hello?" she asked. My heart jumped at the sound of her uneasy voice. "Hello?"

She hung up before I could reply. I clenched my jaw and held my breath. Then I punched in Faye's number. It only took one ring for her to answer.

"Hello?"

She was so tired I could barely hear her. I knew I needed to act fast. I prayed that she could at least hear me. I strained my brain and did everything I could to make myself "visible."

"Hi!" I stuttered, trying out my deepest voice. "Is Meredith there?"

"What?"

Faye heard me. I almost melted right there. Every emotion I could name flooded through me and I had no idea if I was supposed to laugh, cry, or sing. All I knew was that I needed to keep up my façade as long as possible.

"Meredith! I'm looking for Meredith." My voice cracked.

Hopefully, she didn't hear her dead grandson's voice. "This is her phone, right?"

"No, sorry, you must have the wrong number."

"Oh, my mistake." I forced a chuckle.

"It's okay, don't worry about it."

"No, I'm so, so sorry." My chuckling stopped and my voice started shaking again. "I'm sorry."

I hung up before I told her who I was. Because I would have, if I stayed on the line for another second. I shoved my phone into my pocket, pulled my iPod out, and blasted my music loud enough to drown my thoughts. Then, I started jogging. The direction didn't matter. All that mattered was the feel of my feet against the pavement.

A few blocks away from Zinda Mansion, I noticed a familiar face struggling outside an apartment complex. Yvonne Spears stood outside the front door, juggling three bags of groceries and her violin case. I kept walking. I knew better than to stop because I knew I'd try to help her. Right as I passed her, I heard the door open, and Yvonne sigh in relief.

"Thanks, James," she said.

My head shot back, and I would have vomited if I had anything in my stomach. The large Brother with the mousey hair grabbed one of Yvonne's bags and helped her through the door. James let go of the door and followed her in. Before the door shut, I ran up the steps, shoved in my foot, pulled the door back open, and strode right on inside.

Keeping a safe distance, I followed Yvonne and James up the stairs. He was wearing a simple T-shirt and shorts. No backpack, no large pockets, nothing to hide a pair of goggles or a gauntlet in—unless his large stomach was a ploy and he was actually a skinny dude with a bunch of weapons stuffed down his shirt. I remained cautious and channeled a hardboiled detective as I hid behind corners just out of eyesight.

Yvonne took out her keys and opened her apartment door. James handed back her groceries, and Yvonne slid into her room. He walked a few doors down, and I remained on the prowl. He unlocked his own apartment, and I tumbled in before he could close the door. And then I realized I just gave a Brother home field advantage. Goddammit.

"Gabe, I'm back!" he said. "Almost ready?"

Goddammit! But I remained calm. Even if I was invisible, I needed to do my best to *stay* invisible. James headed into his room and shut the door behind him. I kept my hand on the doorknob and studied the apartment. The sound of a running shower permeated the tiny living room. There seemed to be only two bedrooms, but the couch was folded out into a bed, so at least three people were living there. Nothing too fancy popped out to me. A television, a bookshelf, an acoustic guitar by the corner, a simple desk with a ratty laptop on it. An old iPod Nano—nearly identical to mine—was plugged into the laptop with a cable so frayed I wondered how the whole place hadn't burned down. A set of goggles also sat on the desk, but there were no gauntlets in sight. I edged closer to the bookshelf. The only actual books on the shelf were a few Bibles and a pocket Korean dictionary. The rest were cheap notebooks, and all the covers looked so worn they were about to turn to dust. I grabbed the least dilapidated notebook and a pen from the desk. Then, I sat down on the bed, crossed my legs, and opened to a clean page.

James. White male. Late teens to early twenties. Greyish-brown hair. Crooked nose. Patchy beard. I'd call him a bear, but he's probably not gay.

I kept writing down everything I could remember about James, from any distinct facial features to how well he fought in our big parking lot scuffle. The shower stopped and the bathroom door opened. I froze, but morbid curiosity told me to move. I peeked around a corner just in time to see Gabriel walk out of the shower, wearing nothing but a tiny towel that didn't even go down to his knees. I could see almost everything, from his tight pecs to his smooth thighs to the most defined v-line I had ever seen in my life. Without opening my mouth, I screamed like a shrill Muppet.

Gabriel opened the hall closet and pulled out some clothes. He walked closer to me, and I rolled down the foldout couch until I fell into the crevasse between the mattress and the frame. From my new hiding spot, I watched Gabriel as he tossed his clothes onto the bed. Black slacks, black socks, white button-down, black tie. He then tore off his towel, and I shoved my face into the notebook. I sure as hell didn't need to start another fire.

Gabriel. Asian (?) male. Late teens to early twenties. Around my height (I'm taller). Short black hair. Scorpion tattoo. ~~*Muscular and Hot*~~ MY MORTAL ENEMY

A door opened again, and when I looked away from the notebook, Gabriel was fully dressed. He rolled up his sleeves, grabbed the guitar next to the bed, and shoved it in its case. Then he pulled the iPod away from the laptop and gently slid it into his pocket. James walked out of his room, also dolled up and holding a guitar case.

"You ready?" asked James.

"I'm dressed, aren't I?" Gabe snapped.

"No, I mean, like, mentally." James inched closer, but Gabriel didn't answer. "Everyone's gonna be at the Sanctuary. I mean, we weren't close to Paul, but—"

"Doesn't matter if we weren't close. He was still family," he whispered.

James got closer to Gabriel and gave him a one-armed hug.

Gabriel shuddered but patted James on the back. Gabriel and James strapped the cases around their shoulders and headed out the door. I jumped out from the foldout and followed their every step, still keeping a safe distance. They exited their apartment, and I exited as well. They turned a corner; I turned a corner. Unless their guitar cases had hidden compartments, they were without gauntlets. My strides got longer, and before I knew it, I was barely three feet behind them, and I had nothing to worry about.

On another blank page, I scrawled out directions and landmarks as I followed. But as we continued, everything looked familiar. The roads became worse, the buildings grew darker, and the streets had fewer and fewer people crossing them. Within a few blocks, I knew exactly where we were going. I stopped taking notes and instead waited for the "abandoned" factory to come into view.

A gentle tapping sound came from behind me followed by a tiny squeal getting louder and louder. I jumped away from the Brothers, adrenaline pumping. A lime green marble bounced down the ground, rolling toward me, and my adrenaline shot down. A few feet behind it, a white-haired girl slid along the ground on her butt.

"EeeeeeeeeeeeeeeeeeHiAsheeeeeeeeeeeeeeee," she squeaked as she and the marble passed me.

She was careening right toward the Brothers, almost ready to bowl them down. I ran forward and stepped on the marble, stopping it under my foot. Thankfully, neither Brother noticed, and both kept walking. The girl skidded to a halt and stumbled to her feet. Her face was covered with dirt, and leaves were trapped in her frizzy hair. The girl rubbed her oversized sleeve across her face, removing most of the dirt and showing off the smiling freckled face of Teresa. She bent down and picked up the marble from under my feet.

"Thanks for stopping my lucky marble!" she said. "I was looking for you, and then I dropped it. But then it led me to you! And that's why it's my lucky marble." She held it up like a trophy.

"Why were you looking for me?" I whispered, my eyes darting to the Brothers.

"Clementine said you weren't home, so she wanted me to check up on you. She sounded frowny." Teresa shoved her marble into her sneaker. "What are you doing following those Mormons?"

"Espionage." I shook my stolen notebook. "And they're not Mormons, they're part of the Brotherhood."

"Hmm, this sounds like a very, very, very bad idea," said Teresa, pursing her lips.

"Wrong, it's actually a very, very, very good idea," I lied. "I've been planning this all week."

"What's your plan?"

"Those boys are heading to a 'Sanctuary,' where all the Brothers in town will be together." I suddenly realized how very, very, very bad my plan was, but I was in too deep. "I'm gonna take notes on every face I see, every weak spot in their defenses, everything." I sighed, my eyes growing wide. "Yeah."

Teresa peeped a little groan, but said "Okay." She kept her arm around me as we followed behind the Brothers. Whenever I got a little too close for her comfort, she'd pull back, and I'd slow down. I gritted my teeth. If I wanted to, I could have run forward and set both of those defenseless Brothers on fire. It would have served them right. But I just followed behind, keeping my eyes on the prize.

Teresa pulled back again and pointed ahead. We were within a stone's throw of the abandoned factory, and a giant mass of people was outside. A glow emanated from the hoard, but not the intense white glow of gauntlets. Everyone was holding a paper lantern. Teresa and I slid behind a corner and watched as Gabe and James walked into the horde.

"What's going on?" asked Teresa.

I exhaled. "They're mourning."

I crept a little closer to the horde, still keeping myself out of sight, and Teresa stumbled along. We both pressed ourselves against a dilapidated, windowless van mere yards from the horde. Dozens of people were in the parking lot, and for every badass that looked like they exorcized a million Geist, there was another who looked frail and had never even seen a Geist in person. Either they were in nice, church-ready clothes or they were in the nicest clothes they probably owned. One boy a bit closer to us was dressed in a polo much too big for him, with khakis that showed off his ankles.

I took out the notebook and started jotting down notes about every single Brother I could see. Even if I didn't know their names, I knew their faces and I knew who to avoid. But the further I got along in my notes, the more uniform it became. No one looked a day over thirty in the crowd. Some didn't even look like they could shave yet.

"There's no way this is the Brotherhood of Eternity," I whispered, my pen shaking. "These are—" a kid started weeping in the crowd, and an older Brother next to her started to comfort her "—children."

"Maybe they're like Robin. A bunch of little kids who can really kick butt!" she said, as if that was a good thing. "Geist start young, too. I became a Geist when I was six!"

"Oh my God," I stuttered.

"Don't worry, I don't remember dying. It was a long time ago and I was in a coma for seven months anyway."

"Oh my God!"

"Yeah, I dove into an empty pool. I think the doctors said I had 'massive brain trauma.' I don't really know what that means." She smiled off into the distance. "But I didn't mind. It was a very nice time. No stress, no worries, just a long nap."

I stared at Teresa's oddly calm face, absolutely bewildered and wondering if there was anything I could say. Thankfully, a little commotion came from within the Brotherhood horde. The doors of the factory burst open as Dinah made her less-than-grand entrance. Even when mourning, she still wore that horrible army jacket. She was followed by the same meek girl that was with her the night of my crash. She was slouched and a little shaky, but Dinah looked ready for a fight, standing tall on the top step.

"Brothers and Sisters, thank you all for coming together on such a somber night." Everyone was silent, listening to Dinah's every word. "Tonight we are gathered here to remember a Brother who was stolen from us. Paul Daniels, only seventeen, is the latest casualty in our fight against the Geist." She paused, letting her words soak in. "We knew this was coming. Paul's illness had only been getting worse in the past months. But he continued to push on, ready to battle the demons until his dying breath!"

"You have no idea," I mumbled, getting back to my note-taking.

Dinah Jonas. Evil.

"But while Paul's life on Earth may have ended, we must all remember that in the next life he has been given a seat next to God himself." Murmurs rumbled through the horde. "We, the Brotherhood of Eternity, are the modern Apostles! The masses may not believe us when we say that the Geist are the ones killing the holy, but God knows what is true! God does not give His people cancer! God does not give His people AIDS! The Geist are the ones who plant the seeds of death inside our bodies, and when they finally destroy us, that's when they laugh in the face of God!"

I peered up at her from my notebook. No goggles. No glove. Everyone else was holding unlit lanterns. I stood up from behind the car and walked toward the crowd. Teresa peeped and ran with me. She tried to pull me back, but I kept walking toward the preacher. Mourning or not, they were all idiots for leaving behind the only things that could hurt me. Fear flowed through my body, but it pushed me forward. As I walked into the crowd, not a single one noticed me. I stood right between two children, both crying and barely able to hold their lanterns straight. Teresa huddled against me. Even as she tried to convince me to leave, I kept my eyes dead-set on Dinah Jonas.

"But despite the pain and despite the fighting, we must remember that, while we fight monsters, we are only human. When Father Abram formed the Brotherhood of Eternity, he meant that we are a family. And, as the war goes on, we will lose the ones we love." Dinah almost sounded like she was holding back a sob. "Please allow Brothers Gabriel Wing and James Harvey to lead us in song."

Dinah and the frail girl left the steps, letting Gabriel and James take the "stage." They took their guitars out of the cases and strummed. A slow melody filled the somber parking lot, and suddenly, the stars seemed to shine through the clouds. One by one, the Brothers began to light their lanterns, almost in harmony with each note of Gabriel's guitar.

"We sing to you, our Lord, our God, to find our way back home. Give us faith and light our way. No path is set in stone."

In the windy Chicago night, with flickering lights all around him, Gabriel led the Brotherhood in song. Gabriel's rough, gravelly voice turned into something smooth, calming, and almost angelic. James sang in harmony, and around me, some of the Brothers joined in. I closed my eyes and took a deep breath.

"Here we are, showing our love through song. Won't you please fix our shattered lives and show us how to go on?" The melody turned more upbeat, but Gabriel's voice cracked. "Give us faith, our God. Please, give us faith."

En masse, each Brother let go of their lantern. The lanterns began to drift into the air like little hot air balloons. The wind batted around the lanterns, making them dance in the moonlight. As the wind pulled the lanterns toward downtown, Gabriel and James continued their song, and the Brotherhood joined in.

"Give us faith, our God. Please, give us faith," sang the entire Brotherhood.

I rubbed my forehead. "We should go."

I pulled Teresa out of the congregation. We walked away from the concert, and I kept walking until the music was only a little hum in my ears. When I knew I was away from the Brotherhood, I allowed myself to sit down on a stoop and think about what I saw. Teresa sat down with me, rocking back and forth.

"How much do you know about the Brotherhood, Teresa?" I asked.

"Hmm? Oh, not much. They're no biggie," she said, as if she wasn't frightened out of her mind barely a minute ago.

I paused. "And do you know how I got fire powers?"

"Well, we all get special powers. It depends on how you die, though. I was in a coma for a long time, so I make people sleepy." She tapped her heel against the stoop. "I guess you got fire powers 'cause you got in that crash."

I paused again. "What about Revenants?"

Teresa looked at me, scrunching her face. "What're those?"

I sighed and flipped through my notes. Most of the descriptions looked the same. Early teens, early teens, early teens, early teens. I rubbed my forehead, wondering what I even accomplished. Wondering if I could ever accomplish anything. I closed the ratty notebook and stood up.

"You're sweet for coming out, Teresa, but you don't need to worry about me. If Clementine calls again, you can tell her I'm on my way home."

"Okay, Ashy-Bash. Get home safe." She clapped. "Oh! And I planted a new batch of lilies in our greenhouse today! Next time you come by, I should show you around!"

Teresa gave me a loose hug and waltzed away. After a few steps, she slammed into an invisible wall. She turned back to the stoop, bent down, and picked up the marble that fell out of her shoe. Then she left for real, walking like a drunken pirate.

I stood there for a little while longer. My anger toward the Brotherhood was being muddled by the look of terror in the eyes of the children in the crowd. The tears in their eyes. The song they sang. I couldn't even move. I wanted to go home, but my feet were stone.

The wind picked up again, and I heard footsteps coming near me. Gabriel was making his way down the street, walking alone and in a hurry. His guitar wobbled as his steps became more sporadic. He slowed down for a second, reached into his pocket, and pulled out his ancient iPod. He shoved his earbuds into his ears. His steps slowed down, and, slowly, he came to a stop. Right in front of me.

My heart raced. Maybe it was fear. Or maybe it was pity. His eyes were so dark, I could not tell where his irises ended and his pupils started, but I could see how wet they were. His hand quaked as he gripped his iPod. He looked toward the sky and shut his eyes, letting out a deep breath, and then he wiped away any tears before they fell. I gritted my teeth and looked around. I knew I was safe.

"Hey," I said. "Sorry about Paul."

Gabriel shuddered. He turned his head, staring right at me. Both of us stood paralyzed by the stoop, eyeballing each other. He tore his headphones out of his ears and jumped away. My heart skipped several beats. Gabriel inched away from me. His heavy breathing slid through his gritted teeth. His eyes were wider than I had ever seen eyes get.

"Ash?"

Gabriel ran away from me, full-throttle. I could almost see the cloud of dust he left behind. A Gabriel-shaped puff, à la Wile E. Coyote.

A tiny glint on the ground caught my eye. I knelt down and took a closer look. Gabriel's iPod rested on the cold ground. I reached down and picked it up. My iPod and his were practically identical. I had a weird feeling in my gut that I really hoped wasn't guilt. I looked back in the direction where he ran, wondering if I should track my mortal enemy down in a city of almost three million people. I sighed and put his iPod in my pocket, then took out mine and started my journey home.

I made it back to Zinda Mansion well past midnight. I checked the time on my iPod, hoping it wasn't as late as I thought it was. Turned out, it was later. Guilty as a whore in church, I tiptoed my way into the mansion. I shut the doors as quietly as I could and slid up the marble stairs, using my iPod as a flashlight. There was absolutely no natural lighting in the underground manor, so I had no way of seeing anything. The hallways were still unfamiliar to me, so on my way through the second floor, I slammed my hip into every end table there was.

I crept up to the third floor. The second my foot hit the old carpet, a scuffling came from Clementine's room. The door opened and Clementine, still in her nightgown and head wrap, zoomed out. Despite the blinding light inside, Jesse was sound asleep in his separate bed, snoring louder than humanly possible. Clem's face was calm but her body language told a completely different story. The hallway was lit only by the light coming from her room, outlining a dark Clementine in a dim glow.

"You surprised me," she finally muttered. "Figured you wasn't the type for midnight runs."

"Just needed to clear my head," I breathed. "Sorry I kept you up so late. You could've just called me."

"Nah, I wasn't worried." She rubbed her eyes. "I was just readin'."

Even in the dim light, Clementine's face cracked and showed a frown. I walked up to her and wrapped my arms around her shoulders. She did the same.

"You're a terrible liar," I said. "I didn't want to worry you. It's just been a rough day."

"I know." Clementine pulled away from the hug. She stared into my eyes and started rubbing my cheek with her thumb. "No one asks for a life like ours. It ain't exactly a gift. And you'll have a lot of days like this." She took a deep breath. "But that don't mean it can't be great. You can find so much goodness in this life, you just gotta look real hard. Whaddya say you and I have a big day out downtown when we've both got a free day?"

"I'd love to." I flashed her a wide smile. "Get to bed. You've got patrol tomorrow."

Clementine walked back into her room and shut the door. I slammed down onto my bed and stared up at that unfamiliar ceiling. I thought about Clementine's protective lies and the Brotherhood's humanity, and I absolutely hated it. I sat up and rubbed my eyes. My ears perked up when a faint sound came from outside my room. I nudged my door open and the sound became a little louder. Someone was in the music room, playing the piano again. The quiet notes echoed into my room, and I slid back into bed. Within a few minutes, I fell asleep.

Chapter 8
On Patrol

The morning after my espionage, I found a letter written in Clementine's adorably swirly handwriting taped to my door. Clementine had left in the early morning to patrol the city, stressing that she totally wasn't tired or anything. She left ten dollars for me to go out for breakfast. Across the block sat a nice little breakfast café called Dream Bean. Clementine underlined the sentences "Don't bother feeding Vee. She's a grown woman and can fend for herself" several times.

After going through my morning routine, I took Clementine's advice and headed to the café. The café stuck out like a sore thumb and seemed to be the only gentrified building in the neighborhood. Whoever owned the place must've really been pretending he was living in Brooklyn. When I walked into Dream Bean, I was greeted by a really crappy acoustic cover of a Salt-N-Pepa song. I looked up at the menu, and everything looked familiar, only with "quirky" names and cheaper prices than a certain popular coffeehouse that it desperately wanted to be.

I stepped in line. A man strode in through the door and cut in front of me. Either I was still unnoticeable or he was just a giant dick. Focusing on my reflection in the display case, I tried my hardest to do that eye trick again. I tried the same trick I did with Gabriel to get these people to notice me. I was hungry, dammit, and if another person cut, I'd start punching throats.

I made my way up to the front of the line. The barista, a college-aged girl with a purple undercut and giant gauges, stared right at me with dead eyes.

"Nice hair," she said.

"Oh hell yeah!" I glanced back at the display case, seeing a nearly-human-looking Ash staring back at me. "I mean, thanks, you too. I'll have, uh, whatever you guys call a tall mocha Frappuccino."

"A nano choco Frappédaco?" Every word that came out of her mouth must have tasted like crap, because the face she made could've curdled milk.

"That's terrible."

"I know," she said under her breath.

I added a bowl of oatmeal to my order and paid, keeping my eyes on the barista the entire time. She grimaced at me, no doubt creeped out by my constant eye contact. She handed me my change, and I hummed a little victory tune. My first successful interaction with a living person.

A few minutes later, the barista finished my order, and I walked back to the counter. She called my name a few times, droning each syllable. The barista stifled and readjusted her septum piercing. She peered around the room, looking right through me and then continuing on. I grunted, then tapped her on the shoulder. She almost spilled my not-Frappuccino all over her ironic T-shirt.

"Christ! Don't sneak up on me like that!"

"Yeah, sorry, I keep a low profile," I droned.

I took my breakfast from the barista and sat down at a table outside on the patio. I took a sip of my coffee, froze, and then slowly put it down and stared off into the distance. After more than a month of being dead, I had no idea why Geist needed to eat or drink.

Geist anatomy confused me, but I had been putting things together, piece by piece. Even if Geist hair grew white and gray, we could do anything we wanted with it. Judging by all the stuff

Clementine put in her hair, we could cut, sculpt, and dye it any way we wanted.

Geist produced bodily fluids, such as spit, tears, and the other obvious ones. But we didn't bleed. And despite living with three women, I had seen no sign of any tampon, pad, or gross colonial menstrual rag, which meant that Geist didn't get periods and, therefore, were infertile. But, as I learned through my copious amounts of post-mortem alone time, Geist with my equipment didn't have that issue. Either that or I finally learned what ectoplasm really was.

Perhaps most confusing of all were my earrings. Despite getting a "new body" that healed cuts and broken bones instantly, I still had my two piercings. Winona herself always wore a fierce pair of peacock feather earrings. So, even if Geist could have been killed by being ripped apart, eviscerated, and burned, then return with perfectly healed bodies, they could still come back with unhealed holes in their ears.

Geist were crap.

My eyes focused on something in the distance. From my seat in the café, I saw Clementine and Jesse walking to the mansion, holding a little translucent boy in a white robe. I smiled at the cute scene. Clementine and Jesse, with an adorable ghost child, looking like a family. I looked closer. The toddler was crying. From the distance, a tiny "Mama!" echoed. Clementine kept her head buried in the toddler's shoulders as Jesse kept her close to his side. My appetite disappeared.

I still had two days before I had to start my own patrol. To say I was panicking would be to say the Black Plague killed a few people.

My biggest concern was obvious. If I got caught by the

Brotherhood of Eternity while alone, they would serve me to Father Abram with an apple in my mouth. At my disposal, I had a stolen gauntlet, untested fireballs, and a decent-enough right hook. None of those could possibly help me in a real fight against a senior Brother, so I needed to train. Clementine's combat prowess seemed to be entirely ballet and gusts of wind, so she was out of the question. Johanna and I said maybe three words to each other since I moved in. Also out of the question. Jesse was a tall, muscular man with a giant heart and a penchant for bear hugs. If he tried to teach me to wrestle, I knew exactly what would happen. Extremely out of the question. Using all the courage I had, I walked in on Vee while she was in her secret garden. Joint firmly planted in between her lips and erotica firmly grasped, she peered up from her book with bloodshot eyes.

"I need you to teach me to fight," I said.

"No."

"I'll bake you more brownies."

"Brownies first."

Stoned Vee was nicer than regular Vee. Noted. We walked down to the kitchen, and I started my kitchen prep. Vee hopped onto the kitchen island and rested her head on the stovetop.

The joke was on Vee since I could make brownies in my sleep. Melt the butter and baking chocolate, crack the eggs, add the dry ingredients, mix until gooey and decadent. Zack always splashed in extra vanilla. His signature. I put the hand mixer into the chocolate and turned it on low. For her intense aversion to technology, Clementine kept a lot of kitchen gadgets.

"So, what're you gonna teach me?" I asked, licking a droplet of chocolate off my thumb. "Cause I was thinking that maybe karate might be something easy, but I saw this documentary about capoeira a few years ago and that might be—"

"Martial arts are a myth," she snarled. "You think that some gangbanger's gonna let you do eighteen flips so you can kick him in the face? No! What you gotta do is punch him in the face, then punch him again, then punch him again, until finally his skull concaves."

"Ew."

"Yeah, you'll be saying that when you're cleaning his brain off your hands!"

When the batter looked even, I poured it into a brownie pan and shoved it into the oven. Vee reached out for the mixing bowl, desperately wanting it but not enough to warrant movement.

"Lemme lick the bowl," she moaned.

"Careful, Vee, raw eggs are dangerous!" I gasped, pressing my palm against my chest. "What if you die?"

We both broke down laughing. I slid the bowl to Vee, and she went to town on the bowl. The amount of slurping coming out of her mouth was disgusting. I wanted to smash the bowl into her stoned head, and each slurp made the desire grow. But I kept my cool. I knew she was going to help me. She was allowed to make those disgusting, revolting, swine-like sounds. Uncooked chocolate covered Vee's entire face. She looked like a damn toddler. The childish look of satisfaction on her face almost made me want to make her brownies every day.

"You should have your own show," she said, still slurping the beaters.

"Yeah, *Baked Baking with Ash and Vee*. It'll air at three in the morning." I chuckled. "Brownies should be done in about twenty minutes. Can we start with the lesson?"

Vee looked over my arms and shrugged. She shoved the mixing bowl aside. Vee rolled off the burning stove and stood face-to-face with me. She grabbed my hand and motioned it around her body.

"If someone tries to kill you or whatever, aim for the eyes."

She pretend-poked her eyes with my fingers. She then grabbed my fingers and bent them back slightly. "Grab their fingers and bend them as far back as you can. Bite anything you can get your teeth on. And don't be afraid to kick them in the balls. Or the cooter. It still hurts, just not as much." Vee kicked up her knee a few inches away from my crotch. "You got nice legs. Should do some damage."

Vee sat back on the kitchen island. I stared at her, expecting her to kickflip off the countertop and start the real lesson. Instead, she picked up with where she left off in her book. As the timer counted down from twenty, I tapped my foot, waiting for part two. Vee ignored my foot tapping and flipped her page.

"That's it?" I finally asked.

"It's a start," she said. "I mean, eventually I'm gonna make you hit the weights, but you've got forever. No matter what that turd sandwich said yesterday, the Brotherhood ain't gonna do anything to you as long as you play it safe. They're gonna poke and prod you with a few electric forks until you're so buff they'll scream at the sight of you. You know, more so than they do now." She chuckled. "Look, when I see you, I see something. What's the word for it?"

"Potential."

"Second-hand embarrassment. But until I can make you less pathetic, I guess we'll stick with anti-rape techniques."

Stoned Vee turned out to be just as rude as sober Vee. With nothing else to do, I sat on the other side of the kitchen island and stared up at the ceiling. I took in a deep breath and closed my eyes.

"I don't want to go to work," I said.

"I mean, who does?"

"Clementine came back today with a little kid." I toyed with my necklace. "I mean, maybe if I only get people who die of old age, I'll be able to handle it. But if I have to take a kid away from his own dead body and send him into the portal? I don't know."

Vee turned away from her book. She arched her back so she could look down at me, both literally and figuratively.

"We come back with a lot of little kids, Princess. You'll have to do it, too. It's not if, it's when."

"The kid was crying." I sighed. "I mean, of course he was, but he was screaming 'Mama.' I just can't stand seeing kids separated from their parents."

Vee squinted her eyes. She laid back down and covered her face with her book.

"Stop talking."

Clementine threw my curtains open the next morning. The light was like a wasp sting straight in the cornea. For a while, I pretended to still be asleep. Whatever she wanted to do with me, I knew it could wait for a few more hours. From the tiny slit of my open eye, I noticed Clem was having none of that. She pulled the covers off and threw a new outfit onto my faux-sleeping body. The jeans landed right on my dick, which woke me right up.

"What time is it?" I wheezed.

"'Bout 6:30."

"Oh, neat, so are you trying to show me the meal between dinner and breakfast?" I finally rose from the bed. "Seriously, the entire city's asleep, including the ghosts, so why are we up this early?"

"Because, darlin', you've got an early day tomorrow, so I'm gonna have to start gettin' your schedule on track. No more wakin' up at 9:00 for you."

"Why do you hate me?"

I stomped into the bathroom to get myself ready for the

morning. Everything laughed at me. Every droplet of water that fell on my face in the shower giggled. The hairdryer guffawed in my ear. Even my steps sounded like flat hehs. Inanimate objects showed no sympathy for a dead boy who just wanted more sleep.

Clementine and I started our day out. We stopped by the Dream Bean for a nice FrappéDeLorean or whatever they called it, and we sat down outside to enjoy a rare moment of sunshine. As we chatted, I noticed Clementine acting a little slower, a little more subdued. Agitated as I was, she needed the day out more. Clementine was noticeably shaken up after our encounter with Paul. That, plus my misadventures around town and the previous workday, probably planted a seed of stress under her flowery Southern Belle façade. No amount of "y'alls" could cover up her shaking knees, and it was my job to make her feel better.

"I saw you bring back a little kid yesterday." Failed step one. "I mean, uh, no, never mind."

"Yeah, I did. Poor kid. He'd been sick for a while now." Clementine added a tiny bit of cream to her coffee. "Sometimes this all feels like just a job, but when you have to take care of crying kids, everythin' feels strange again."

"You ever see a kid you really wanted to give a Spark to?"

"You only get one Spark, hon, and I gave mine away to the man I love." She bit her lip. "But death is an important part'a life. Without death, life can't be cherished. I know that every kid that died is up in Heaven, and I don't cry for happy angels. I cry for the ones they leave behind." She swirled around her coffee. It took her a bit to speak again, almost as if she was waiting for me to respond. But I had nothing to say. "We're all trying to figure out God's plan, Ash. And I still don't know why He causes so much pain."

I closed my eyes and tried my best not to snarl.

"You think that kid's death was part of God's plan?"

She stared at me for a long time. "What do you want me to do? Mope?"

I thought I singlehandedly ruined the day, but Clementine's plans for the day continued. Once we finished eating, made our way to the first stop, a place called Bijou Beauty Salon. Clementine made reservations for me under the name "Marley Farley." Hers were under "Carly Farley." Because, clearly, we were twins. For two hours, a stylist snipped at my hair and a manicurist took care of my nails. They talked to me through the entire thing, as if I was a normal, visible, living customer. The stylist said how "cute" my white hair was and then asked if I wanted it dyed "something more youthful." I made another enemy that day.

Cue the shopping spree. I knew buying clothes would be pointless. Clementine, master seamstress, could make clothes better than any store sold. Instead, we bought enough shoes to last me eight lifetimes. As expected of a ghost without an identity, Clementine paid in cash. Seeing us handle stacks of twenties must have made the salespeople think we were drug dealers.

"Hey, do we sell Vee's weed?" I asked.

"No!" she screamed.

As the day ticked on and noon turned into dusk, Clementine and I got ourselves a table at a very small, very crowded Argentinian steakhouse for dinner. And while all the other businesses in Chicago were going all out for Independence Day, the steakhouse decided to celebrate by placing a tiny American flag next to their giant portrait of Eva Peron.

It was hard to fully enjoy the setting since apparently everyone in the damn city decided to eat there that night too, but something inside my heart felt a bit aflutter. No matter how many times I reminded myself I was dead, I couldn't seem to make myself depressed. Clementine was right across from me, tearing into a steak like a damn hyena, with her fresh new haircut and a bunch of shopping bags from our day out. And as we talked, the people around us seemed to get quieter and quieter until all I could hear was the two of us.

Out of the blue, I said "Thank you."

"Hmm?" Clementine wiped her lips and placed her napkin back onto her lap. "Oh, no need to thank me, hon."

"I've never—" I thought about stopping before I went in too deep, but I went anyway. "I never did anything like this before. My grandma took me out all the time, but I never really had," I stopped to think about what word to use, "someone like you."

Clementine cocked her head to the side and leaned in. Her silver eyes glowed in the dim light, and I tried to keep a straight face when I noticed her growing concern.

"What do you mean, darlin'?"

I took in a little breath. "It's just, um—" I bit my lip and tried to hide a cough. "No one could even look at me after Zack died."

My face twitched. I made sure it didn't do anything worse. I wasn't entirely sure how much I wanted to share with her. The generational gap would make a few things confusing, and I didn't want to ramble on about gay ennui during dinner. But, I saw my best friend across from me, and I felt safe.

"I was always a pretty closed-off kid, so I never really had any friends. Zack was my only real friend. So, when Zack died, I just became the depressed kid no one wanted to talk to." I closed my eyes. "But they were talking about me. Of course they were. No one could look me in the eye, but they were just fine saying I was going to kill myself, t—" I stopped. I saw Clem make a face from the corner of my eye, but I ignored it. "I just had to focus on being better. If I was hotter than them, if I got better grades, if I ran faster, then I was the real winner. Because it's better to look good than feel good, right?" I faked a smile. "But that didn't matter to them, because I was just some pathetic little faggot who cried in the bathrooms during lunch."

"Oh, Ash. Please don't think that."

I still couldn't bear to look at her face.

"Didn't matter. Not like I'd see them after high school. I had a scholarship to a nice college out of state, and I was going to be a big wig lawyer in New York while all of them were gonna get trapped in pyramid schemes." My fake smile faded. "And now I'm dead, and they're all probably lying on Twitter about how much I meant to them."

I stared at Clementine for a while. I wasn't crying, or screaming, or even shaking. I was just looking at the Geist seated across from me. Clementine sighed and slid her hand over mine. Before she could try to console me, I smiled again, that time for real.

"So, thank you. For showing me what it's like to have friends."

Clementine smiled with me. "Always."

The dim room grew brighter, and I never felt safer.

Night fell, and our day out came to a close. Clementine and I returned to the mansion, and I got ready for bed. But sleep never came. Minutes turned to hours as thoughts of everything that could go wrong filled my head. I tried counting sheep, but the sheep yelled at me and said I was ugly. I found a new position to sleep in and, bam, terrorist attack killing hundreds. My breathing finally settled down and, whoops, one-versus-fifty fight with the Brotherhood.

Finally, I found peace. My eyelids settled. Everything felt

wonderful in my bed. For the first night in a long time, my dreams carried me to safe, happy places. I was so serene, I didn't notice Clementine walk into the room.

"Ash, sweetie. Time to get up!"

The pterodactyl screech I made shook the planet.

Five-fifty in the morning. A time when mating birds and still-partying co-eds were the only things awake. Once again, my daily routine laughed at me. As I walked out of the bathroom, I wondered if I could defenestrate myself, run away, and join the circus to avoid Geist duties. Then I remembered all of our windows were fake and the only ways out were the front door and the portal to Hell. My thoughts of escape stopped when I heard my name being whispered in the music room. I stopped and leaned against the door.

"I don't know if he's ready, Jo. He's still so young."

"I have faith in Ashton, Clementine." Johanna lowered her voice. "If it will make you feel better, I will be sure to patrol extra thoroughly tonight, just in case he missed anything."

I tried not to think about that too much as I headed back into my room for supplies. My iPod, my stolen notebook, and two novels would help keep me occupied during my downtime. A water bottle and various blah-flavored granola bars were going to help me not dehydrate or starve, which were apparently things that could happen to Geist. Deep in the back pockets, Gabriel's iPod rested. I still had no idea what I was gonna do with it, but it felt good to keep it on me. When I got to the front door, Clementine was waiting for me, and she gave me fifty dollars, just in case. She noticed a giant lump in my messenger bag, unzipped it, and confiscated my stolen gauntlet.

"You won't be needin' this," she hummed.

"You don't know my life!"

She laughed, but I could tell it was hollow. The air around us felt still as she stared up at me.

"Listen, Ash. Sometimes, it might be hard for you to go save a spirit. It might be behind a locked door or trapped in a cave or…" She stopped herself and sighed. "You're probably going to see some bad stuff today, so don't hesitate to ask for help. If you have any trouble at all, call me and I'll take over for you."

I nodded and readjusted my bag. "I've got this."

Without another word, I left the premises of Zinda Mansion and walked into the world of the living. Taking into account Vee's five-seconds worth of training, I headed toward the hospital. When Clementine, Johanna, and every other competent Geist in town went "on patrol," I imagined that they literally circled their section of the city for hours on end. Vee's method, despite being lazy as holy Hell, seemed significantly more efficient.

By the time I got a block away from the mansion, my head cleared a bit. I was no longer scared. The more I walked, the more I realized that patrol duty was not a "job" per se. Salespeople made calls to potential buyers, surgeons split conjoined twins, and Geist walked a few miles every couple of days. Granted, the fate of the world was probably resting on our shoulders, but if Geist roamed the Earth since the dawn of time, I knew there was no way one boy could eff up spectacularly enough to cause the apocalypse.

Even if it was early, people were going about their days, heading off to work, and enjoying the dawn. A man sidestepped me. As I kept walking, everyone kept subconsciously avoiding me. I stopped for a second. If all I needed to do for people to see me was expect them to, I could go through the entire day like a normal person. I decided to do it. From that point on, everyone in town would see me.

I marched down the sidewalk, repeating in my head that

everyone could see me. Sure enough, I caught a few glances coming my way. No one said anything to me, but their glances meant the world. I was one step closer to normalcy.

A group of men in camo pants stood by the corner of an intersection passing out religious pamphlets. They didn't look like the Brotherhood, but I remained on-guard. I walked on by, noticing one look at me. He smiled, and I tried to look away as quickly as I could. He stepped closer to me.

"Do you have time to talk about Jesus Christ?" he asked.

"Sorry, not right now."

"He had time to die for you!" he scorned.

"Oh my God."

I went back to being invisible.

Barely ten minutes later, my necklace started to glow. My heart plummeted. I knew that, somewhere close by, someone was dead. I closed my eyes, took a breath, and held my necklace out in front of me. The magnetic pull beckoned me to keep going forward. With each step, the mental pull intensified and the light got brighter.

The light led me to a three-floor apartment not too far from Yvonne's place. I stood outside the building, knowing full well that something bad was in there. Best case scenario, an old man died in his sleep. I did not want to think about the worst-case scenario. The only important thing was that there was a ghost inside that needed my help. A tiny tinge of righteousness coursed through me. It was time to save a soul. I marched up to the front door of the apartment complex, grabbed the handle, and realized that it was locked.

I screamed like Homer Simpson. The ghost might as well have been inside Fort Knox. Somehow, I needed to find a way inside a locked apartment complex. And once inside, I would need to find a way into a locked apartment. And then, possibly, into a locked room. My phone sat in my pocket, and Clementine's number was right inside. I could have called her, but I knew that would be too pathetic. "Hi, Mommy? The door's locked, and I can't get in." There was a large brick on the side of the glass doorway. My shoulder devil told me to a hero. Ash smash. I cast aside that idea when I saw an open window on the second floor.

The distance between the steps and the open window was not too far. If I stood on the arm rails, I could jump from there to the first-floor window's ledge. From there, it would be a simple pull-up to get to the open window. Simple enough. I was trained for this. I stood up on the railings, jumped to the window, missed entirely, and fell onto the sidewalk. My nose shattered again, then popped back into place. I groaned for five minutes straight.

Plan B commenced. I jumped, grabbed the ledge of the window, and pulled myself up. I hadn't done a pull-up in months, but I gave myself leverage by walking up the wall at the same time. Standing on the tiny ledge was more difficult. The open window was still one floor up and I needed to do a second pull-up, somehow. I stood, pressed myself against the window, looked up, hoped that nothing terrible was about to happen. I reached up for the ledge. It was an inch out of my reach. I sighed, knowing I needed to jump again. I felt like the world's most pathetic burglar. Ghosts in movies would have been able to glide through the wall, but Geist needed to climb through windows like teenage boys sneaking into their girlfriends' bedrooms.

I jumped again, barely catching the ledge with the tips of my fingers. I pulled myself up to the window using all the might my arms had. I tried to use my legs again, but they kept slipping on the window. With a huge amount of wheezing and a tiny amount of confidence, I made progress. Little by little, I inched my way up. Finally, I could see into the apartment. I could feel the soul was close. I reached into the window and grabbed the couch close by. I pulled myself through and fell into the apartment, flat on my face. If I had to do that for every ghost, I was ready to put in my two weeks' notice.

The ghost was close. My necklace's light was pointing straight ahead. Its pull was so strong, it must have been coming from within this particular unit, thank God. A sudden ringing came from my pocket. I jumped. I pulled the phone out of my pocket and saw that Clementine was calling me. Knowing that there was a soul close by, I answered the phone with my hand blocking my mouth.

"Hello?" I whispered.

"Hi, darlin'!" said Clementine. "Just makin' sure you're doin' good right now."

"Yeah, I'm fine, it's good, nothing's wrong, I'm perfect." I monitored the room to make sure the ghost wasn't anywhere near. "Superb. Marvelous. Tubular."

"You sure you're good? You don't need me to rush out and help you, right?"

"Clementine, are you watching me on the skull board?"

Static.

"Yes," she answered.

"Don't."

I said goodbye to Clem and continued following the light. Steam filled the hallway. Water slipped out from the cracks of one of the rooms. The sound of a shower covered the tiny whimpers coming from the bathroom. I stopped walking. Inside the bathroom, shrouded in steam, was a crying soul. I knew that, in a few steps, I'd be standing face to face with a recently deceased person. There was no turning back, that's all I was sure of. I had a duty, so I opened the door.

The shower poured hot water into the overflowing bathtub, the drain covered by a ripped-down curtain. A thin coat of pink water filled most of the bathroom. The pink turned into a deep maroon the closer it got to a woman lying naked by the toilet, which was covered in her blood. The large, open indent on her temple showed just how hard she must have hit her head. Huddled over the body, a translucent ghost waited, almost catatonic.

The ghost's head slowly turned to see me. I could barely see her eyes in the steamy room, but I could still see the transparent tears running down her cheeks. I walked closer to the woman and kneeled in the bloody water. Even if my jeans became stained, I didn't care. The woman mattered more. I thought about how Clementine looked at me when she found me and tried my best to give the woman the same expression. She deserved as much warmth as I could give.

"I'm sorry," was all I could say.

The woman slammed her hands down onto the tile, making the bloody water splash all over us. She wheezed out a few inaudible words before giving up. Her sobbing broke through the hum of the shower and filled the room with a horrible lament of misery and confusion. I knew I couldn't join her. At that moment, I needed to be the strong one, and I knew I always needed to be the strong one.

"What's your name?" I asked.

The woman stopped her sobbing and looked at me again. Her eyes wandered around the room, looking for an explanation. She sniffled, finally able to form words through her weeping.

"Natalie."

"Natalie, my name's Ash."

Ripples coursed through the water around the woman. Her ghostly body shook the room. I reached my hand out to her. She recoiled and backed closer to her body. I pulled back my hand, knowing she needed more than just a fake hug.

"I'm a Geist," I explained. "I guess you could say I'm kind of like a Grim Reaper. When people pass, I help them move on."

"No!" she cried. "No, I can't be dead! I only hit my head. It couldn't have killed me!"

Blood continued to trickle from her body's head wound. Even if the hit did not kill her, the blood she lost must have finished it. Natalie grabbed her former body and rocked it. She slapped its face, covering her translucent hand with opaque blood.

"I died alone! Oh my God, I died alone!" she screamed. "No one's going to find me! I'm going to be stuck in this puddle until someone downstairs complains about the smell!"

"Natalie, that's—that's not something you need to worry about," I stuttered. I tried to reach out to her again. She didn't back away. "The only important thing is how you are right now."

"I can't die yet," she wept. "I was just getting things right."

Everything looked familiar. The circumstances were different, but I was sitting right across from someone who died in a freak accident before her time. Looking at Natalie, I made a terrible realization that she was not unique. The realization that my life's work was to see people like Natalie every time I left the house. Every hour, a new Natalie.

"I just got out of grad school, and I just started working at a law firm," she said, her eyes getting wider. "And I'm going on my first date in years tomorrow. We're going to go see a movie. It's not going to be anything big, but—" she stopped herself before she could go any further. Her face showed she had a billion other things in her future and all for naught. "I spent so long trying to get where I am now. You can't tell me it was all for nothing."

My mouth dried. "I'm sorry."

There was nothing else I could say. Clementine or Johanna or Jesse would have given her a speech about Heaven. Vee would have picked her up off the floor without a simple hello and dragged her back to the portal. In good conscience, I could do neither. Nothing inside me could form a rousing speech or a heartfelt goodbye. All I could lend her was my hand.

"It's time to go."

Natalie grabbed my hand. We left the body, the overflowing bathtub, and the blood for someone else to take care of. Together, we walked out her door, went down the steps, and left the building. We did not talk on the trip back to the mansion. I tried to keep a step ahead of her at all times, knowing that it would hurt too much to look at her. The Brotherhood never entered my mind on the trip home. Nothing did. The only thing I cared about was getting Natalie to the portal.

I walked Natalie down the steps of Zinda Mansion. When I saw her face, I did not know if it was full of wonder, fear, or both. Inside, I motioned her toward the doors between the two staircases. I opened the basement doors and pointed her down the steps, telling her that her next step is at the very bottom.

"You'll go through the portal, and then you'll come out on the other side," I said.

"What's on the other side?" she asked.

No clue. But I knew I couldn't say that. Not to someone as terrified as Natalie. I also knew I couldn't lie. I wasn't going to tell her that Jesus was waiting for her with open arms. All she needed was a gentle nudge.

"Go on through and you'll find out," I said, winking.

I felt disgusting, but then Natalie smiled. Not a huge smile.

Just a twitch in the right direction. Natalie stepped into the darkness and did not turn back. Her outline faded into black the further she walked down. I did not linger. I shut the door and sat down on the tile.

One soul, all by myself. And it hurt. Sitting there, I thought of a million things I could have told her, a million things I could have done differently. But I knew I needed to ignore those thoughts. To me, she was only the first in a long line of people I needed to send away. To Natalie, I was the last thing she saw before leaving. My breathing became heavy. The strange magnetic pull I felt toward Natalie wasn't getting any weaker. Holding my breath, I stood back up, reopened the door, and went back into the darkness, so at least Natalie had someone with her for a little longer.

Chapter 9
Turncoats

I had gotten a few blocks away from Zinda when my phone rang again. Judging by how many phone calls I had gotten in the first few hours, I worried that I'd be out of minutes by the end of the week. I looked down at my phone and, to my surprise, it said Winona Iron Cloud. I answered the phone, not even able to get out a hello.

"Oh my God, Ash!" Winona sang. "Guess what! Me and Farrah got back in town and we're so, so, so happy to be back in Chicago! Oh, Aruba was so fun, but let me tell you, I missed you so much! And Farrah is just dying to see you!"

"That's—"

"I could not stop talking about you while on vacation! I still can't believe you're finally hanging with all of us! And I just got off the phone with Clementine, and she said it's your first official day on the job! I'm so excited for you! But we neeeeeeeeeeeed to meet up for lunch! I don't think Farrah can wait another second to see you!"

"Uh-huh."

"Listen, I know you have that wonderful café right across the street from Zinda, right? Well, we can just head over right now and have a wonderful meal together. We only just dropped our bags off at La Maison, we're that excited to see you! We'll be there in a few minutes! Oh my God, I can't wait! Bye!"

"B—"

She hung up. Putting my headphones back on, I turned my ass around and headed toward the Starbucks clone. Confusion overtook any other emotion I could have been having. I was alone reaping dead people a month after my own death, but Winona and Farrah were allowed to take an almost month-long vacation. Demons, all of them. The Brotherhood was right.

The Dream Bean was practically empty, despite having super special red, white, and blue Frappédacos that probably tasted like crap. As I waited for the Geistbians to arrive, I picked a seat next to a window and took out my notebook. Wistfully flicking through my few pages of notes on the Brotherhood, a few weathered pages fell out of the notebook. I tried to read them, but they were covered in the worst handwriting I had ever seen. I went back to my own, much prettier pages.

I turned up the volume on my music. The volume remained the same. I looked down at my iPod and saw my greatest fear coming to life. Low battery. My iPod powered down, leaving me alone and music-less. It was fine. This was fine. Just a few minutes without music. Completely fine.

The girl at the table next to me kept sucking on her straw, even if ninety-nine-point-nine percent of her drink was gone. Some man in line was loudly complaining about the names of drinks to the barista, who looked like she was two steps from kicking him in the taint. A middle-aged woman a few tables down, in her best Irish whisper, mentioned something about menopause turning her vagina into rice paper.

This wasn't fine! I needed a solution. Something to fix my problem. Something that wasn't setting fire to the entire café, even if the barista would've loved that. I needed music, but the only music I had was my dead iPod.

The problem found its solution when I looked through my bag. Gabriel's iPod shined like a beacon of salvation. I took the tiny piece of outdated tech, plugged in my headphones, and blocked out all the horrible sounds around me.

I flipped through several of Gabriel's songs. At first, I ran into some melodramatic gospel and emo rock. Not a damn Top 40 anywhere, but a whole lotta Nickelback. I kept skipping through his songs, but I stopped when I heard a somewhat familiar song.

"We sing to you, our Lord, our God, to find our way back home…"

The narcissistic asshole had an iPod filled with his own music. I surfed along, hearing a bunch of covers, religious schlock, and alternate covers of his religious schlock. I looked back at the weathered papers that fell out of the notebook, then rapidly flipped through the earlier pages. The first half of the notebook was filled with his song lyrics and sheet music.

"Oh shi—"

I flipped to the next song. Instantly, the sound of trumpets filled my ears. Instead of Gabriel's gravelly voice, I heard some out of tune rando trying to be quirky. I tore off my headphones and shoved the iPod into my bag.

"No! No! Suck my dick, ska-punk!"

Thankfully, the front door flew open and Winona strutted into café. Everyone's eyes turned to her, because, of course, she wanted an audience. Dressed in a fur coat in the middle of summer, she ripped off her huge sunglasses and shrieked. I braced myself just in time for her to grab me, swing me around, and give me several cheek kisses.

"Ash! Bon Bini! How have you been?" she bellowed. "Oh, it's been too long! I barely got to meet you and then I had to up and leave! How me," she huffed. "But no matter! I'm here now! And so is Mrs. Farrah!"

Farrah followed Winona, much slower and equally ill-dressed for the weather. Somehow, despite coming back from a beach resort, Farrah seemed paler than I last saw her. And she looked much less excited to see me than Winona implied, but I already knew that'd be the case.

The two wasted no time getting their food and even took the liberty of ordering me a coffee. When they brought it back, I didn't ask what it was. Instead, I paid attention to the two women sitting across from me, one super eager to tell me everything about her trip, the other bored.

"The ocean is so blue out there! And clear! It's absolutely amazing! If you looked into it, you could almost see right to bottom!"

"Well, you could if the rich Dutch bastards didn't fill the water with their yachts." Farrah tilted her head toward me. "Ash, how familiar are you with the term 'neocolonialism?'"

"Not very," I mumbled.

"And you'll never guess who we met!" Winona said, completely ignoring the discourse. "Go on, guess!"

"It was Cher, wasn't it?" I asked, pushing aside the crappy notebook.

"Oh my God, I wish!" she exclaimed, raising her hands as if praying. "But, no, keep guessing!"

"It was Geena Davis," answered Farrah.

"Oh boo, he was so close," huffed Winona.

Winona continued gushing about the trip to Aruba, and Farrah said maybe five slightly positive things about it. Part of me really wanted to talk about my day, particularly Natalie. Every time they mentioned anything about the scenery, my mind drifted right back to the bloody water. But I wasn't going to mention it. I spent too many years ruining conversations with depressing crap. Plus, Winona was not about to let me get a word in edgewise because apparently she learned how to talk without having to breathe. So I just kept my mouth shut, nodded when I needed to, and did my best to be the friend I assumed Winona wanted.

"We need to take you on our next vacation as a welcome present! Ugh! I cannot wait for us to hang out more often, Ash!" Winona exclaimed. I started to wonder if she ever used a period at the end of sentences. "I can't believe we had to wait so long to meet you, but just seeing your face enter La Maison made the wait worth it!"

I smirked. "That's sweet, but, I don't think you had to wait that long to meet me."

"Oh, you have no idea!" she laughed. "But you really left an impact on Clementine." I blushed. "I even offered to drop everything and come to Zinda the second she told me about you, but Clementine told me to keep my distance. Especially after what happened with Carson and Lily."

I blinked. Farrah's head shot toward Winona. Failing to be inconspicuous, a tiny shhh left her mouth. I almost felt like I misheard her.

"What do you—?"

A bell jingled as the door opened. Three people entered the café. I glanced toward them for a short time, then turned back to Winona. I had a double take and looked back at the people entering the café. Gabriel walked in the front. James trailed Gabriel, all while using his phone as a mirror to check out his new haircut. Finally, the girl with the multicolored hair pulled the door shut behind her. No sign of Dinah.

I made an ugly guttural noise. Winona and Farrah looked back at the group. Both of them clearly recognized them as well, judging from Farrah's sneer and Winona's annoyed grunt. None of us said anything as we watched the people go up to the counter. The three Brothers each ordered, and James took out his wallet to pay.

The Brothers walked to a table on the other side of Dream Bean. Winona tried to start the conversation again, but it died after two words. We were all busy watching the three. I pulled Gabriel's iPod out of my backpack, shuffled the notebook back together, and stood up.

"I'm going to do something really stupid. If I die, tell Vee it's all her fault."

"Don't!" said Farrah.

I did it anyway. I walked across the café, pulled up a chair, and sat down at the same table as the three Brothers. Winona and Farrah both made exaggerated, desperate hand motions at me from across the room. I signaled for them to chill. In reality, I was not chill in the slightest. But I had my excuses for sitting with them. Espionage was the main excuse. The real reason was in my hand. I toyed with the iPod, dancing it around in my fingers and waiting for the right time to sneak it into his pocket.

"You really didn't have to do that," Gabriel said to James. "I can pay for myself."

"When Harmony's better, you can pay me back," said James.

Gabriel looked down at his coffee and frowned. Their voices sounded too human. I hated it. I needed them to be evil. I needed them to be faceless, Satanic cultists, not kids still fresh off of mourning a dead friend. Gabriel's voice, when he wasn't trying to kill me, had a raspy cadence, and when he was sad, it got gravely. James's voice was almost hilariously nasally, like he had a perpetual cold. It was almost like James's huge, hairy body was just a puppet and a toddler was somewhere behind a curtain controlling him.

"Rosa," Gabriel said to the girl. "How're you holding up? You haven't said a word all day."

The girl added a pack of sugar to her coffee and stirred. She did not look up at Gabriel. Her thick eyebrows pressed down on her eyes. I pulled a pen from my pocket and added her name to my notes.

Rosa. Tan, probably Latina. Late teens to early twenties. Scrawny. Wavy, dark hair. Kickass pink bangs.

"I'm fine," she snipped.

That was a blatant lie. Neither she nor Gabe looked fine. I could almost see little thunderclouds over them. James wrapped his arm around Rosa's shoulders and took a huff of his e-cig. The vapor cloud went straight into my face.

"You know," he said, "I think I have an idea of how to cheer you up."

"Does it have to do with your birthday?" Gabriel raised an eyebrow. "Because you've only been talking about that for forty years, so I can't remember when it is."

"It's tomorrow, and we all need to celebrate!" James said. He pulled Rosa even closer and nuzzled his nose against her nose. "I'm turning twenty-one, and that means I can finally get wasted in public!"

"You already do that," said Gabriel. "Or are you just going to turn up the dial and straight-up piss yourself in front of some cops tomorrow?"

I chuckled. Gabriel's ears perked up. I covered my mouth. Gabriel glanced my way, then looked back at James.

Gabe's face was, for once, not masked by goggles or moonlight. His hair was a little longer than it was when I first saw him, and he was desperately in need of a shave. Also adding to his disheveled-ness, it turned out he wore contacts, because he wore slim glasses that morning that magnified his already huge eyes. He was, and it pained me to even think of the word, beautiful.

"Being twenty-one isn't going to change our worlds, it's just going to be a number on our IDs," said Gabe. "Once the novelty of legal drinking wears off, you'll realize that everything's just one day after another."

"Oh my God, shut up," I said as I added "Pretentious" to my notes on Gabriel.

Winona and Farrah rushed over to the table and squatted next to me. Both women glared at me, pouting in the exact same way, as if years of marriage had unified their facial expressions. Winona put her head on the table and duckfaced at all the Brothers, making a *pfft* sound at each of them.

"Learning anything interesting?" asked Winona.

"I'm learning jack and crap. It's all birthday planning and faux-philosophical bull."

"Well, what did you expect?" asked Farrah, putting her hands on her hips. "You thought they'd talk about their WMDs while in a public coffee hut?"

"I mean, kinda. They're trying to fight the concept of death. They can't be too high on the IQ charts."

The Brothers rambled on about birthday planning, which basically amounted to "Someone buys the beer and someone rents a movie." Not exactly a Kardashian affair. I often thought about what my own twenty-first would have been like, but after the whole death thing, I kinda stopped caring. I suddenly felt bad. Not because of my situation, but because I low-key agreed with Gabe's pretentious monologue.

"What about a cake?" peeped Rosa, finally unclenching her jaw. If she wasn't so adorable, I would have been terrified of her perpetual scowl. She put her hand on James's thigh, finally reciprocating his affection. "I was on Facebook last night and someone shared a story about an eight-year-old that won a baking competition with a strawberry cake."

"Whadda we gotta get?" asked James. "Because if we gotta

buy some naturally grown strawberries from the mountains of Nepal, we ain't doing that. Birthday on a budget."

"Didn't read the whole thing," Rosa answered. "I can't go on Facebook too much anymore. Everyone keeps on talking about the, uhh, you know." She winced. "The guy that died in the crash."

Winona's hand glided over to mine. I avoided it, and I kept my eyes on Gabriel.

"Oh right, the guy that stole all of our fliers?" asked James. "Yeah, I remember seeing it all over the news the next day." He shook his head. "Real messed up. I saw an interview with the dude's mom and she couldn't form a sentence."

"His name was Ash," mumbled Gabriel, looking into his coffee. "Killed in a drunk driving accident a few months before heading to college. And yeah, it is real messed up how his family seems to use every opportunity they have to get an interview. I'm shocked they haven't given his grandma a reality show already."

Suddenly he was less attractive. Even if he couldn't see me, I made sure my glare went into his soul.

"Dude, they've got two dead kids."

"Yeah, and they make sure we know it whenever someone's got a camera ready. Plenty of people out there have dead family, but they're making sure we don't forget theirs." His lip twitched. "You see anyone trying to interview me about my parents? Or what about Paul?" The others' faces fell. "No, because we aren't rich shits with a sob story, but right here in Chicago we got a family who's going to keep milking their son's horrible death for airtime until the day they d—"

I kicked back my chair, reeled back, and punched the back of Gabriel's head. His glasses flew onto the table. Gabriel looked up at me, his teeth bared and his eyes wide open. His quick breaths slid out his mouth like a snake hissing. No one moved.

Faint groans escaped Farrah and Winona. James and Rosa sat at the very edge of their seats, clutching anything they could grab onto. While everyone else in the café was none the wiser, I broke the ice with the Brotherhood of Eternity.

Gabriel reached down for his backpack. Before he could even touch a strap, I batted his arm away, grabbed the bag, and tossed it to Winona. Gabriel got up from his seat and reached for Winona, but I pushed him back, pointing at his face and scowling.

"Farrah! Winona! Bags."

Winona, without hesitation, and Farrah, with much hesitation, grabbed the bags of the others at the table. They searched the bags and found a gauntlet and a pair of goggles in each bag. Farrah gasped, re-zipping the bags right away. She glared at me, as if to ask "What the Hell did you get me into," which is when I noticed that only one of her eyes was silver and black. The other looked completely human. Winona's were the same and, in all likelihood, mine were too. It didn't even occur to me at the time that the Brotherhood could see us, but we were invisible to the rest of the coffee shop. I was far too rattled to take more notes about Geist anatomy.

All the Brothers stood up. James walked past me, reached for his backpack, and snatched it right out of Farrah's hands. Farrah was pulled forward from the force, falling against the table. Winona grabbed James's collar and pulled the two-hundred-plus-pound man right off his feet. He dangled in the air while Winona's puppy disposition fled. Underneath her vibrant personality and flamboyant clothes, a wolf stirred.

"Watch it, little boy."

Winona dropped James and took his bag back. James backed off, standing tall next to Rosa. Rosa's head darted around the room. But I didn't look at the others for too long. My attention was focused on Gabriel. Standing face-to-face, he was about an inch shorter than me. My feet shook and I could not tell if it was from anger or fear. Gabriel's body quaked all in the same places. My same anger and fear stood mirrored in front of me.

"How long have you been here?" Rosa said. She was possibly the only person there ready to talk without screaming.

"Long enough," I replied.

"Do you really want to start a fight in this place?" She leaned forward. "There are a lot of people here that don't know about what you are."

"Oh, we all know they can't see me."

"Please don't do this," Farrah whispered to me.

"You're acting really harsh right now." Winona put her hands on my shoulders and dragged me back. "We should leave."

"You both can leave, but I'm not leaving until I get an apology."

Winona let go of me. She and Farrah backed away a few steps, keeping an eye on me but keeping themselves out of whatever the Hell I was getting into. With the Brotherhood of Eternity right in front of me, I stepped closer to Gabriel again. Any possible attraction was gone, and all that was left was Murphy-brand fury. Never in my life had I felt that angry, and it took everything I could to make sure I didn't set the entire coffee shop on fire.

"What do you all think I am, exactly? Just a ghost? Or a demon?" I tilted my head a little so I could look down on all of them. "Am I a god to you? Is that it? Do you want to kill us because you're scared of us?"

Gabriel's face contorted. He looked toward the other Brothers for help, but they looked just as disturbed. Everyone stood locked in place. Even I couldn't move. Every bone in my body was going in a different direction. One leg wanted me to go forward, while the other wanted to run away, and my fists wanted to punch Gabriel while my arms stayed by my side.

"We should really take this outside." James finally moved away from the table. "I don't feel comfortable talking to you with this crowd."

"Great, yeah, because the other times we met up away from the crowd, it worked out so well for all of us," I sneered.

"Well, we're leaving. If you want to keep on harassing us, you can catch us on the way home."

"Harassing you?" I almost had to laugh. "Are you serious right now?"

James ignored me. He held out his hand to Farrah. Farrah hesitated. Then, with a huff, she tossed James his bag. James put it over his shoulder, took a drag of his e-cig, and left the café. The others followed suit, taking their bags from Winona and Farrah and leaving. Gabriel took one last angry look at me before closing the door.

I gripped my hands hard, pinching them on what I was holding. In my rage, I forgot I hadn't given that jackass his iPod back. Winona put her hands on her hips and *tsk*-ed a few times. Hopefully, I thought, it was aimed at them and not me. Farrah pulled a cell phone out of her skirt pocket and dialed a few numbers.

"What're you doing?" I asked.

"Calling Clementine!" Farrah said, huddling next to her wife. "This is getting way out of hand and you know it."

I froze again. "Don't worry, they're gone. I won't follow." I put on my most sincere smile. "It was fun, but I gotta get back on patrol. See ya later!"

Blatantly lying, I decided to follow the Brotherhood. I threw everything back into my bag and rushed out the door. Whatever the two of them were gonna do afterward didn't matter to me.

Gabriel, James, and Rosa had disappeared and I needed to catch them. A bunch of pedestrians passed me on the sidewalk, but none of them looked like Brotherhood material. I stepped around the front of the Dream Bean, looking for any sign of them. I ran back and forth, from one end of the café to the other. No sign. I took a quick peek in the tiny alley between the café and its adjacent building. I proceeded to fall into the most obvious trap outside of a Road Runner cartoon.

James grabbed me by the face and pulled me into the alley. Already equipped with his goggles and gauntlet, his fist sparked with a current that shocked me down to my toes. He tossed me against the bricks and pressed my shoulder against the wall. Electricity jolted through every section of my body, not giving me any room to react. I thought back to Vee's half-assed self-defense lesson.

"If someone tries to kill you or whatever, aim for the eyes."

While James was concentrating on my shoulder, I pushed up his goggles and pulled them off his forehead. He cursed, then I went for the simple eye poke. The man almost twice my size winced and covered his face in pain.

Gabriel flipped around the squirming James and jumped at me with his gauntlet ready. I, too, was ready. Gabriel lunged at my waist and pulled me back, farther into the alleyway. Gabriel sidestepped right up to my face, gauntlet directed straight at my head.

"Grab their fingers and bend them as far back as you can."

I reached for Gabriel's exposed hand. In the confusion, I shoved his index and middle fingers and far back as I could. Two loud pops echoed through the alley. Before I could run again, he grabbed my wrist, twisted me around, covered my mouth with his exposed hand, and grabbed my neck with his gauntlet.

Gabriel shot his current straight into my throat. My

necklace started pressing into my chest, pulsating as if it had its own heartbeat. Eighteen heart attacks went through my chest in the span of three seconds. I was completely frozen in his grip. It was like the entire world turned black and white. The only thing I could make out was Gabriel's fingers eskew across my face.

"Bite anything you can get your teeth on."

I opened my mouth and bit down on whatever was around it. I felt two fingers slip in and lodge between my teeth. Gabe flinched, but he kept his electricity flowing. I bit down harder and his blood trickled down my throat. Gabriel finally let go of me and fell back, cursing and grabbing his hand. I pulled off his goggles while he dealt with his bleeding hand.

Both looked around the alley for me. Gabriel cursed and punched the wall. James still rubbed his eyes, looking like a child who just woke up from a nap. I realized right there that I took down two well-trained assassins, and I was incredibly proud of myself. I almost felt like gloating. Gabriel and James, both defeated by an inexperienced turd with next-to-no fighting skills.

"Wait, where's the other—"

Rosa jumped down from a fire escape and slammed her sparkling fist onto my cranium.

Everything that happened after that was a blur. I only vaguely remembered the Brothers getting their goggles back and propping me up against the wall. By the time I came to, all three Brothers were staring down at me. None of them were trying to strangle, punch, or electrify me. They only stared.

I shifted and slid up the wall until I was at my feet again. All the pain I had left my body, not leaving a single scratch. The memories stayed, but the stinging left as soon as it came. Of course, I expected more pain to come. Winona and Farrah flew to goddamn Bangkok for all I knew and left me alone with the Brotherhood of Eternity. It was time for me to stand my ground.

"There a reason you aren't trying to kill me right now? Why'd you stop?" I wheezed. "I shouldn't still be here right now. You all know that. Something's stopping you from straight up killing me."

"We just want to talk to you," said James.

He held his hands up, acting completely innocent.

"Oh, I guess it was my fault for starting the fight, then! I'm sorry my hubris got in the way of the roundtable you wanted with me!" I shook my head violently enough that a deaf man could hear my sarcasm. "Jesus Christ, look at all of you. Beating up a poor, defenseless ghost. I swear, is your whole cult filled with school shooters and wife beaters?"

"Where do you get off coming up to us and harassing us like this?" exclaimed James. "We weren't bothering you until you barged in and punched Gabe!"

And I snapped. Every single bit of rage I had about the Brotherhood of Eternity shot out of my mouth at light speed. No fear, just fury. I took a step forward, and James took a step back, pressing up against the opposite wall.

"You bash my skull in, shoot me full of lightning, and try to kill me every time you see me, but I punch one of you for running your damn mouth and you start to cry? Go to Hell!" James flinched. Neither of the others reacted. "Was I bothering you when I was alone on the street? Or when I was having a nice day out with my friends? No, because I was just some lost kid who got assaulted by a bunch of gangbangers!" Spittle flew out of my mouth as I screamed. "How dare you? What do you think I am? Am I some evil Satan thing or just some kind of stupid beetle you can squish whenever you think your penis isn't big enough?"

Rosa crossed her arms and looked at the ground. James wheezed a long "uhhhh" under his breath. Gabriel showed no change in body language and said nothing. He kept his face directly at me. I would have said it was a stare down if I could have seen his eyes.

"You talk way too much."

In all my years on Earth, I had never met a person I wanted to stab as much as Gabriel. Stab his throat to shut him up. Stab his face and turn beauty into horror. Stab anything at all to make his bratty little mouth leave my afterlife forever.

"Oh, no no no, out of everyone in this crack-addled city, you're the last person who gets to talk back to me!" I screamed. "Go out and pretend to be the Avengers all you want, but don't you dare pretend to be deep and brooding by saying that my family is benefitting from my death!"

His lips twitched again. "What the Hell are you talking about?" he glared.

"I'm Ash Murphy!"

With my mouth almost frothing, everyone took a step back. Even if I couldn't see their eyes, they were all visibly confused. They looked at one another, bemused. Gabriel's eyebrows basically went on a journey around his forehead. Gabriel stopped his shock and leaned forward.

"Bullshit."

"You're bullshit!" I said.

James took out his phone and started typing. Rosa looked over his shoulder, taking minute glances at me to make sure I was still against the wall.

"That's impossible, there's no way that one of the demons could be—" James stopped and make a melodramatic gasp. "Oh my God, he is." He shoved the phone into Gabe's face. "Gabe, lo—"

Gabe pushed it away. "I know what he looks like."

James lifted his goggles to get a better look at the picture. He put the phone right next to my face for a side-by-side comparison. Gabriel gave me a side-eye. I mouthed a big "blow me" at him.

"So what?" Gabriel said, his voice cracking. "They can already turn invisible and shoot fire, how do we know he can't change appearance, too?"

If I could have changed my appearance, I would have tightened my waist, thinned down my face, lowered my body fat percentage to about zero, straightened my teeth, defined my ass more, whittled down my nose, and given myself an eight-pack. Not that I thought about it too much.

"I mean, who wouldn't want to morph their body to look like this?" I said, framing my face. "But if I wasn't actually Ash Murphy, why would I have punched you?"

"Easy, because you want to kill us anyway, and you're looking for an excuse!"

"I wanted to kill you so I pretended to be a dead brat, walked up to you in a coffee shop, and sucker punched you?" I made a fake surprised face. "God, that sounds like an amazing plan, but don't give me that much credit! I'm not like a skience-tist!"

"Well, then why'd you come up to us in the first place?"

I tried to hold my real reason in until, oops, it burst out. "Because you dropped this, dumbass!"

I reached into my pocket and shoved his iPod into his hands. Gabriel's face became softer. The harshness of his eyes dissolved, and he suddenly looked exactly like the scared boy I saw when he first dropped the player.

"Gabe, we—" started Rosa.

"Hold on," he interrupted.

"Your music taste is crap, by the way." I started twirling my hair. "If I ever have to listen to anymore ska, I swear to God."

Another twitch. "What did you say?"

"I said ska is for forty-year-olds who still wear flame print!"

Gabriel gripped his iPod and shoved it into his pocket, trying to mask his shaking hands. The two others, confused out of their minds, no doubt, decided it was time to put a stop to this. James stepped between Gabriel and me, basically plastering both of us against the bricks. He put his hand on my shoulder, gentle enough not to hurt me but hard enough to show me that he was a big, strong man who was about to teach a petulant little kid a lesson.

"You honestly can't expect us to believe that, out of the goodness of your heart, you wanted to return a cheap iPod."

"I felt guilty. There. That a good enough explanation?" I smacked his hand. It did not budge. "It was my fault he lost it, so I brought it back."

"It's a trick," said Rosa. "He's going to kill us the second you let your guard down."

"Oh, shut up. Get your own heads out of the sand and think about what you're doing."

It was hard to pinpoint the emotions on all of their faces. Mostly because of the huge goggles. But their bodies betrayed them in some way. Rosa, looking as intimidating as a scarecrow could, trembled in all the wrong places. James kept pressing me against the wall, but the rest of his body stayed as far away as our close quarters allowed him. The entire cult was as terrified of us as we were of them.

"Has any Geist, any at all, ever tried to hurt you without being provoked?" I asked. I tried to add a little tone of caring in my voice, but everything always came out more accusatory than I wanted it. Family trait. "And do I honestly look like a demon?"

"Yes," replied Gabriel.

"You are, by far, my least favorite." I turned my attention back to James. "And who the Hell is Father Abram? You all keep talking about him. He one of Manson's kids?"

"We're not in a cult!" He tightened his grip a bit. I glared and he loosened it again. "Father Abram trying to save our lives! From you!"

"Right, sure." I glared at Gabriel. "Let's say, hypothetically, that every death in the universe is caused by these demons. Which they aren't. You think that, during wars, there are Geist shooting bullets and dropping bombs?"

"Of course we know that people kill people," said Gabe, shaking off whatever was going over him. "We're not stupid."

"Debatable but, yeah, go on."

"But you're connected. Everything you do revolves around death. You're creatures that feed off death. Every time someone dies, you're there and you steal their soul away. That's not natural!"

"Well, it's not like I want to clean up after people die!" My mouth dried up. "Just earlier today, I saw a girl who cracked her skull open on a toilet! I don't want to do this! But I didn't have a choice, and no one else will!" I forced James's hand off my shoulder. "I'm doing you all a favor. Without Geist, everyone would be stuck on Earth. I'm the one doing God's work, goddammit!"

Hyperbole, perhaps. Embellishment, absolutely. But I needed to play to my audience. The three Brotherhood members briefly slid their goggles onto their foreheads. They exchanged glances, saying more than words could. Gabriel gritted his teeth a bit and coming closer to me.

"Let's say, hypothetically, you aren't a demon and really are the ghost of Ash Murphy—"

"Which is the truth, but, sure, hypothetically."

"Will you stop interrupting? Rude."

"You're rude."

"Shut up. So, you're not a demon and you go around saving

the planet from whatever! What happens when you don't get the souls?"

I crossed my arms. "I don't know."

"That's it? You're not even going to think up a better lie?" he asked.

"It's not a lie!" I yelled. "No one tells me anything!"

"So, for all you know, you could be a demon? You just don't know it?"

"I know I'm not a goddamn demon!"

James and Rosa looked less and less involved by the second. Gabriel and I were practically nose-to-nose, creating a tiny tornado of anger between us.

James threw his hands up. Awkwardness turned into exasperation. Gabriel still stayed right next to me, but James and Rosa stepped out of the crowded alleyway and onto the sidewalk. James took off all of his equipment and placed it in his backpack. Rosa followed suit, but stopped before she took off her goggles. Both looked down the sidewalk, frowns growing.

"James! Rosa!"

Another shadow across the sidewalk. Dinah walked into view, already wearing her goggles around her neck. I started panicking again. Even if I talked away the others, there was no way Dinah was going to leave without murdering me. Not after the head trauma I gave her.

"Oh, great, which one of you called in Patty Hearst?" I muttered.

"Wasn't me," whispered Gabriel. It sounded he was just as excited to see her as I was. He put his gauntlet and goggles back into his bag. "Don't let her see you."

Dinah, still a fashion nightmare, pounded her boots across the pavement and stood face-to-chest with James.

"There a reason you told me to, and I quote—" Dinah took

out her phone and showed it to James. "'Come to be Dream Bean right now!'?"

"I didn't send you anything," said James.

"It was Rosa." Dinah motioned toward Rosa's goggles. "Why're those out, Rosa? Is there a demon around here that you aren't telling me about?" She glared at James. "Because that would be stupid."

"There's no demon," said James. I was taken aback. Rosa was too. "We thought we heard something, but it was nothing."

"I asked Rosa!" shrieked Dinah, going from zero to ten real quick. "Is she such a useless bitch that you have to answer her questions, too?"

"I'm not a bitch!" Rosa screamed. A few people on the street turned their heads toward her, but kept walking.

"Then how about you grow some balls and tell me why you made me come halfway across the city to some goddamn coffee shop!"

Rosa and Dinah spat at each other for a hot second, shooting useless words at each other that I could barely make out. James stayed on the sidelines, trying to say a word but only getting half of one out before someone else cut in. Rosa kept defending herself instead of actually saying why she texted her. Her voice cracked almost every other word. With the Brotherhood's in-fighting, my gay ass could slip away unnoticed, assuming I could slip past the three-person wall blocking my exit.

"Is this normal?" I asked Gabriel, my forehead wrinkling.

"Stop talking to me like you know me!" he said through his teeth. "Just get out of here before she notices you. I'm not in a Dinah mood today."

"Then bye." I started walking toward the people-wall. "Au revoir. Arrivederci. Auf Wiedersehen. Never speak to me again."

Thus, I turned my back to the bastard. Trying to find a way

through the barricade, I grabbed James's shoulders and hoisted my way up. James's back stiffened, and I could see him break out in a cold sweat. I just crawled along James's shoulders like a gymnast on a pommel horse, trying my best not to touch Dinah. I flipped down from him, and I was finally free from the alley. James let out a faint "Ehhhhh" and Gabe let out a faint "Christ," and I tried to ignore both. Dinah shot a glance toward them, and James mumbled something and forced a laugh.

Dinah, fed up with the angry small talk, finally gave the ultimatum. She put her fingers on her goggles.

"You're a bunch of dirty liars and—"

"I thought you could help us prepare for James's birthday!" blurted Rosa.

I stopped. Either from my nervousness or actual enjoyment, I burst out laughing. Everyone looked like they had been hit with a frying pan. James's eyes screamed, even if his mouth didn't. He looked over at me. Dinah cocked her head to the side.

"You lie about as well as you give out pamphlets."

Dinah slipped on her goggles. She turned around faster than I could react and stared right at me. I yelped and took a step back. All the others bowed their heads.

"Hey, Diiiiiiiiiii-nah." I waved and let out a nervous chuckle. "How's your head?"

"Burn in Hell," she hissed.

"You're supposed to say 'Haven't had any complaints,' but, okay, you do you."

"Shut uuuuuuuup," wheezed Gabriel.

Dinah, like a pro, slipped her hand into her pocket, pulled it back out, and grabbed my neck. She now had a brand-new gauntlet on her hands. This one was rose gold. I would have been more impressed if she wasn't choking me with it. Dinah kept her attention on the other Brotherhood members while she kept hold of me.

"So, you thought you could keep this monster a secret?" she spat. "Why? Is it because this one's a cute boy? You want to fall in loooooove with this one?" She glanced toward Gabe before looking back at me. "Idiots. Every single one of these things is the same. So just because you want to hump this one doesn't mean you can hide it from me!"

Rosa and James did not argue back. They both inched back toward the alley, getting away from the shrieking woman. Gabriel even came out of the alley to get closer to the screaming.

"He said he was Ash Murphy," peeped James. "You know, the guy that stole all of our pamphlets?"

"Our pamphlets get stolen every day. Do you have any idea how little that narrows it down? Also, are you listening to it?" Dinah looked back at me, sending another shock into my throat. "This thing will do anything to get into your head. Was that not the first thing we taught you? Never trust demons! They only know how to kill and lie!"

"But he looks exactly like him!" said James, standing a little taller. "Here, let me show you!" He took out his phone. "There's a pictu—"

James held out his phone to Dinah. She smacked it right out of his hands. The phone's glass shattered the second it hit the sidewalk. Before James could pick his phone back up, Dinah grabbed him by the collar.

"I was wrong. Rosa isn't the weakest Brother in the city. It's you, you giant rat!"

Gabriel grabbed Dinah's hand and pried it from James's collar. James backed off again, picking up his phone and huddling behind Gabe. Gabe did not scream, punch, or bite. He only glowered at her with bared fangs.

"Don't you touch him."

Dinah scoffed, unfazed. She looked back at me again. Her squinting eyes shot daggers into mine. I thought about any options of escape. Dinah helped me out on that one. She let go of my neck and pushed me into James. James grabbed my arms, keeping me close to his chest.

"Turncoats, every one of you," hissed Dinah, shoving her hand in all of their faces. "Should I kick you out of the Brotherhood right now? Should I call up Father Abram and tell him that there are three fewer Brothers in our midst?"

"Don't!" cried Rosa.

Dinah laughed a single "Ha." No matter how much power that woman had, it was too much. Gabriel stepped between me and Dinah, pushing her back with his shoulder.

"We were milking him for information. He talked, and we got all the info we needed." He was lying. Or he played me. Either way, I respected that, in a stupid way. "We made a compromise, so we let him walk. We didn't tell you because we knew you'd freak out like this."

Dinah sneered at Gabe. She slumped back, crossing her arms. A cloud passed overhead, covering everyone in a shadow. For a long time, Dinah stared. Everyone waited with bated breath to hear her response. Rosa's breathing shook her entire body.

"Fine," Dinah finally said. "I'll buy it. What did you get out of him?"

"They don't know if they're demons or not," said Gabriel. "They think they're doing God's work."

Dinah fiddled with her gauntlet. An evil little smile crossed her face.

"That's what the other ones said, too." She held up her gauntlet. "Hold him tight while I find his weak spot."

James tightened his grip, letting tiny jolts of plasma course through me. I panicked. With every heartbeat, my body temperature rose. Chicago might as well have been on Mercury. Every breath I inhaled only burnt my insides. I was in the burning car again. My heart stopped beating. All the noise around me muted. The only thing I could hear was the tiny pulse inside my necklace.

Dinah pushed Gabriel aside and scanned my body with her gauntlet. She lingered around my necklace, but kept searching. I needed to think of something to do. Anything at all.

"And don't be afraid to kick them in the balls. Or the cooter."

I shot my leg up as far as I could, can-canning her right between the legs. All the air in Dinah's body escaped. I could almost hear her lungs collapse. Dinah's knees buckled, and she said a few cuss words with whatever breath she still had. She propped herself up against the wall, took in a deep breath, and aimed her gauntlet at me.

"You piece of sh—!"

I put my hands up. The next thing I heard was a loud *fwoosh*, followed by several screams. I looked down and saw a large circle of blue fire around my feet. James let go of my arms. Everyone stepped back. I stared down at the fire, shaking. The ring of blue fire danced around me and snapped toward the Brothers.

Surrounded by blue flames, I stared down at the Brotherhood of Eternity. The four faces stared back at me, all anger replaced with terror. My heart continued to race, and as the fire flickered around me, I decided it was time to flee. I leaped above the circle of fire and onto the street. None of the Brotherhood moved, but several passersby started to yell as they finally noticed what was going on in the alley. I weaved past the rubbernecking cars, stopped in the center, and turned back around.

Staring at him right in the eyes, I slowly raised my middle fingers at Gabriel, and then I ran home.

Chapter 10
Part of Something Unexplainable

My iPod charged next to my bed. I sat on the sheets, looking at the little picture of the battery fill with green juice. Time passed slowly. I thought about occupying my time with something else, but there was nothing. An eternity of days exactly like this. Watching people realize they're dead and getting in fights with cultists. Every single day. Forever.

A violent pounding hit my door. I broke out of whatever trance I put myself in. In an instant, I remembered everything. Despite all that happened, I still had a job to do, and someone was on the other side of that door, wanting me to get back to work. Vee wouldn't care at all and the Js were nowhere near confrontational enough, leaving one remaining.

Stowing my iPod and the charger into my messenger bag, I opened the door. Clementine stood on the other side, clutching her brick phone like a stress-ball. She wasn't making any eye contact with me, instead staring at the door frame.

"I thought you were still on patrol," she said, her warm trill gone.

"Forgot my charger," I said, equally as cold. "You could'a checked the skull board."

"I did, and it said you're locked in your room." She decided to look up from the doorframe. "Farrah called. She told me that you were causing trouble with the Brotherhood." Her stability wavered. "You walked up to them and punched one unprovoked? What in God's name happened?"

"Nothing, Clementine. Nothing happened."

Lying was easy. Lying became my favorite pastime when my brother died. "I'm fine." "Nothing's wrong." "I'm not hungry." Sometimes, I lied to myself so well, I forgot what the truth was.

Of course, Clementine had her own form of untruth. I thought about the fire I started on the pavement. I thought about what Dinah meant by a "weak point." I thought about who Carson and Lily were. I thought about everything I had to learn myself. I clicked my tongue and stared at her dead in the eyes.

"No. Actually, a lot happened," I corrected. "I punched one of the Ghostbusters." I nodded, smirking with pride. "They left, I went after them, and we got in a big fight. And then Queen Ghostbuster came along and tried to kill me. Said something about 'aiming for my weak spot.' Then I used my magic fire powers to get away from them. The sidewalk's probably still on fire."

Clementine dropped her phone. It clunked against the wood, almost leaving a dent. For the first time, I saw Clementine angry at me, and I could not care less.

"You goin' out pickin' fights now?"

"They started it."

Clementine's eyes grew wider. I could see every vein in her eyes. She let her phone sit on the floor while she shook. Every vibration looked like an earthquake through her body. Clementine looked like she was about six seconds away from backhanding me.

"What's been goin' through your head that says you should be proddin' at the Brotherhood? Walkin' into a lion cage with a dress of meat!" She stared at me for a second, silent and fuming. "That's not rhetorical! Answer me!"

"I wanted to—"

"To what? Get yourself killed?" She didn't wait for an answer. "We have no idea what these people can do! Just a few months ago, all they had was those goggles! Now they got those gauntlets, and they been sayin' they found a way to get rid of us!"

"Oh, so suddenly they're a threat? I thought that you said they couldn't do anything! Was that a lie or are you just 'protecting' me again?"

Steam flew out of Clem's nostrils. I was an incompetent matador, and she was a bull with her horns right at my throat, but I kept on showing her red.

"I don't know what can happen!" she snapped. "Anythin' can! Don't you get smart with me and pretend you ain't afraid of them! I know you quiver in your socks just thinkin' about them."

"Yeah, and I'm the only one doing something about it!"

"Something?" she snapped. "From what I've heard, all you've been doing is runnin' around like a chicken with his head cut off! If you've got some master plan, it sure ain't workin'!"

I slipped past Clementine and headed for the front door. Clementine kept on my tail, but I did not make eye contact with her. My head was aimed ahead. With my bag around my shoulder and my iPod fifty percent charged, I was ready to get as far away from people as I could. Clementine, of course, had different ideas and followed me all the way down the steps.

"What is wrong with you? Talkin' back to me like a snotty child!" Clementine yelled. I wasn't looking at her face, so I could only guess what kind of contempt she was throwing my way with her eyes. "Don't you try to pin any of this on me! Out of the goodness of my heart, I came to you when you needed me! And now you think you can give me lip?"

My steps muffled her words. I didn't want to say anything else. I didn't want to retaliate. I said enough. We skittered down the steps to the foyer, me keeping a distance between myself and Clementine. Clementine kept making little comments at me until we finally made it to the front door. I reached for the door handle, clenching my jaw so hard I could crack my teeth.

A huge gust of wind swept through the foyer, causing the curtains to almost rip away from the windows. The current flowed around me and made me turn around one hundred and eighty degrees. I stared at Clementine's deep red face, clenching my jaw even harder.

"I ain't your dang mother, Ash, but I may as well be, and I'm doin' the best I can!"

I knew she was right. Clementine Leigh was my best friend and the only person who ever bothered to visit me. Guilt welled up inside of me. If I kept walking down the path I was going, I could sully the only good friendship I had since I was fourteen. I knew that. But I was in no mood to dance around my feelings anymore.

"Who are Carson and Lily?" I asked.

The wind died. The curtains slapped back down against the walls. Clementine stared at me with sunken eyes. And I kept running head-first into a brick wall.

"What?" she breathed.

"What's a Revenant?" My knees shook. "What happens when a spirit isn't taken into the portal?" With every question, my voice rose. "What the Hell am I?"

"Ash, stop." Her tone shifted. Losing its authority, her voice quaked a little. "Don't do this."

I continued. My body shook violently. I leaned forward, backward, sideways. I flung my body around and waved my hands. A morning's worth of fury crossed paths with weeks of anxiety and created the worst storm it could have. My chest started burning again, but I ignored it. The air around me twisted and contorted with the heat coming from my body.

"I was killed, Clementine!" I screamed. "I was murdered and

I have no idea who's to blame! And I barely even got time to cry about it because now I have to worry about everyone else!" I waited a second. Something inside me wanted to stop. It didn't get its wish. A single tear escaped my eyes. I wiped it away before it went down my cheek. "Do you even care?"

No answer came, despite how much I needed one. Dry air escaped Clementine's throat. I wanted so badly to leave, but my feet wouldn't move. When Clementine finally spoke, only two words left her mouth.

"I'm sorry."

Those two words should have left my mouth, too. Instead, I buried myself deeper. Eyes pointed elsewhere, I spoke to the floor.

"I'm getting back to work. Someone's probably dead."

I turned my back and left the mansion. With no destination in mind, I started walking. Across the street, the ring of fire vanished, along with the four Brotherhood thugs. I kept walking in a straight line down the sidewalk. No Geist instincts or magical lights pushed me forward. Just shame.

All the clouds in the sky disappeared, and the sun made the entire city glisten. Nature continued to find new ways to taunt me. People strode by, busy living their lives, celebrating America's independence. Each one of them had a story, and each of their stories would eventually finish. It was my job to help them close their books. And, by God, I wished it wasn't.

I must have walked ten blocks without stopping. The people stepped aside for me. Even cars came to a halt when I crossed the street. Everyone pretended I wasn't there while still moving around to accommodate me. It felt like how people treated me after Zack died. No one would look at me, but they still knew how to avoid me.

If I wanted to, I could appear to them all. They would all

notice me, and I could have done something stupid or hilarious and they would see it. I could run around naked in the streets, and I had the power to let them react. Instead, I kept moving. I was done with talking to people for the day. It felt good, being alone in public.

The feeling dissipated when I realized the same footsteps had been following me for several blocks. Calculated footsteps, each one trying to mimic my own. The tiny delay between my feet and the stalker's feet gave everything away. Someone was following me. It didn't take too much mental gymnastics to figure out it was either a Geist or a member of the Brotherhood.

Perhaps I was too rash to think I had a stalker. Chicago had a population of millions, so it was entirely possible I was just hearing things. If I really had a stalker, he would follow me anywhere. I could turn corners, run through buildings, run across busy streets, anything to get away. If I did all that and the footsteps still remained, I had a stalker.

Instead, I decided to forgo that crap and turn around.

Gabriel was a few steps behind me. He stopped the second I turned. He didn't act surprised or scared or angry. He only stood there like a statue. Neither of us moved. We stared at each other as people passed us by. I was already one hundred and fifty percent done with whatever was about to happen.

"Hello, demon," he said.

"Hello, dipshit," I replied.

Gabriel took a few steps forward. He held up his hands, showing that he was unarmed. While he lacked his gauntlet, his goggles were firmly back on his face.

"You don't have to worry about me," he said.

"First time for everything," I muttered.

He took another step forward. His backpack was missing. Without his gauntlet, he couldn't harm me. I knew that. I kept repeating that fact in my head. He couldn't touch me. He couldn't touch me. Another step. Too close.

"I'm here to talk," whispered Gabriel. "Just to talk." He shook his head. "I'm not gonna hurt you."

"Oh, I'm not up for this. Not today of all days," I snipped.

Gabriel took a step back. He kept his hands up. I honestly had no idea where he was going with anything. It could have been a trap. Even if he was unarmed, James could have been somewhere in yet another nook that was too small for him, ready to snatch me in when I let my guard down. Or he could have had a gauntlet-like shank in his socks.

"What could you possibly want to talk about?" I questioned. "You all seem to have a pretty set-in-stone idea of what I am."

Gabriel sighed. He slid his goggles up his forehead, and I allowed him to see me.

"Maybe you look kinda like a guy I met a couple weeks ago. He offered me some lemon drops, and we talked about music. And, maybe, I woke up the next day and found out that same guy died in a fiery crash barely half an hour after we got in a fight. And everywhere I went, I saw his face and kept hearing about how he died." Something in his voice felt too innocent. "Maybe if I talked to him for a bit longer, he'd still be alive."

I gritted my teeth before I could show any real emotion.

"What's your game, little man?"

"I want to hear what you have to say."

"And how do I know your Brothers won't jump from the roofs and kill me?"

"You don't." He raised an eyebrow. "How do I know you won't burn me alive again and drag me to Hell?"

"You don't."

I groaned internally and closed my eyes for a second. Gabriel wanted a heart to heart about what a Geist was. If only he did that before trying to kill me on three separate occasions. I knew it was naïve of him to ask me that, and I knew it was equally naïve of me to accept. Perhaps this was Gabriel's white flag or even a cry for help.

Faith never came easily to me. My parents stopped making me go to church when I was eight, and Yvonne made sure I stopped believing in God way before that, despite Faye's wishes. I never trusted anyone outside of my family with anything important.

So, I asked myself, why was I putting my life in the hands of the least trustworthy person I know? Maybe it was my fight with Clementine or maybe it was my burning need to finally know who Father Abram really was. But the voice in my head repeated itself. We were doing this.

I opened my eyes. "Every time you ask a question, I can ask you one. We're doing this in a public place and not that goddamn coffee shop. I've had enough of that place for today." I crossed my arms. "I'm not going to set you on fire because I'm a good boy who knows better. If you try anything funny, I will scream, people will hear, and you'll be in for a world of trouble. Deal?"

He slowly nodded. "Deal."

Against my better judgment, Gabriel and I headed off to find a good area to talk, not that that was going to be easy to find. It needed to be secluded enough so some uninformed rando didn't hear something about my secret ghost sect, but still populated enough so that I could get help if Gabriel tried anything funny. On top of that, most dining areas around us were closed for the holiday. There were a few fast-food places, but I was not about to step foot in one of those. This, of course, led me to one conclusion: McDuffie's.

We strode into the tavern. There were a fair few people day-drinking, but no sign of Yvonne. In some ways, I was thankful. I already knew she was neighbors with my mortal enemy, but I didn't need to know if they were friends. We sat down at a table at the very back end of the tavern. Far enough away from other patrons, but close enough so they could hear me scream. Still, I made sure to be invisible. Didn't need anyone recognizing me. A waitress came up to Gabriel and asked if he wanted to order anything, but he lied and said he were waiting on people, so she went on her way.

I reached into my bag and pulled out the notebook I stole from him. I tore out my few pages of notes, then slid it across the table to him. He grabbed the notebook, flipped through a few pages, and shot a very confused and very pissed off look my way.

"Don't ask how I got it. You won't like the answer," I said. "But I figured you'd like it back."

Gabriel kept a tight grip on his notebook, probably to make sure I didn't swipe it again. He drummed his fingers against it, then rubbed his forehead. McDuffie's had all of its TVs on mute, and the music overhead was so quiet it almost sounded like static. I could hear every strained exhale coming from Gabriel's nose. A short gulp. His leg bouncing up-and-down against the hardwood floor.

"If you really are Ash Murphy, do you remember what we talked about before you left?"

"Our conversation was hardly the most memorable thing to happen to me that day." I drummed my fingers along the table.

"You're trying to convince me that you're not a demon." He glared at me. "Try harder."

I raised an eyebrow. "'Discreet.'"

Gabriel's leg stopped bouncing. He kept glaring, but I didn't know if it was out of anger or shame. His gaze shifted away from me, so I assumed the latter. I thought I could hear his heartbeat, but it could have just been my own. The lighting above us started to flicker. Its humming felt like tinnitus.

"My turn." My lips twisted. "Who's Dinah? And James? And Rosa?" I glanced toward my notes, but those were the only Brothers I knew by name.

"Dinah manages the Brotherhood in Chicago. She does her best to keep everyone together and tries to, uh—" it took him some time to find the right word. "Recruit." He blinked. "James is a good friend. He joined the Brotherhood a bit before me, but we've known each other since we were kids. He's basically my big brother. Rosa's his girlfriend. She moved to town a few months ago, but doesn't really like talking about stuff before that."

My chair squeaked as I pushed it out a little.

"And Father Abram?" I asked.

He looked around the room. The other patrons were getting up to leave, and the waitress had retreated to the back room. He furrowed his brow and scooted his chair back a bit.

"Father Abram is a good man. That's all you need to know about him."

"Coulda guessed that myself," I hummed. "Dinah's a disaster. She's far too uncharismatic to actually run a cult. I'm sure whoever Abram is, he's as charming as they come."

As much as I would have loved to say something like "Dinah's incompetence is the only reason you're second-guessing anything," I didn't want to twist the knife too deep. Or praise Father Abram, for that matter. Gabriel didn't seem to take my backhanded compliment too well, but I wasn't sure if my words or my presence was making him uncomfortable. The front door opened, and another customer entered. Gabe's spine relaxed. Presence it was, then.

"My turn," he said. "If you don't really kill people, then what do you do?"

"I walk around the city and wait for someone to die. Then I pick up their ghost and bring them to a magical whirlpool in my basement so they can go to Heaven." I huffed. "I'm sure there's a better name for it, but we just call it the portal."

"So then if you think you're taking them to Heaven, you think you're an angel or something?"

"I'm just a scared little boy who's in way over his head." I brushed my hair out of my eyes. "And I'm sure you don't believe a word I'm saying, do you?"

The lights above us flickered again.

"I'm trying to keep an open mind."

"What makes you think that Geist cause death?" I came off a lot more accusatory than I meant to. "How do you explain cancer?"

"How do you explain the first-degree burn on my stomach?" He cocked his head to the side. "How am I supposed to know that you can't give someone Ebola just by looking at them?"

"Touché," I said. "But do you think that there's one Ebola Geist going around giving everyone Ebola? Or a million different Geist with Ebola powers? And what about accidents? If a plane crashes and everyone dies, is it the pilot's fault, or was there a Geist hovering over his shoulder? Was every terrorist attack in US history caused by magical demons?"

His fingers twitched. "Am I supposed to answer that?"

"You're supposed to think."

Gabriel stopped talking again. He leaned in closer. His face looked rather blank, but his eyebrows traveled up his forehead. He laced his fingers together and rested his chin on them.

"Why'd you give me back my iPod?"

"Because I'd feel like complete crap if I lost mine, and I don't want other people to feel that way."

He smiled a bit. Seeing him smile sent a little spark down my spine, and I didn't know if it was good or bad.

"I feel like I should thank you," he admitted. "I've, uh, I've been doing my best to listen to Dinah when it comes to you guys. We don't know what all of you are capable of. When I finally got a good look at you, it, uh, it kinda…" he stopped himself.

I rubbed the back of my neck. "Shook your faith?"

He didn't react for a bit, but nodded. "Y-yeah."

"My turn. Who's Harmony? She some other Brother I haven't had the chance to fight yet?"

His eyebrows did a little dance. "Harmony's my grandma."

He glanced toward the other people in the tavern. The question clearly made him uncomfortable. But I decided to press. If that ass could find out my life's story in a tabloid, it was time I pried.

"Same question, part two. Tell me about your family."

"That's not a question."

"It might as well be. Talk."

I crossed my arms. Gabe folded his hands and sighed.

"My dad was Second Lieutenant Christopher Wing. He died in Afghanistan after being there for nine months." A scowl crawled across his face. "Someone shot him in the stomach. All we got was a Purple Heart and his dog tags. Took the military three years before they said it was friendly fire." His scowl grew. "My mom died a few months after my dad. Now it's just me and Harmony, but she's, uh, she's not well." He took a deep breath and tried to erase his scowl. "So, to answer your question, the Brotherhood is the only family I have."

I leaned in. "Do you blame Geist for their deaths?"

"No." His voice gained the same authority it had earlier. "My dad died in a stupid accident. I don't know who killed him, but

I'm not going to blame some ghost. And my mom?" He paused. "Everyone knows how she died."

My pity was limited, but I still had it. Poor boy, I stupidly thought. His dad died overseas, but his mom may have died right in Chicago. I didn't know how she died, despite his assumption, but I hoped a good Geist helped her in the end. Someone like Clementine, or Johanna, or Winona. Basically, anyone but Vee.

"So, you with the Brotherhood because you believe Geist are evil, or because you've got nowhere else to go?" Or because he was a closeted homosexual overcompen—I stopped before that thought developed too much. He was in a doomsday cult-slash-street gang. Being in the closet was the least of his problems.

"I think it's obvious why," he said. "A Brother came to me, taught me how to see you, and told me all about what was going on." Gabriel tapped his goggles. "Father Abram developed these himself. They can pick up orgone energy. Every living thing gives off orgone energy, and that includes half-living things like Geist. So, when I first got to see you people taking ghosts of the dead to God knows where, of course I wanted to stop you. Invisible creatures with the ability to shoot fire from their hands?" His mouth twitched. "It's ungodly."

The lights stopped flickering, turning off altogether. Most of the day-drinkers left the building, and the waitress went to the back room again. We were alone again, but Gabriel didn't take his eyes off me. His brows wrinkled. His mouth twitched downward again.

"Ungodly. My ass." I grimaced and looked away. "Can I have one goddamn day where I don't have God shoved in my face?"

"Shoved in your face? How the Hell can you say that?" His scowl returned. "God's everywhere. Even someone like you should know He's with you. How can you not believe there are beings out there that're making this happen? We're both a part of something unexplainable."

"Everything's explainable. This isn't ancient Greece where they made a new god whenever they found a new lake." I clicked my tongue. "You see something you don't understand, and your instant reaction is to blame Satan and join a cult? Get a brain."

I hated being the angry atheist who complained about God. Of course, my patience was dead and so was I. Years of hearing about God's mercy and love from everyone around me all while dealing with constant emptiness left me bitter toward someone I didn't believe in. And dealing with a cult that thought I was a demon who fed souls to Satan was the exact opposite of what I needed. That said, I shouldn't have been too shocked by the amount of fanaticism around me. Gabe was right, and I didn't want to admit it. We were a part of something unexplainable.

Gabriel didn't take my sacrilege well. He got up from his seat and leered down at me. I got up from my seat so he didn't have to strain his thick neck with his condescending gaze.

"You say you aren't a demon? Show me," he demanded, pointing to the door. "Show me what you do with the souls. Show me how you find them, where you take them, where they go, whatever!"

"What if I don't?" I asked, looking back at him.

"Then we're stuck doing the same dance for the rest of our lives."

I tilted my hips to the side and chuckled.

"Wrong. The rest of your life." I took a step toward the door. "I've got all the time in the world."

Gabriel wanted me to drag him so deep into the rabbit hole he'd be neck-first in front of the Queen of Hearts. Of course, I knew the analogy went both ways. If I kept seeing him, Father Abram would scream "Off with his head." But, once again,

Gabriel was right, and I needed to figure out if the light at the end of the rabbit hole was the sun or its reflection off the guillotine's blade.

"Fine." I sighed and forced a fanged smile. "Have it your way. But if I prove to you that I'm not a demon from Hell, you owe me a present."

"A present?"

"Yeah. A present. I don't care what it is, just something to show that you're sorry and I'm perfect and always right." I smirked. "Unless it's your goddamn gospel music." My smirk turned into a scowl. "I never want to hear another acoustic guitar in my life."

It was time for me to get back to work, and apparently it was Bring Your Mortal Enemy to Work Day. I didn't want to think too hard about all the terrible things that could have happened. There was still a huge possibility of an ambush. Any other Geist could see me fraternizing with the enemy. Both could happen at the same time, leading the Brotherhood and all the Geist in the city to have a giant gang fight à la *West Side Story*. Song and dance included.

Gabriel and I left McDuffie's. He looked at me expectantly, as if I'd take out my ghost dowsing device. Instead, we started walking. No lights shot out of my necklace and nothing magnetized me in any direction. I explained the basics to Gabe as we walked around aimlessly. He almost looked disappointed. He probably wanted something more "unexplainable."

The two of us walked down the arid streets together. He usually stayed a few steps behind me, watching my back. I kept waiting for some kind of instinct to tell me where to go, but nothing came. I focusing so intently on my necklace, I almost didn't notice the vibration in my pocket. Pulling out the phone,

I saw Clementine's name across the screen. I let it keep ringing. My apologies could wait.

It was a horrible feeling, honestly. Waiting for someone else's death. I didn't want to see someone dead on the cold floor again, despite having an eternity of that ahead of me. But I also needed it. Gabriel was watching me, and every second there wasn't a soul reaping, he was growing more suspicious. I had found a crack in the Brotherhood's armor, and if I didn't convince him of Geist innocence quickly, the crack would reseal, possibly forever.

A giant bang rang through the air, followed by a trickle of hushed sizzles. I shuddered and let out a tiny yelp. Just fireworks, Ash. It was nothing. Just someone setting things off early.

As we walked, we didn't talk too much. Occasionally, Gabe would ask me if I felt anything. It hurt every time I said I didn't. It felt good every time I said I didn't. I was having a lot of feelings that day and needed a goddamn break. We kept winding by the streets in Zinda's territory. Time crept. Minutes went by and still nothing happened. Clementine called again. Someone else set off an early firework.

Gabriel grew more impatient. Over the hour we walked, the frequency of his questions increased, and they became much curter. His sentences whittled themselves down to the bare essentials. "Anything?" "Got something?" All the while, I got two more phone calls from Clementine. Still unanswered. Eight more burst of fireworks rang in my ears. Things kept coming at me from all sides and still nothing to show for it.

"Dammit, this is Chicago!" I cried. "Aren't people supposed to die every ten minutes from gunshots or cocaine or—"

"I've gotta leave."

I turned around, eyes widening, and stared at Gabriel. I stopped breathing but still tried to speak. He stayed in place, shifting his body around and pointing his shoulders away. I took a step closer to him and he took a step back.

"No! No, you're not leaving!" I said, waving my arms. "I brought you out with me so you could see what we do! If you want to see what's up, you're going to have to be goddamn patient!"

"Shut up!" he spat. "You're taking me on some wild goose chase around the city just so you can pretend you're really some angel of death. Well, I got news for you! It's not working! And even if you are helping them, this is gross. You're all a bunch of vultures."

"Oh-ho-ho-ho! Nonononono!" I laughed, edging toward hysteria. "You wanted to come out with me, boy! You said you wanted to see what it's like to be a Geist, and this is it! It's wasted time, emptiness, and waiting for the world to die around you!"

"That's disgusting."

"Well, I didn't want this! None of us wanted this! You think I wanted to die?" I screamed.

"Well, you sure do act like it," he said to my feet. "Bragging about your immortality, like it's a joke that you get to watch everyone die."

His face looked vicious, but it could not have been more vicious than my face. The air around me burned. It hurt to breathe the smoking air. Embers formed around the edges of my clothes. My collar glowed bright blue. The fire ate away my shirt. And I screamed like Hell.

"Shut up! Shut up! Shut up!" My head felt like it was going to fall off. "You don't get to pretend you know who I am! You wanna know how I got this way?"

I took another step forward, pulling the burning air with me. Pedestrians looped around us, ignoring the two people screaming in the middle of the sidewalk. Tiny flecks of my clothes blew away in the wind. Gabriel's face shifted again with a look of growing concern crossing it. I didn't know if it was fear, or pity, or empathy, but I didn't need any of those from him.

"Because, after you decided to show your true colors, some Geist decided to hitchhike in my ride home and grill me about Father Abram and then decided to turn me into a Geist. So, when my body burned up in the car fire, I got a new body, and this new body woke up only a few feet away from the entire scene." Another step. Little charred bits of clothes collided with his skin. He didn't avoid them. He was too focused on me. I was so close, I could have bitten his face off. "You wanna know what it's like to look down at your own burnt cadaver, Gabriel?"

Gabriel took another step back. I didn't bother to step forward. I was done. Done with Gabriel, done with stupidly trying to get his approval, done with the horrible Chinese water torture that came with patrolling the city. My pocket vibrated again. I let it keep vibrating. Another firework shot off into the air. The entire world became fuzzy, and the only things I could see were Gabriel and the tiny flecks of burning clothes spinning around my head.

"Just go. Go on and have fun with your stupid cult. Get wasted at your friend's big birthday. And then, when you're all just a bunch of drunk punks ready for a fight, go out and find a few Geist to harass." My voice lowered. "Because, no matter how many times you gouge out our teeth, burn our skin, and electrify us, eventually, you will die. And we'll be the ones dragging your screaming soul away from your corpse. And there's no way to stop that."

I walked away. The world became clear again. My clothes stopped burning. Gabriel was out of my line of sight, and I didn't need to look at him any longer. I started walking away. I could not hear any sound coming from him. The entire city seemed to quiet down just for me. No cars honking, no birds squawking, no fireworks exploding. All I could hear was the sound of the Earth rotating.

And then, a light. A blue light shot out of my necklace, pointing me right toward a fresh corpse. I closed my eyes, took in a deep breath, and turned back to Gabriel.

"I found someone."

Gabriel didn't say anything. He walked up to me, jaw clenched, and started following me again. Neither of us said a word as I followed the light. Another phone call came from Clementine. But I didn't let myself get distracted. I just followed the light toward the spirit.

The fireworks got more frequent. I couldn't see the explosions in the daylight, but the sound burned in my ears. I forced myself to keep following the light, but every few seconds, another explosion shot into the sky. And with each explosion, I saw fire. I saw the red truck crash into me. I saw the smug face of the Geist that gave me my Spark. I saw my own death. My breathing grew faint. All I could do was follow the light.

I stopped. I was close to the ghost. The light was pointing me toward an apartment, and it dawned on me how familiar it was. Gabriel and I were standing right outside his apartment, and the pull was pointing me inside.

"This is my—" Horror dawned on Gabriel's face. "Harmony!"

Gabriel pushed past me and ripped the door open. I stood in shock, my knees shaking. Another firework shot into the sky, and the explosion almost ripped my heart open.

"Yvonne!"

I ran in.

Chapter 11
Feel Human Again

Gabriel was already miles ahead of me by the time I flew through the door. I jumped up the steps five at a time, terrified out of my mind. The horrible image of Yvonne's body bleeding on her carpet haunted me. My foot caught the tip of the final stair. I tumbled to the ground, but I clawed my way toward Yvonne's door. I kicked myself up, grabbed her door handle, and realized that the light was pointing a few doors down the hall.

A scream permeated the hallway, and my head turned to Gabriel's open door. My breathing stopped, and it was like all sound was erased from the building. I put one foot in front of the other. With each step, I grew closer to Gabriel's apartment, and the light pointed me inside.

I pushed open the door. The small living room was empty, but two doors ahead of me were ajar, and both had thick moans coming from them. I crept toward the door without light and peeked inside. With only the light from the living room, I saw a floor covered in old magazines, newspapers, and pill bottles. Someone laying on a large bed, wrapped in blankets, and her strained breathing rattled my bones.

But another moan came from the other door. I inched away from the dark room and walked toward the bathroom. Thoughts of Natalie ran through my head. When I looked inside the room, it was much worse, and I ran back and pressed myself against the wall. I covered my mouth and nose to keep myself from screaming.

Gabriel shoved the door wide open, teeth bared and eyes

filled with tears. I tried to keep my eyes on him and not the scene inside the bathtub. Gabriel slammed the door shut and stood between me and the doorway. His legs were shaking so intensely, the entire building shook.

"G-get away from him!" he shouted.

I couldn't move. I was shaking almost as much as he was. Everything behind that door was a nightmare I didn't want to see again. Even if I only saw it for a second, even if it was through my periphery vision, I saw the entire scene every time I blinked. The bathtub. The bloody wrists. The barely-formed ghost laying catatonic next to his former body.

Gabriel ran past me and jumped toward the closet. He pulled his gauntlet from the top shelf and slipped it on his quivering arm. Another moan came from inside the bathroom, and my hand moved toward the knob. Gabriel grabbed my fingers with his gauntlet and zapped my entire hand.

"Get out!" he screamed. "Get the hell out!"

He shoved me to the ground. Another moan came from the bathroom, and another vibration came from my cell phone. It wasn't until another loud explosion rang through the sky that I finally found the strength to move. I stumbled toward the exit, and Gabriel chased me the entire way. But I was faster. No matter how hard he tried, I was already out of the building before he reached his own door.

Without looking back, I ran as quickly as I could back to the mansion. Nothing felt quiet anymore. Every step on the pavement sounded like cymbals clashing. The cars passing me sounded like they were skidding against the road. The fireworks above me seemed like they were exploding only inches away from my face, and I could feel their heat. I closed my eyes and kept running.

I opened my eyes, and Zinda Mansion was within my grasp.

My breaths became quicker, and I slapped my necklace onto the lily. I fell down the steps and pushed the door open, causing it to crash against the wall. My breaths echoed through the giant foyer. I took a step in, and the door creaked closed behind me. Everything felt quiet again, but my heartbeats kept pounding.

"Ash?"

I looked into the living room. Clementine sat on a couch with Jesse, Winona, and Farrah right by her side. She got up from her seat, but before she could step forward, I was already in the living room next to her. I crashed into her chest and started crying. She fell back onto the couch as I wept into her dress. Jesse reached his arms around both of us, shushing me.

"I'm sorry!" I cried. "I'm sorry, Clementine!" I kept repeating it. "I can't do this! I—I can't do this! I'm sorry!"

Clementine tightened her grip around me and stroked my hair. She and Jesse kept their arms around me as I laid on top of them, sobbing my way through a million apologies. Winona tried to whisper a few "It's okay"s into my ear, but I ignored them.

It became hard for me to call something "the worst day of my life." I had a lot of crappy days. The day I found out Zack died was terrible, as were the following few months. Of course, the day I died was terrible. But that led to a question that I didn't want to ask. Was it possible to have a good day anymore?

I should have expected that. I was dead. There was no beating around the bush with that. No matter how many times people told me I was immortal, Ash Murphy was legally dead. What I was experiencing was not purgatory. We weren't waiting for any judgment. What I was experiencing was a parody of life.

I laid face-down on the couch for a while. Sobs escaped me when I couldn't stop them. Clementine rubbed my back the entire time, and all the others cooed little words of encouragement to me. Each one felt like a lie.

"The first day's always the hardest, Ash," said Farrah.

"You ain't gotta tell us what happened, hon," said Clementine. "Just sit here and breathe for a few, 'kay?" She rubbed my scalp again. "You did a good job today."

"No, I didn't." I slid up from her lap and put my back against the armrest. I rubbed my eyes, trying to remove the dried tears but only ended up making them redder. "One of the Brotherhood guys killed himself, and I couldn't get him. James's wrists…" my sentence was drowned out by my own sobs. "I couldn't get him."

"Wait, James? The big one?" Winona piped in, her words unsteady. "But we just saw him this morning." Winona looked toward Farrah. "Oh my God, did I—"

"No," Farrah hushed. "This is not your fault. None of us are at fault here!"

"That's not what Gabriel said," I mumbled. "I tried—I tried to show him how Geist work, and all I did was make him think I made his best friend commit suicide." I looked at Clementine, my black eyes still bloodshot. My mouth contorted into a smile. A scared, wide-eyed smile. Like I was telling a joke and I was the punchline. "I thought I could take down the Brotherhood all by myself." I tried to calm myself. I didn't want to set fire to anything. "What if I could have changed their minds? What if I could have shown them the good we do?"

"Buddy, there are people out there you just can't reason with," said Jesse. "There ain't no use tryin'a be nice to 'em."

Jesse's giant hand rubbed a tear away from my cheek. My entire body felt cold. There was no chance of burning the mansion down because my veins were pumping ice.

"Then we saw James, I—" My hand grabbed my head. I huddled on the couch, slowly rocking in place. "When I saw James, I saw my body in the car. I can still taste the fire. Why do we even pretend this is okay?"

Clementine's shoulders collapsed. She edged closer to me, giving me a big hug. She made direct eye contact, not breaking it for a second.

"Oh, sweetie." Her words barely registered. "I'm sorry you had to go through this today."

"Today?" Nothing seemed funny anymore. My hysteria disappeared. "We spend every day waiting for people to die, and then we pretend that we're just a bunch of happy children partying it up!" My eyes burned. "Why can't you all see we're living a damn joke?" I stopped breathing. "All of us are dead!"

"Ash, come on!" huffed Winona. She got up from the couch. "We may all be dead, but we can at least make the best of a bad situation! I'd rather party like a child than drown in my feelings all day!"

"And we ain't livin' no joke!" exclaimed Jesse. He got up from the couch too and looked down at us, a mix of anger and panic on his face. "We're helpin' those people get into Heaven! And we got a good deal outta this. We can live forever if we just take some time outta our week to get these people home."

I sunk further into the couch. Everyone's anger pierced my skin. I couldn't look them in the eyes, so I just covered my face and nodded.

"I'm sorry. I just—I just thought I could fix this. I wanted to help. And I failed on the first goddamn day."

No one else said anything. Winona and Jesse slowly sat back down on the couch. Jesse patted me on the back, and Winona reached around to give me a hug that was, as always, too tight. Then, my heart stopped. I looked at Clementine, pleading.

"We need to go back! James's ghost is still there!" I gasped. "What happens? What happens when we just leave them? Why won't you tell me?"

Clementine lowered her gaze and stayed silent. My spine

shook. I could feel her judgment. I was a brat who mouthed off to her, disobeyed her, and never gave her the friendship she deserved. Clementine closed her eyes, got up from the couch, and patted my cheek.

"You said it was a suicide?" She put her hands on her hips. "That means we got time. Ash, you stay put and rest up. We'll go out and make sure that boy gets to the portal safely."

I told them where to find James, and Clementine, Jesse, Winona, and Farrah headed out the front door. I stayed on the couch, sinking even deeper into it. An Ash-shaped groove formed. Getting up and heading to my room seemed too hard. Even putting on my headphones was too much for me. I wilted in the huge living room, alone with my thoughts.

I lost track of time, but no matter how long I stayed on the couch, the front door stayed shut. At least an hour must have passed before I heard footsteps click through the foyer. The steps were light and delicate, unlike Vee's constant stomping. Even if I barely heard them, I knew they must have been Johanna's. The footsteps came closer to the living room, but I still didn't turn around. I kept my face toward the cushions.

"Ashton? Why are you not out on patrol?"

I turned my head, seeing Johanna wearing the same expression she always wore. I propped myself up on the couch. Even if I was out of it, I didn't want to seem rude. Johanna was the only person I knew who didn't see me eff up majorly, so I needed to be on my best behavior. Still, my head hurt and I couldn't keep my foot out of my mouth.

"Because I screwed the pooch, Johanna. Clementine and her friends are out looking for a ghost I couldn't bring back." I shook my head, forcing a smile. "I think it's been an hour and I haven't moved from this couch." Johanna's face stayed blank. "Screwing the pooch means that I—"

"I am aware of what it means."

Johanna sat on the chair across from the couch. Her posture was straight against the chair's back, her hands were placed gently on her lap, and her legs stayed completely straight. She almost looked like an old porcelain doll. I tried to mimic her posture, but ended up looking like a sleeping giraffe.

"How exactly did you mess up?" she asked me.

"What a question." I laughed. My laughter stopped as soon as it started. I wondered how much I wanted to tell Johanna. More so, how much I was able to tell her. "Well, today, I was having coffee with Winona and Farrah." My face soured. "All of a sudden, three Brothers show up, and I stupidly decided to go up to them. One of the guys said bad things about my family, so I punched him. Then I just kept making an ass of myself all over the place. And we got in a fight."

Johanna didn't respond. She only nodded. She was thinking something, and I wanted to know. Judgments were being made about me. Johanna had the perfect poker face, but I knew she was judging me. Everyone was.

"And is that what caused you to come back?"

"No. I came back for a bit, got in a stupid, stupid fight with Clementine, and then went out again." Everything sounded so simple when I said it out loud. "And before long, a Brotherhood boy came up to me. He wanted to watch me go on patrol. He wanted to see what we really did." I desperately wished I could have finished the story there. "And then we came across the dead body of his best friend."

Johanna looked off to the side. She got out of her seat and went over to the window. Keeping her gaze toward the outside, she gripped her right wrist with her left hand and squeezed.

"Perhaps it was foolish of me to want you to go on patrol so early." A chill went through my spine when she looked at me. No matter how many times I saw her, it was a special occasion whenever her frigid gray eyes looked directly at me instead of around me. "I had been dead for decades before I knew it was my duty to gather souls. In those decades, I was able to cry. I was able to mourn my own death. And the death of—" there was a slight stutter in her usually robotic voice "—my husband, Nathaniel." Johanna blinked and walked toward me. "We gave you no time to recover, did we?"

I tried to respond in some way, but I couldn't. Not a "No," not a shake of my head, not even a blink. I had been dead for barely a month. And in that time, I was expected to completely upend my life, relearn everything I knew about the universe, and do my best not to think about everyone I left behind. Johanna walked closer to me, and I finally snapped out of my daze.

"Clementine will bring back the soul of the Brother soon. There is nothing for you to fret over." Johanna almost glided over to me. As if she wasn't moving her legs at all. "Tomorrow the cycle starts again. In a few days' time, it will be your turn again. I understand if you want us to make a compromise. Perhaps you could only go out every seven days instead of every four, or you could only go out for half a day like today."

"I'll have to think about it."

I glanced away from Johanna, toward the bottom of our grand staircase. The door to the portal was only a few yards away from me. Natalie was on the other side of that portal, along with countless others. Zack, too. The only people who had the option to never see the other side of it were the Geist. Johanna, Vee, Clementine, Jesse, Winona, Farrah, Teresa, Olive, me, and however many else there were in the world. All we had to do was throw the real dead people down the drain, and we were allowed to continue with our quasi-lives.

Johanna walked toward the foyer and beckoned me to follow. I stood up, unsteady on my feet, and chased after her. She opened the front door. The two of us continued walking and stood at the top step of the cold, ghostly stairs. Dozens of people were waiting on the tracks above us, yet none of them had any idea what they were standing over. Just an unnoticeable stairwell going into an impossible building.

"Clementine may have told you this already," Johanna started, "but I do not sleep. One thing I prefer over sleeping is walking. Do you find joy in taking walks?"

I nodded. "I used to do cross country."

"I recommend you start walking again, Ashton." She stepped the ground of the real world. "Every day, leave the mansion for a while and jog. Above all else, it will clear your mind. Perhaps, by the time we return, Clementine will be back with the Brother. Do you wish to walk with me for a spell?"

Nodding, I took a step into the real world too.

Johanna and I started walking. Neither of us talked for a while. Johanna, nowhere near dressed for a jog, clicked her flats across the sidewalk while keeping a snail's speed. I kept my pace slow, trying to match hers. At times, I had to stop moving and wait for her to catch up. She noticed my constant stopping and restarting and started talking again.

"Feel free to walk ahead, Ashton. You do not need to stay to chat. I will probably be on this walk for a long time, so you can just run ahead and come back to the mansion whenever you desire. And feel free to listen to your music player. Clementine told me how much you enjoy it."

I told her thanks and then walked ahead. I put my headphones on, turned on my music, and started up a jog. The weight of death was lifted. I wasn't outside to patrol the city, I was outside to walk and only walk. Within a minute, I was several blocks away from the mansion and keeping up a brisk pace. The only thing on my mind was the next step I was going to take. I pretended I was wearing horse blinders. The buildings next to me did not exist. My music was loud enough to block out the sound of the explosions. There was only a sidewalk and me.

Of course, me being me, I went back to thinking very quickly. All Geist died at one point. And even though Johanna and Clementine gave me no time to recover, I didn't know if I'd ever really get better. From what little I heard, Johanna's death still haunted her. No one who avoided sleep could possibly be free of trauma. Other Geist seemed less haunted. Jesse died. Winona, too. Neither of them acted like people who had a traumatic, life-ending experience. Not that outside emotions mattered. Anyone could fake a smile and pretend everything was fine.

The city kept moving. As I got further from the mansion, things became more peaceful for me. I had forgotten how much jogging with music calmed me. I forgot about most of the things that made me happy. The vibrations my body got from my feet slamming on the ground, the wind blowing against my sweat, everything felt amazing. I didn't have to think about the Brotherhood or James or Zack or death at all. For the first time in a long time, I started to feel human again.

I returned to the mansion a few hours later, out of breath and covered in sweat. I tried not to think of James when I looked toward the doors to our basement. I wanted to open it, hoping that I'd see a glimpse of James's head as he receded into the portal. Or maybe see Clementine come up the steps with a cute smile on her face. The door stayed shut, and I didn't bother opening it. I headed upstairs, walking as quietly as possible.

I stopped mid-step right as I reached the third floor.

Mumbling was coming from inside the music room, and I held my breath.

"We searched everywhere, Jo. He was gone, body and spirit." Clementine's voice was so quiet, but I could still hear her panic. "There was blood everywhere, but they must have moved the body."

"It is possible that another Geist found the soul before you did," reassured Johanna.

"There's a snowball's chance in Hell that actually happened, but I'll make some calls to check." Clementine sighed. "We can't tell Ash we couldn't find him."

I sat down outside the music room, keeping my ear close to the door. Every good feeling I reclaimed on my run disappeared, and all my fears returned. Somehow, on my first day, I managed to cause a crisis not even Clementine could fix.

"Is he positive it was a suicide?" asked Johanna. "If it was a murder, we will have to act very quickly. The soul could turn before the end of the week." The way she said turn sent a chill down my spine.

Clementine paused. "He said it was suicide. I trust him."

"If he left this world willingly, then we have a fair while before we have to worry. I will go searching tonight, and I will not return until I have found him. Do not let Ashton do anything foolish."

Footsteps came toward the door, and I scattered toward my room. Barely a second after I closed my door halfway, the music room opened and Johanna headed downstairs. Clementine left as well and shot a glance toward my door. We made eye contact, and my heart sank.

Clementine slid my door open. She grabbed my hands and whisked me over to my bed. We sat there, not breaking eye contact, with Clementine's tight grip keeping my hands from shivering. Even when more and more fireworks ignited the sky, I felt her hands on mine, and I didn't hear a thing.

"Everythin's gonna be fine, Ash." Clementine shook my hand and gripped it tighter. "Do you trust me?"

I thought about all the things Clementine kept secret from me. I thought about all the lies of omission. But when I looked at her, all I saw was the woman who was there for me during my darkest hours.

I nodded. "Yes."

Chapter 12
Sanctuary

Johanna didn't return that night. I woke up the next morning and went straight to her room. I knocked. No answer. The music room was silent. I headed into the bleak room with the skull board. Johanna's red skull was far away from Zinda Mansion, still wandering around the city. Inch by inch, it traversed, no doubt still looking for the missing ghost. I ran my finger around the other skulls and told myself not to worry.

After a bit of rescheduling, I was relieved of my duties for the foreseeable future. It was Vee's day to monitor the city. Clementine and I had a small lunch by ourselves while Jesse took care of some errands around town. Clementine either completely forgave me for my stupid outburst or just didn't want to talk about it. I guessed the latter. She spent the rest of the day in her fashion room, while I meandered around the mansion trying to find something to do. I checked in on her occasionally, seeing her sketching out new designs or comparing fabrics. Each time I popped in, I noticed her little glass of whiskey was always full, no matter how many times she took a sip.

Johanna was still gone. I told myself not to worry.

The next day, it was Clementine's turn at bat. I took another jog in the morning, not seeing any sign of the Brotherhood. When I came back, I checked on the skull board again. The red skull was still a little ways away from the mansion. My anxiety grew, and I needed a way to quickly calm myself down. I spent the rest of the day reading through one of Vee's romance novels, *Help! I'm Locked in the Minotaur's Sex Labyrinth*. I made a meatloaf for dinner that night. Vee took one look at the meatloaf, gagged, and left to pick up a pizza.

"Are you trying to kill me?" she said as she flipped me off.

Johanna's day came. Vee went off to do her own thing while Clementine, Jesse, and I headed over to La Maison. Before I left, I checked the skull board. Johanna was still out and about. On the trip to La Maison, I still saw no signs of the Brotherhood. We spent the day hanging out with Winona, Farrah, and Teresa, with Olive popping up once before running off. None of them mentioned anything about James or my breakdown. It was as if they had forgotten anything had happened.

Around eight, I suggested to get dinner at McDuffie's on the off-chance Yvonne was playing that night. Winona voted for my idea before I even finished saying it, and we headed off to the tavern, still free from the Brotherhood. McDuffie's was hopping, which was to say that there were more than ten people in the bar. Yvonne was, sadly, off that night. Our waitress refilled our drinks exactly once. The stage was barren, and it seemed like I was the only one that noticed.

Our walk home was nice and Brotherhood-free. When we made it back to the mansion, we were greeted with a giant cloud of dank smoke and Vee sprawled out on the living room couch with her bong. Johanna was nowhere to be found.

Jesse's day came. Still no sign of Johanna. Clementine took advantage of our alone time by taking me to a play. We ended up finding a production of *A Midsummer Night's Dream*, one that was "experimental" and also steampunk for some reason. Like a good lady, she actually paid for our seats. I asked if the play reminded her of her childhood in ancient Greece, and she gave me a massive side-eye. We spent most of the day downtown, still free from the Brotherhood. When we came home, Vee was once again simmering in a cloud of pot. Johanna wasn't home.

Vee's patrol came around again. Johanna was still unaccounted for. Clementine didn't go into her workshop that day. She stayed in the living room, sometimes reading a book, but mostly just watching the front doors. Every so often, I ran back to the skull board. Johanna's skull was still on the map, a good distance away from the mansion. I measured the distance between her skull and mine with my thumb and index finger. Vee came home more frequently that day, dropping off at least one soul per hour.

Clementine left early the next morning for her patrol. Johanna still never returned. I grew more concerned, so I checked the skull board again before breakfast. Her skull was still a fair distance away from the mansion on the board. It looked like it was in the exact same spot it was the day before. I measured the distance between her skull and mine again. Same distance. I called Clementine. She told me not to worry.

Suddenly, it was Johanna's day again. I hadn't seen Johanna in days, but Clementine assured me she was the most professional woman in town and would never slack off on duty. She proceeded to go on a long rant about the differences between Johanna and Vee.

Clementine and I left the mansion that afternoon to pick up a year's worth of fabrics from her favorite craft store. All the way there, still no Brotherhood. Clementine rummaged through the sale rack, as if she didn't have at least seven Benjamins stuffed in her purse. I leaned up against the rack, brushing my shoulder against a hideous floral fabric. Clementine compared a few different fabrics, putting them against me to see if they were "my color." A bell rang from the front of the store, and I half-expected Gabriel to pop in, looking for supplies to make a cozy for his gauntlet. Instead, it was a random middle-aged woman, probably not associated with the Brotherhood. I sneered.

"It's been a full week since we've seen anything from the Brotherhood," I said. "Don't you find that weird?"

"I'm almost a hundred years old. I don't find many things weird no more." Clementine put a swatch of dark blue velvet against my skin. "They lost two of their own within a few days. Brotherhood or not, they're human, and they need time to rest after that."

"Don't you think they could be planning something?" I asked.

"The Brotherhood can plan all they want." Clementine plopped the velvet into her basket. "They're tryin'a play God, and God don't like that, so He ain't helpin' them out any."

"And what about James's ghost?" I asked.

Clementine kept her attention on the different fabrics. Feeling them, checking the price, and comparing them to the sketches in her sketch pad. I got bored and started playing around with the spools of ribbon. I noticed Clementine pull a ream of pea green silk from the bottom shelf.

"That's the most hideous color I've ever seen," I said. "Don't use it."

Looking me directly in the eyes, she dropped the fabric into her cart. Her eyes widened, and she tilted her head. Satan was in her eyes. A petty, spiteful Satan.

"I'll make an amazing cocktail dress out of this, and you'll eat your—"

The front door slammed open.

"Clementine!" someone screamed. "Clementine!"

Vee stomped toward the back of the store, and she was more sober than I had seen her in days. Her eyes looked red, but more from rage than weed. She elbowed past an over-tanned soccer mom and stomped up to Clementine. With the crappy lighting, her biceps looked even more jacked than normal. Clementine remained unimpressed and continued on with her fabric.

"I've been calling you for ten minutes. Is it really too hard for you to answer your damn phone?"

Clementine handed me her basket and took her giant phone out of her purse.

"Oh, this dern gizmo. It just makes my ol' arthritis kick in." She dialed a few numbers and put the phone up to her ear. "Want me to call you back?"

Vee's phone started to ring. She didn't pick it up. Her beeping ringtone filled the store with awkward, pixelated tension. I kept my distance, watching the two women just stare at each other with mildly pissed off glares. Clementine dropped the call, put her phone back into her purse, and went back to her shopping.

"Johanna's not on patrol," Vee said. "I was getting lunch and, on the way, there was some dead old guy locked in his apartment. He was screaming that he died yesterday. He was like four blocks from the mansion. She should'a gotten him the second she left."

Clementine gripped the pea-green fabric. Tightened her grip. Loosened it. Tightened it again. Her eyes were clenched shut so tightly it looked like her eyelids were about to burst.

"That's it! We're checking in on her!" she exclaimed.

Clementine threw her basket of fabric to the ground and rushed out of the store. Her feet weren't even touching the floor. Vee and I chased after her. I told myself to worry.

Vee didn't look too nervous. She looked more annoyed than anything, sneering that she had to ferry a soul on her off-day. Clementine tried to keep her cool, only nodding and make affirming grunts when Vee complained about something, but I saw the fear in her eyes.

Every step I took, I thought of a new horrible thing that

could have happened to Johanna. Step—What if she fell down a bottomless pit?—step—What if she fell into a lake and froze? In summer.—step—What if some religious nut wanted to talk about Jesus with her, and she's still talking to him? In a lot of ways, I exaggerated my fear. It was all a hyperbole to distract me from the actual possibility. What if the Brotherhood got to her?

Clementine called Jesse and asked him to check the skull board. After about a minute of her trying to reteach him how to use it, she called Farrah instead. Farrah pointed us in the right direction, acting as a quasi-living GPS. The further we got on our journey, the more familiar a few things got. A gas station, a specific pothole in the road, tiny things that jogged my memory. Before long, I told Clementine to hang up. I knew exactly where we were going. Within a few blocks, we were right outside the Brotherhood's Sanctuary.

"If Johanna's really inside that building, that means that the Brotherhood's got her."

"Johanna couldn't have been kidnapped," Clementine said, with zero confidence backing anything she was saying. "She knows how to take care of herself."

"Well then, let's head on in and find out what she's doing in there." Vee started walking toward the Sanctuary. "Hope it's a surprise party. Any of your birthdays coming up?"

The old factory's front door was ajar. That was our first bad omen. Our second was the light coming from inside. Vee pushed the door open, giving us a view of the allegedly abandoned factory's inside. Like a geode, the factory's dilapidated outside hid a comely interior.

The large room was deserted, but everything still looked fresh. The walls were lined with arcade machines, pool tables, and bar paraphernalia. All the electronics were plugged in. Vee walked over to a refrigerator. She opened it, pulled out a beer, and drank it. I knelt beside a vintage arcade cabinet. The wall behind it was completely dust free. Not only was the factory populated, it was freshly populated.

Vee tossed her empty beer can onto the floor. Clementine picked up the can and placed it in the recycling bin. She stopped in her tracks. She knelt down, putting her head right by the floor. Vee and I stepped closer as she pulled out her pocket watch.

Clementine looked like something other than a Brotherhood man-cave was bothering her. I sat down next to her, and suddenly, I felt her unease. A thin, barely visible purple light was shooting out of her pocket watch. Vee pulled out her dog tags and I pulled out my necklace. Weak lights all shot right toward the floor below.

"I think we found James," said Clementine.

Clementine shot back up. Without another word, she headed for the closest door. Vee and I followed her, and I knew exactly what was going on. Somewhere in the giant factory, Johanna and James hid. If the factory really was the Brotherhood's Sanctuary, there really was a dead body somewhere in the basement, and Johanna really was trapped here, that meant only one thing.

We were boned.

Clementine pushed open the door to the next room. Everything looked a lot crappier beyond the threshold. We walked into a hallway, and it was as dirty as I expected an abandoned factory to be. A fine coating of dust muffled our footsteps. Paint chips fluttered down from the ceiling like petals in a breeze. Were I alive, I would have worried about asbestos. A sliver of lighting slipped through broken windows, giving us just enough visibility to see a few feet ahead of us and just enough to make me want to cry in terror.

I flipped open my phone and used the screen as a flashlight.

Thin paths free of dust and clutter led to different doors. Clementine opened a door next to us, leading to what used to be a small office. We tried another door, leading to a similar room. Every room in the hall seemed to be barren. At the very end of the hall, we opened the final door. It led to a pitch-black stairwell descending into a void.

"This is dumb. This is so dumb." I reached my phone over the railing. It illuminated nothing. "I'm crapping myself, Clementine."

"Yeah, what if this place is haunted?" said Vee. "Wouldn't that be scary?"

"Bite me, Virginia."

"What's wrong, pussy?" she hissed. "Didn't you say you wanted to take down this cult? Now's your chance."

"You two better pipe down before I sew your mouths shut!" Clementine spat. She took a step onto the stairwell. Somehow, they looked even more rickety than the stairs down to the portal. A giant creak echoed through the room. "Johanna's somewhere in this building with a lingering spirit. The Brotherhood could be anywhere. We gotta get in and out without causin' a ruckus."

"Hey, Brotherhood!" Vee screamed into the darkness. Her own voice echoed back. Clementine and I jumped. "Y'all got Johanna?"

"Virginia Zhang," said Clementine, folding her arms.

"What?"

"I'm prayin' for you."

Clementine, Vee, and I descended the stairs. Our footsteps echoed down the empty chasm. Every little creak sounded like a potential disaster, and every time my foot reached another step, I felt like I was going to fall. I looked behind me and saw Clementine's apprehension, and I forced myself to hide my fear.

When we finally reached solid ground, I had no idea how

far underground we were. We exited the dark stairwell and found ourselves in another hallway. Fluorescent lights flickered above us. While nowhere near as well put together as the opening room, it still looked slightly lived-in. People had been through the hall recently.

The magnetic pull seemed stronger. Still feeble, the sensation came from the end of the hallway. All the doors had been ripped off the hinges except the one door at the very end, which, undoubtedly, was where James's soul stayed. Clementine walked down the hall and grabbed the knob. I stopped her from pulling it open.

"Clementine, there's three of us and God knows how many Brothers. Why don't we call Jesse or Winona or any of the hundreds of Geist in this city?" I pleaded. "This is a trap. It's gotta be a trap."

"We can take care of this, Ash." Clementine pulled my hand away from hers. She stroked a strand of hair out of my face. "No matter how many times they punch or shock us, we'll get up and keep walking. Let them trap us."

I stared at her, then nodded. Clementine slid the door open. The three of us stepped into the next room. Everything was pitch black. I could barely see Clementine or Vee in the darkness. Near the ceiling, a blue glow waned and waxed. A buzzing sound resonated around us. We took a few more steps. From behind us, I heard a slam. The door shut behind us, and we stood there in darkness.

"Surprise, it's a trap," mumbled Vee.

"Oh, godda—" I started.

A spotlight turned on, highlighting the blue light. My eyes widened. Johanna dangled from the ceiling, as unmoving and straight as a steel girder, with thick wires twisted around her neck. Sparks shot out from the bindings wrapped around her arms and legs. Electricity streamed through every part of her body, but she still remained motionless.

About seven feet below her, her Bible floated in mid-air. With her neck latched to the ceiling with electric wires and her Memento pulling her toward the floor, Johanna's immortal body was being pulled in two different directions, unable to be ripped apart but unable to fight anything.

Clementine screamed and ran forward, stumbling on fragments of broken cement along the way. I chased after her, avoiding the few obstacles I could see. Clementine and I stood directly below the hanging Johanna. Clementine screamed her name, but Johanna stayed motionless. A whimper escaped Clementine.

"How could this happen?"

Blue glows sparked all around us, like thousands of eyes opening at once. My heart plummeted. All the lights in the room turned on. We were inside a huge room large enough to fit a jumbo jet. A labyrinth of catwalks hung above us. Religious decorum scattered around the room with rows of pews leading to a giant cross. And in every direction, from every angle, the Brotherhood of Eternity surrounded us.

Clementine and I spun around, taking in everything. More Brotherhood members than I had ever seen enclosed us. On the ground floor, at least sixty members crowded around us. The catwalks above us overflowed with more members. Each one wore their goggles, turning themselves into a faceless mob, and whatever age, or height, or weight they were, it didn't matter anymore. Vee crept forward and joined us under Johanna. I huddled next to Clementine, clutching her hand. She clutched mine even harder.

"What the Hell is this?" screamed Vee.

From a catwalk, a familiar army jacket poked its way out of

the faceless masses. Dinah loomed over us, hocking a giant wad of phlegm toward our feet. It missed me, thank God. Next to her, I could make out the silhouette of Rosa. In the crowd, I could make out a whole host of other Brothers I recognized. But I saw no sign of Gabriel.

"You did this!" screamed Dinah. "You tried to pry your way into our family. You tricked our Brothers. Manipulated them! And the second they let their guard down, you stole one of them from right under us!"

"What's she talking about?" growled Vee.

Dinah stepped onto the railing. Two stories above us, a crazed woman was using a rickety metal fence as her stage. If the Brothers weren't staring at us, they were looking up at her. The ones still intent on us stepped closer, shrinking our cage.

"This is what we fight!" shouted Dinah to her mob. "Every day, these things steal the ones we care about and feed them to whatever it is they call God! These are the creatures that cause innocent lives to end themselves! These monsters! These demons! These—" She squatted down, perched over us like a gargoyle, "—Geist."

"No, really, what's she talking about?" repeated Vee, a slight shake in her voice.

"Who knows what would have happened if we let them roam without our intervention? But by helping purge the world of their filth, we have made sacrifices we never could prepare ourselves for!" A roar of agreement came from the mob. "We managed to capture one of theirs before she was able to abscond with our Brother! And now we have in our grasp two of our prize targets! And they even brought a third! Don't give them an inch! Attack them until there's nothing left!" she bellowed. "And aim for whatever looks important."

Like a swarm of fire ants, they all attacked at once. All sixty-plus Brotherhood members on the ground lunged forward with their gauntlets at the ready. I yelped, and Clementine pushed me between her and Vee.

Vee didn't need to be told what to do. As soon as the Brothers came close, she attacked. Vee slammed her fists into the faces of everyone within reach. Several Brothers grabbed her arms and tried to pull her to the ground. Vee roared and shards of ice flew out of her body in all directions. One shard nicked me across the face. All the Brothers around her jumped back, picking the shards out of their bloodied skin. But when they withdrew, more charged in their place.

One particularly large woman smashed her gauntlet onto Clementine's forehead. A giant bomb of electricity pushed her into me, and I fell to the floor. Vee, in between punches, pulled me to my feet by my neck, then attacked another Brother. Her devilish smirk made it look like she was almost enjoying the chaos. Clementine blew in the giant woman's face, making her entire body flip backward into a mass of her Brothers.

Clementine grabbed my arm and ran. When she came within a foot of the mass of Brothers, she shoved out her palm. A rush of wind flowed through the stale air and pushed all of the Brothers away from us. A clearing formed and, in the far end of the room, a door looked ajar. Clementine pushed me in the direction, and I didn't have to be told twice what to do.

"Vee and I got this. Find the boy!"

I ran down the clearing. More adrenaline ran through my veins than ever in my life. The clearing closed down, and people started clawing at me. A very spindly Brother kicked my kneecap, and I fell right to the ground. All of the Brothers around me buckled down and clawed at me. Their hands searched everywhere around my body. I screamed and kicked. A scrappy one slammed her foot onto my head, digging my face into the cement to keep me from screaming. The spindly Brother finally put a finger on my necklace. The necklace heated up and shook.

"It's the necklace!"

Another giant gust of wind came from behind me. Every Brother around me flew aside, colliding with each other and slamming against the walls. The wind threw me forward several yards. My head slammed onto the cement just feet from the open door. I rubbed my face, got up, and ran through the door, locking it behind me. Vicious pounding came from the other side, but stopped after a few seconds. Everything became quiet.

The magnetic pull was weak, but I knew it was close. I was in a storage room. Nothing was in the room except for a few dilapidated pews, candle holders, and a worn down, brown piano. But when I took in a breath, my nostrils filled with possibly the most rancid thing I had ever smelled in my life. I gagged, but tried to keep quiet. I walked toward the piano. The magnetic pull became slightly stronger as I moved closer. The light from my necklace intensified. I craned my head around to see around the piano. A white tarp was covering something, and it didn't take me long to make out what was under it.

Behind the piano, James's ghost huddled close to the tarp. He twitched, but remained catatonic. His eyes, with pupils like pinpricks, stayed on the body under the tarp. I tried to keep my eyes on him and not whatever was under the tarp.

Something was off about his ghost. His skin was less transparent than other ghosts. He almost looked whole, except for the tiny bits of the wall I could see through his flesh. Instead of being drained of color, he only looked slightly gray. I could even see the blue in his eyes.

A scraping echoed around me. My head jolted around. Gabriel came out from behind the pews, shaking with rage. I could hear his frantic breathing from across the room. He ran closer to me, gauntlet already sparking.

"Don't touch him!" he screamed.

Gabriel pushed me against the wall. He dug his hands into my shoulders. Tiny jolts of electricity shot into my torso. In the scuffle, the tarp moved away from James's body, revealing his bare feet. His skin was green and his feet were so bloated they looked twice the size of a normal person's.

Gabriel dug his hands deeper. "This is your fault! All of this is your fault!"

He threw me to the floor, then crashed to the floor on top of me. He shot my stomach full of voltage, and I felt only a tiny jolt. His body felt limp and weak. He put his arms around my neck, but I could still breathe. He stared down at me, tears streaming from under his goggles, and I stared back.

"I trusted you!" he screamed. "Why'd you make him do this? You could have taken any of us, but you took the only family I had left!"

He picked me up off the floor by my collar. Every move he made seemed so strained. He had to use his whole body to pick me up. Gabriel pressed me against the door, unable to look at me anymore. From the other side of the door, screams and thuds seeped through the cracks. From my side, all I could hear was whimpering.

"He wouldn't have done this if you people didn't make him. I don't care if it was you or one of your other friends, you're all responsible for this!" He looked back at me, tears trickling out from his goggles. "You made my best friend kill himself!"

I stopped blinking. Muffled screeches still roared from outside. James's ghost never moved away from his body, still barely conscious. Gabriel's entire body trembled, and I could feel mine tremble as well. Gabriel pushed me against the door harder, but it felt like he didn't even touch me. I only stared at him. I moved my hand up to his face and covered his mouth.

"Get off me before I weld your fucking mouth shut."

Gabriel roared. He unlocked the door and opened it. We both fell onto the hard concrete on the outskirts of the giant gang fight. Clementine and Vee still kept themselves under Johanna, barely able to keep the Brotherhood away from them. All of the catwalks were empty. Every Brother in the room was attacking Clementine and Vee.

I punched Gabriel right in the Adam's apple. Gabriel fell over, and I pushed him off of me. He wheezed and twitched against the ground. Without any time to think, I ran to the closest set of stairs. I dashed up to the catwalks, my feet clanking against the steel grating. Many Brothers below noticed me and shouted in my direction.

Clementine and Vee were outnumbered. No matter how powerful they were, the Brotherhood had them surrounded. Clementine shot nonstop gusts of wind, but each one became weaker. The first one knocked out an entire group of Brothers, but the ones she shot after could barely knock over one. Her legs shivered and buckled under her. Vee had much more endurance. Even without using her powers, she could knock out a Brother with a single punch. Still, she only had two fists, and there were almost a hundred Brothers attacking her at once.

More clanking resonated around me. Several Brothers started climbing the stairs back up to the catwalks. Gabriel, still feeble and limping, practically crawled up the stairs and pulled himself along the railing to get me. Johanna was only a few feet away from me, dangling from the ceiling. I weighed my options and decided that the dumbest option I could take would be the best.

I took a few steps back. Only a few feet. Simple enough. I

broke into a sprint and jumped. My foot landed on the railing, and I took a second leap. Thirty feet in the air, I flew above the chaos and reached my hand out to grab Johanna. With the tips of my fingers, I caught Johanna's bindings and, with all the might I had in my body, I pulled myself closer and circled my arms around her. Using her bindings as grips, I climbed up Johanna. Even though the bindings pulsed with electricity, I grinded my teeth and forced my hands to hold on tight. If I ignored the pain, it wouldn't be real.

I placed my hand on the wires binding Johanna to the ceiling. People screamed all around me, Brothers reached out to attack me, and I tried my damnedest to do what I did best: burn. I stared at Gabriel, still limping along the catwalk, and I gritted my teeth. Son of a bitch. The wires got hotter. Droplets of melting plastic and metal trickled down my hand. A giant discharge of electricity shot out of the opening and the entire wire caught fire. The wire snapped.

Everything slowed down as Johanna and I fell to the Earth. Everyone looked up at us. Johanna's Bible fell right into Clementine's hands. Clementine, looking more exhausted than I had ever seen her, shot one last gust of wind up at us. Johanna and I slowed our decent and landed right next to Vee. Vee shot a giant chunk of ice at Johanna, slicing through the cords tied around her body. In an instant, Johanna's eyes opened, and they were completely red.

Johanna rose up into the air. Every Brother in the building suddenly started glowing the same red. Without any time to register what was happening, everyone shot backward. Each Brother slammed against the wall and stuck to it as if it were made of flypaper. Johanna towered above us like an angry goddess, and none of the Brothers could get away from her grasp.

And barely a second after it happened, Johanna fell back to

the ground, along with every member of the Brotherhood. Johanna was unconscious again. Clementine slapped her face, but she was unresponsive. Several members of the Brotherhood got to their feet and started limping over to us. Vee grabbed the Bible from Clem, picked up Johanna, and booked it toward the door.

"Leaving!" she called.

"But the ghost!" I said.

"It'll still be here when you come back!"

The Brotherhood came closer. I grabbed Clementine's clammy hand and pulled her with me. Together, we ran to the exit with Vee. Not stopping to look back, we all ran through the hallway and up the stairs. Clamoring came from behind us, but it became quieter as we ran. We sprinted out the Sanctuary, barely a breath left in us.

Chapter 13
He's With Me

Three hours later, and Johanna was still asleep. When we got back home, Jesse tucked her into his bed. We all stayed by the bed, holding vigil for an immortal woman. Clementine sat slumped on Jesse's lap in their vintage scoop chair, barely able to keep her eyes open. Vee stayed by the window, brooding like a stoner Batman. I paced the room and tried to keep my mind off of the horrible thing that happened.

"She gonna be okay?" I asked.

"She hasn't slept since America had a king. She's just making up for lost time." Vee sat down on the windowsill. "Shit, might be days until she wakes up."

I shook my head. Two things on Clementine's bedside table caught my eye. One was an old, black-and-white photograph of a family. A grandmother sat in a small rocking chair in the center of the picture. A mother and father stood next to the grandmother, both standing tall and smiling. A son stood next to the mother, barely taller than her. Huddled next to the patriarch was Clementine, looking a bit younger than I knew her, with natural, dark hair. I decided it would be best not to talk about it.

Right next to the picture was Johanna's Bible. With no one else looking, I picked it up. It had been years since I even touched a Bible, but the main thing on my mind was that I was touching Johanna's Memento. I thought about how convenient it was for me to have a necklace and not a clunky old book to carry around twenty-four seven. Unlike mine, Johanna's Memento was cold. It lacked the heartbeat mine possessed. It felt like a book and nothing more.

I turned over the book and did a double take. The front still looked the same, barely yellowed since the days of the Puritans. The back cover was burned at the bottom edge. I flipped through the book backward, seeing the burn go through multiple pages. The entire second half of the New Testament had some form of damage on the very bottom. I touched one of the scorched pages.

Johanna screamed. She woke up with a jolt, her blanket flying right onto me. I put the Bible back onto the end table and kept my hands as far away from it as possible. Clementine jumped out of Jesse's lap and ran over to Johanna. After a slight bout of emotion, Johanna's face returned to normal.

"Johanna!" exclaimed Clementine, sitting down right next to Johanna. "Are you okay?"

"How long was I unconscious?" she asked.

"Probably a hot second, Jo." Jesse flipped their desk calendar around to show Johanna the date. "What was it like to finally sleep again?"

"As unpleasant as I remember." She picked up the calendar and looked harder at the date. "This is horrific."

Johanna put the calendar back on Clementine's table and grabbed her Bible. She caressed the back cover, looking down on it so intently to see every little scorch mark. She reached her finger out to touch a burn, but retracted it before she could feel it.

"I was foolish," she started. "A few days ago, the lingering soul seemed close, and I entered the Brotherhood of Eternity's hideout. Before I got to the boy, the entire Brotherhood attacked me at once. I never had time to stop them." She passed the Bible to Clementine. "They tortured me for hours before I finally lost consciousness."

Everyone leaned over and looked at the Bible. Clementine started shaking and covered her mouth. Jesse tried to open it, but accidentally touched the back cover, making Johanna scream in pain again. Jesse jumped back and refused to touch it again.

"Did the Brotherhood burn your Bible?" Clementine asked, looking both terrified and disgusted. Johanna nodded.

"When the Brotherhood pinned me down, they said something about my necklace." I entwined my necklace around my fingers. "Oh my God, they really do know how to kill us."

"That does not matter." Johanna left the bed. "What matters is that we take care of the lingering soul trapped in their hideout."

"Goddammit, they both matter! They know how to kill us!" I cried. Everyone's eyes shifted to me. "If we don't do something, the Brotherhood will keep attacking us until they finally end up burning every page in your Bible! What happens then?" I turned my head to Clementine. "Clementine, what happens when a Memento is broken?"

Clementine stuttered. Johanna, Jesse, and Vee remained silent. I felt lightheaded. I clasped Clementine's dresser and tried to keep my balance.

"I've only been with you all for a month, and I've had it! How are you all numb to this? Why am I the only one that cares about stopping them?"

Johanna, motionless, looked me in the eye. "The Brotherhood of Eternity will not matter in the long run, nor will they kill us. I made a mistake that I will not make again."

"What if I make that mistake? What if another Geist makes that mistake?" I asked. "Those cultists took your Memento—probably the one thing keeping us from outright disappearing—and found a way to burn it. We need to attack them at the source and make sure that never happens again!"

"The day I listen to battle strategies from a dried-up fruit is the day I die," mumbled Vee. She walked toward the door, opened it, and looked back at me. "And, like, die-die, not Geist-die."

"What're you gonna do, then?" I snapped. "Just sit back and watch us get killed?"

"No. I'm going to sit in my room, read some porn, smoke some weed, and wait for you to move out. Because none of this shit was happening until you decided to show up!"

Vee slammed the door behind her. Jesse tried to put his hand on my shoulder, but I shook him off. Instead, I ran to her bed, grabbed a pillow, and screamed into it. And kept screaming. I screamed until my voice grew hoarse, and no one stopped me. Then I collapsed onto the bed, face-down in the pillow. Clementine rubbed my back in a circular motion.

"We need to go back there." Clementine sounded worried. "We can't have much time left."

"If it really was a suicide, that means we have at least a few more days before his soul becomes restless. We can regroup in the morning."

"No, Johanna, this needs to be done now!" she said, sounding even more worried. "We can't let that boy stay there for much longer, or he'll—"

"Clementine," interrupted Johanna. "Please. Let me rest."

Silence. Johanna hobbled out of the room. She collapsed onto the doorframe and tried to hold herself up. Jesse ran up to her and helped her get her footing again, then guided her back to wherever she was going to waste her time. I tossed the pillow across the room and saw Clementine shaking on the other side of the bed. Her hands dug into the corners of her sheets. I tried to find any words to comfort her. And that's when I realized I couldn't do anything.

Clementine was showing a crack. I realized right there that

I never learned how to help her. Our relationship was simple. I would be down about something, Clementine would distract me. The life of a Geist was a life of diversions, where fashion, poetry, and trips to Aruba distracted us from the one thing truly connecting us: we were dead.

I needed to step up. It was my turn to be the distraction.

"It's going to be okay," I said, knowing that those words meant nothing. "We can head back tomorrow with a huge army of Geist, and the Brotherhood will have no choice but to give us James. Johanna just needs some rest. When—"

"Ash, can—" Her words weren't forming. "Can you not—I wanna—please. Come upstairs with me."

Clementine grabbed my hand. She led me all the way upstairs, into the fake clock tower. The strange, moving gears above us ticked in such an awkward tempo, they sounded more like a heartbeat than an actual clock. Clementine and I sat down on the couch facing the clock. We both knew we were just looking at a fake clock with a fake light coming from the other end, but we kept staring at it as if we could see something worthwhile. Clementine fingers tapped her knee in tune with the gears.

She pulled out her pocket watch, holding it up to her ear. The ticking of the watch and the gears almost lined up perfectly. Two ticks from the gears, one tick from the watch. In attic, everyone was silent, and everything had a heartbeat.

"What's the point of having a giant clock on an invisible underground house?" I asked. Clementine flinched at the broken silence. "Sorry. I just don't see the point of this place."

Clementine placed the watch onto her lap. She edged closer to me, but kept her eyes on the clock. Her gray eyes were wet, but no tear fell.

"I come up here when I'm sad." Clementine fiddled with the

watch. Opening it, closing it, flipping it upside-down. "Having a sad spot helps me. If I stay sad in my room or my workshop, that means that, when I'm happy, I might remember something that made me sad in there. This way, I can keep everythin' that bothers me in a tower high above the streets."

"That sounds aggressively unhealthy." I shook my head.

"I don't know how else to live." I could barely hear her voice over the gears. She looked at me, finally taking her eyes off the useless clock. "I'm sorry I never told to you about anythin'. You're right. You deserve a better friend."

"You took care of me when I needed you, and you gave me everything I needed. You were the best friend I could ask for." A mysterious breeze came through the room. "I know you don't want to talk about anything that's worrying you. I get that. But you can't bottle everything up like this. You have to trust me."

Clementine closed her eyes. She took a deep breath.

"I try to pretend nothin' happened before we died." Her voice cracked. She tilted her head upward to keep the tears from falling. "But I can't. None of us can. Most of us in this city've been dead longer than alive, but it never matters." The tears fell anyway. They fell onto her watch, pinging off the surface just like the rain. "You were right. We're all dead, and it's so hard to look someone in the eye, knowin' that they've been through somethin' so terrible. Sometimes, I still feel like that scared sixteen-year-old in Alabama, and it's a feelin' I try to bury deep, deep down inside me. But I can't all the time."

Clementine broke down. She fell into her own lap and sobbed. That's when I saw it. She was right; those were not the tears of an ageless ghost. Those were the tears of a teenage girl, terrified of her own death. I nudged closer to her, knowing exactly what to do. Gently, I moved her head from her lap to my chest. I ran my hands across her back and gave her the tightest hug I'd ever given anyone.

"Of course not. If you bottle up everything, nothing'll ever get better," I whispered.

"I know that it can get a whole lot better. But for that to happen, it's gonna get a whole lot worse, and I don't think I'll ever be able to handle that. I've kept everyone at arm's length for so long, I don't even know if Jesse knows the real me." She moved her head away from my chest. "I've made so many mistakes, I don't think I'll ever be able to correct them."

"You can start now." I rubbed the back of her neck. "No more keeping people at arm's length, alright? That goes for both of us."

Clementine pushed the watch off her lap. Her hand touched mine, and her tears slowed. She rested her head on my shoulder and closed her eyes. Our breathing synched. I knew, right then, we needed to use the time we still had to its fullest.

"Tell me about your family," she whispered.

I thought for a long time. Remembering all the wonderful moments I had with Mom, Dad, Faye, Zack, and Yvonne. Remembering all the terrible moments. Remembering the moments that seemed meaningless at the time, but I looked back on with an unexplainable fondness.

"My mom, Betsy." Words came to me easier than they ever had. "I—I loved her a lot. She always had this frankness about her that I loved. And whenever my dad got too uppity about something, she could shut him down with one word." I laughed. "Been a while since she's had to shut him down, though."

Clementine's shoulders relaxed. "What about your daddy?"

"Loved him, too." My smile grew. "He was kind of like a big kid. He'd get excited about little things, but he'd freak out over them, too. And he loved my mom's desserts more than anything else in the world. After the divorce, he still told me that we always had to sneak some of her desserts over to his house. He was an only child, so I guess my grandma never let him grow up all the way. God, I wish you could meet Faye. You'd love her."

"I bet I would," Clementine hummed. She gripped my shoulder. Her eyes started to dry.

"She and my grandpa had trouble having kids, so my dad was their only one. It's weird, since I know we were supposed to be a huge family. I mean, Irish Catholic, come on. But we were fine being a small family. It was cozy."

Clementine stayed silent. Her mouth twitched into a forced smile. I knew what she was thinking. Even when trying to get closer to me, she still couldn't ask the big question. So, I decided to answer it anyway.

"Yvonne kinda joined the family once grandpa died. She and Faye just connected on a spiritual level, which is probably why my dad never really liked her. Faye played favorites and everyone knew that. And Zack—"

Suddenly, words stopped. I knew what I wanted to say. Simple words couldn't come out of my mouth. They bottlenecked in my throat and clogged my airway. I couldn't breathe. Everything terrible about Zack flooded back to me. I couldn't think of any of the good things about Zack. None of the late-night marathons of horror movies we weren't allowed to watch, or the times we made our own action figures out of clay. Nothing about how I idolized him. Just how my life was ruined.

"My brother killed himself."

Shock dawned on Clementine's face so slowly, I could see the exact moment she registered what I said. The heartbreak in her eyes, the way her hands became limp, it all showed that she wasn't ready to hear what I said. But my back was strong, and my breathing was steady. I wasn't going to cry.

I told myself that I was done crying about him. I went through periods of hating Zack. For months, I wouldn't even mention his name, pretending he never existed. It never worked. Zack would come back to me, randomly and without warning, in the smallest ways. Every day I'd see someone on the street who looked a bit like him, or hear a voice on TV that sounded like his, and he'd return to me.

"He was going to college up in Boston, and he'd only been gone for three months. I'd call him every day to see how he was doing. I missed him. So much. One day he didn't answer me. And he—he died." I rubbed my eyes with my index finger and thumb. I knew there weren't any tears, but I felt like there should have been. "We got a call at two in the morning. My parents dropped me off at Faye's so they could fly out to Boston. And none of us stopped crying until they got back." My lips curled from keeping in a cough. "And then the same thing happened with me."

Clementine and I held each other for a long time. No words, no sobs, just the rain splattering against the glass and the quiet ticking of her watch. My grip would tighten and loosen, depending on what memory was running through my head. We broke free from our hug, and Clementine wiped my eyes again. She kissed me on the forehead, and her lips made the damp, cold room feel warm.

"Maybe, in the next life, God'll let us live the lives we wanted." Clementine nuzzled my forehead with hers. "Heaven'll be a big ol' town, and you and I can live right next to each other. Jesse and I'll be married, and we'll have a whole bunch'a kids that you can babysit. Johanna can be the schoolteacher, and my lil' kids will love her, and she'll finally be able to see Nathaniel and her kids again. Winona and Farrah will never need to travel, since our town'll have everythin' they'll ever need. Teresa can take care of all the flowers and make the town look gorgeous. And Vee—" she paused. "Vee'll be with her husband again. And she'll be so happy."

I gave her a half-hearted smile. She was being helpful in her own way, I knew that. Clementine must have noticed how fake my smile was, because hers faltered. She cocked her head a bit.

"Do you believe in God, Ash?" she asked. "You can say no. I won't think any less of you."

I shook my head slowly. "No. I'm sorry." There was a lot I could have said. But I needed to find the right way to say it. "It's—uh, it's not easy for people like me to be religious."

"I figured," she said. If she was disappointed, I couldn't hear it. "Things in this world don't make a lotta sense, 'specially for people like us. It helps a lot, knowin' He's with me." She shook her head. "Guess I'm not sayin' anythin' helpful, then. Probably sounds like a bunch'a mumbo jumbo to you."

I rested my head on Clementine's shoulder. We stared out the frozen clock together. Slowly, the rain cleared, only leaving a fine blue mist across the city. I half-expected a rainbow to pop up somewhere, with a ray of God's light shining through the glass to give me a sign. The rain's clearing was enough of a sign for me. I squeezed Clementine's hand.

"Everything you're doing is so, so helpful, Clementine. I'm sorry about how I exploded on you last week. It was uncalled for." I gulped. "Can I ask you a question, though?" I looked for the right way to ask my question. "Who are Carson and Lily?"

Clementine's hand tensed around mine, but the rest of her body stayed tranquil.

"Carson and Lily were two Geist I tried to help out. It was a while ago. I met Carson about fifteen years ago. And Lily—" a surprised look crossed her face. "I guess she wasn't long ago at all. Neither of them knew who gave them a Legacy Spark. They were alone. And I tried to help them. Get them accustomed to the Geist ways. But they left.”

“What do you mean left?” My voice almost disappeared mid-sentence.

Clementine looked at me from the corners of her still-wet eyes. Little gears ticked inside her head. She was hiding another secret from me. She finally relented, letting everything fall out.

“For a Geist to finally move on, they only need to do two things.” The heartbreak in her voice killed me. “They need to give their Legacy Spark away, and then they just gotta walk into a portal.”

I knew exactly where this was going, but I couldn’t bring myself to stop her. She was struggling her way through painful memories, and all I could do was hold her hand. I hoped it was enough.

“Carson was a wanderer. He’d spent a few months running around the country before Johanna and I took him in. In the few weeks he stayed in the mansion, I told him everythin’ he needed to know about Geist. Eventually, I made the mistake of tellin’ him what I just told you. And the next day, I woke up and saw a note on his door. And he was gone.” She held back a sob. “Lily was different. Lily never left her old home. She never even left her bed. I’d come every day to check on her and try to get her out of the house. And every time I’d see her, she’d say the same thing. ‘I want to die.’” She looked toward our reflections in the clock. “And so, after a few months, I showed her what to do.”

Clementine rubbed her face. She fiddled around with her pocket watch again. She did anything to keep her hands moving. Finally, she rested her head in her hands and stayed motionless.

“I felt like such a failure,” she whimpered. “The only reason I never told you anythin’ was because I was scared. I just wanted you to be safe. And not end up like the others.” A tremor flowed through her voice. "I try to be the strong one. I figure, if I can be the one to keep the secrets, and work a little harder than everyone else, we can all live normal lives. And no one would ever want to go through that portal again." A little shake. "Every day, I wake up and worry I'll see a note just like Carson's, except it's from Vee, or Farrah, or you."

I pushed Clementine's hands away from her head. I sat her upright, held her hands, and gave her the same kiss on the forehead she gave me.

"I'm not leaving you."

Grief always hung over Zinda Mansion. But for a brief moment, Clementine and I did something amazing. In sharing our stories, we defied nature. Like two negative numbers combining into a positive, we found a sparkling shard of something tender inside the terrors life threw at us.

"I love you, Ash."

"I love you, too, Clem."

We left the clock tower behind us. With our spirits cleansed, it was time to return to the less miserable parts of the mansion. Clementine headed straight for her workshop, telling me that she was going to spend the rest of the day sewing. The rest of the day was mine, and I could fill it with meaningless interruptions. At that moment, James was tomorrow's problem.

I went back to my room. Before I even got to my bed, I stepped on a tossed pair of jeans. My entire room had clothes scattered around the floor. Clementine would kill me if she knew her clothes were gathering dust on the hard carpet. I bent down and, like the responsible adult I should have become a long time ago, I started cleaning.

Every article of clothing on the floor flew right into my hamper. Everything was inside-out, but that was a problem for future Ash. I picked up a sock that was next to my bed. I looked for its sister, but couldn't find it. Using my rusty critical thinking skills, I looked under the bed. Sure enough, the sister somehow traveled under my bed. I got to the floor, crawled a few inches under the bed, and reached for it. A loose nail dug into my shirt. A faint rip stopped me in my tracks.

"Aw crap," I mumbled.

I got up. There was a giant hole in the side of my shirt. Clementine was not going to be happy, especially after I burnt half an outfit to cinders. I put on a different shirt and left my room. Without knocking, I went into Clementine's workshop.

"Clementine, I ripped a hole in…" No one was there. "Clementine?"

I placed the ripped shirt on her empty work desk. A normal person would have thought "Oh, she's in the bathroom." But I was not normal. I went to her room and knocked on the door. I took a look inside, seeing no one. I went down to the living room and saw no one.

Then I ran up to the skull board. My skull, along with Johanna's, Jesse's, and Vee's, sat on Zinda Mansion. Clementine's purple skull slowly slid away from the mansion, directly toward the Sanctuary. I waited for a bit, praying that the skull would turn around and head back to the mansion. To my not-surprise, it did not.

"Goddamn lying hillbilly!"

I broke into a sprint. I ran down the stairs, I ran through the foyer, and I ran out the door. Clementine was on her way back to an obvious trap, and I needed to stop her. Or help her. Just like everything else in my life, I had no idea what I was doing, but goddammit I was doing something.

Chapter 14
Secrets You're Allowed to Keep

Bravery never came easily to me. I grew up a passive, well-off guy who didn't need to fight for anything. Life was easy. For the most part. Zack's death was a kick to the face. High school bullying wasn't easy, either. But I never had to work eight minimum wage jobs to support my family. I never had to work, period. I grew up in a country without war. Most importantly, I never had to fight a cult bent on eradicating Death. But that was what was on my plate, and I needed to fake a brave face. All alone, I headed into battle.

Every inch of Chicago was covered in a thick mist. The entire city changed, turning from an urban squalor to an otherworldly abyss. It made my run absolutely terrifying. I was in a horror movie. Occasionally, people would emerge from the mist, but would get swallowed up again before I could see their faces.

The Brotherhood of Eternity's Sanctuary materialized from the mist. The front doors of the factory were held open by cinderblocks. Clementine was nowhere to be found. Both of those things added up to something horrible. I crept closer to the building, each step getting slightly bigger than the last. I stood in front of the doors. I paced in front of the doors, clawing at my forehead.

There were basically no good decisions I could have made. If I went home, that would mean I left Clementine to fend for herself. If I went in, I'd be going knee-deep into a trap that I had gone through mere hours before. Plus, I didn't know one-hundred percent if Clementine was in there or not. I only knew that the worst decision I could have made would be to pace around outside.

So, I made the dumbest, most proactive decision of my life, and I ran through the front doors. My feet hit the hard ground of the factory, and it echoed through the entire room. My other foot froze mid-air. I glanced around, looking for any sign of life, Clementine's or otherwise. The factory was empty.

Within the span of hours, the entire room was stripped barren. The only light came from the semi-boarded up windows, leaving slivers of blue light to show the nothingness. The arcade machines and pool tables were gone. The posters lining the walls vanished. All that was left was an empty minibar and piles of trash. The inside matched the outside. My heartbeat quickened. What if they were gone? What if they captured Clementine and skipped town? I put my head close to the floor. While my necklace didn't glow, I still felt a barely-there pull coming from the basement. The Brotherhood was still in the building.

I wandered around the room, still looking for any sign of Clementine. My steps were almost silent, but I needed them to be quieter. If anyone heard me, I was as gonna end up like Johanna. My eyes glanced toward the front doors again. I still had a chance to leave.

A muffled yell came from across the building. A deep, masculine yell, not filled with fear, but with anger. I turned my attention to another set of doors and slid my way to the next hallway. Using only one finger, I pushed the door open. Seeing no one on the other side, I squeezed on through. I pressed myself up against the wall and glided through the hallway, checking every door I went by. Still no Clementine, still no Brotherhood.

The loud voice became clearer as I went down the hall. As he kept talking, I realized who it was. Gabriel, in the middle of a huge tirade, screamed loud enough that I could stomp my way down the hall unnoticed. I slid closer to the source of the screaming, keeping my eye out for any sudden movements. Another voice fired back at Gabe, this one trying and failing to be as loud. Dinah's. All the voices came one room over from the stairwell. I pressed my ear up against the closed door, praying no one would open it.

"I've been guarding James nonstop for a week!" Gabe screamed. "Do you know what you're making me do? You're telling me to stare at my best friend's body and watch it rot!"

"You want to talk with the demons, then you'll be there when they try to get James!" Dinah screamed back. "That idiot decided to off himself, so don't even try to imply this is my fault. He killed himself because he was weak, and unless we harden you, you'll be soaking in your own blood in your bathtub, too!"

"You're a sick bitch, Dinah," growled Gabriel. "Do you know how it smells in there?"

"Is that not good enough? Should I head down to Bath & Body and pick up some candles, faggot? Grow up and shut up. You should have known this was coming the second you became a Brother."

A chair squeaked. Footsteps came closer to the door. I panicked and almost fell to the ground.

"I became a Brother because I had nowhere else to go!"

The footsteps stopped. Then, they moved farther away from the door.

"Then you should be on the streets, because we're not here to take in the homeless! We're here to save the world from these Satan worshipers! But somehow I got straddled with a bunch of bums! How is that?"

"Because it's exactly what you want. If you don't want scared kids, then why are we hanging outside of tenements and graveyards when it's time for a 'recruitment drive?' If you really wanted soldiers, you'd let the world know about Geist instead of keeping it a secret in this stupid little—"

"Don't you dare!"

I held my breath. Sayitsayitsayit!

"Cult."

I mouthed a huge yes. A loud shuffling came from behind the door, followed by a flurry of expletives from Dinah, plus some racial slurs I was not allowed to say. My hand went toward the knob. I stopped myself from opening it. I backed away. Nothing I could do would help in that situation.

A hand grabbed me. Before I could yell, another hand covered my mouth. My assailant pulled me into the stairwell, pressed me up to the wall, and revealed herself to be Clementine. Clementine kept a look of determination on her face as she looked up at me. Beneath her eyes, fire burned. She gently pulled my hands away from her shoulders, using only her thumb and forefinger. She looked away, a sudden shake appearing in her hands.

"Clementine!" I said. "What the hell?"

"You shouldn't be here." She brushed the dust off my clothes. "I can take care of this myself."

"You saw what they did to Johanna! You want them to do the same thing to you?" I scream-whispered. "What makes you think this is a good idea?"

"This isn't the first time I've had to do this." Just like Johanna, Clem's eyes stayed away from mine. "You need to go home right now before someone finds you."

"What's that supposed to mean? You mean you regularly nosedive into cults and try not to get evaporated while you scoop out some dead guy?"

Clementine's fire dimmed. I broke her confidence. She

grabbed her elbows and huddled next to the door. She still couldn't look at me. I moved into her line of sight, and she shifted her eyes again.

"People mess up, Ash. A lot. There are times when Geist don't do their jobs, or there's a spirit that no one can get to. So, Johanna and I weed out the ones everyone missed before bad things happen."

I narrowed my eyes. "You mean, weed out the Revenants?"

Clementine kept her mouth shut. She glared at me, but slowly, she nodded.

"And so you two stay the only Geist in the city to know what a Revenant is?" I scoffed. "Stop that! You can't clean up all of our messes! Let us take responsibility for ourselves and show us what happens when we mess up!"

"No, Ash." She finally looked at me. "Everyone in this city is so fragile. If they knew what happens when a spirit is left alone for too long, I don't think they could handle living anymore."

"Clementine, stop!" I stomped my feet and leaned forward. "Why do you insist on doing this alone like a damn martyr? Because if something goes wrong and I'm not there to help, you could die! And I don't want to lose you!" My voice cracked. "I can't! Your life matters to me and Jesse and Winona and everyone else much more than whatever will happen if that ghost goes unchecked! So let me help."

Clementine looked at her feet. Her body swayed slightly. She perked up, looking back up at me. That mother look was in her eyes again.

"If things start headin' south, I need you to run as fast as you can out of here. Don't worry about me. Just get out of here and run back home."

"Clementine." I grabbed her shoulders. "We both know I'm not going to do that."

A door creaked open. Clementine and I froze. She pulled me down to the floor, and we both hid in the corner of the stairwell. She kept herself a little closer to the door than me, hands sprawled out like Spider-Man, ready to get up if someone found us. Footsteps pattered closer to the stairwell, and she rose up like an alley cat ready to pounce. Dinah entered the stairwell, her goggles around her neck and her stringy hair tussled. A smear of bright blood ran from her nose to her upper lip. She sniffed, pulling the trail back into her nose. She stomped down the stairs, not noticing us.

Gabriel walked in after her, looking angry and battered. One eye on his goggles was shattered, while the right eye was perfectly fine and staring right at us. He didn't react at all. Clementine pushed me back a little. As Dinah kept stomping down the steps, Gabriel mouthed one word.

Follow.

He made his way down the stairs with Dinah. Clementine and I stayed on the floor for a second. Obvious trap. Of all the obvious traps I'd fallen into, this was the most obvious. I stood up. Clementine grabbed my hand and pulled down, but I responded by pulling her to her feet. I followed Gabe's obvious trap, and, after stomping her foot in a huff, Clementine followed, too.

Dinah descended to the bottom floor. Then Gabe, then me, then Clementine. Dinah, unaware of the Geist behind her, kept snapping little insults Gabe's way. Tiny snips of things like "incompetent," "failure," and "dead friend." Gabriel kept his lips shut the entire time.

"And where exactly else would you go, Gabe?" continued Dinah. "If you quit, you might as well say goodbye to everyone. I'll make sure they hate you by the end of the week. Believe me, feelings of betrayal? Easy seed to plant. And who else do you have? A drug addict grandma that can't shit without you having to wipe her ass?" An ugly, smug smirk crossed her lips when she looked back at him. She lost it when he still gave no reaction. "Because who else wants you? Your mom didn't, clearly. And we all know that God doesn't!" Steam almost flew out of her nostrils. "So play fair, and maybe God will find it in His heart to forgive your bullshit before you get killed by some disease-ridden rapist!"

Dinah opened the door to the giant storage room. Gabriel inched backward, subtly pushing his elbows against Clementine and me. Dinah walked in, turning her attention away from harassing Gabriel and toward fifty-or-so people waiting inside the giant room. When she was far enough away, Gabriel cocked his head in our direction, still keeping his eyes on Dinah.

"Every Brother that isn't down here is clearing out the place. This is your last chance to get James before we move him to the new Sanctuary." He whispered so quietly I could barely hear him over the dripping pipes. "The catwalks are empty. There's a set of stairs you can run up not far from here. I'll make sure no one else sees you while you climb. You just get James out of here."

"Well, well, look who decided to switch sides," I chuckled.

"I'm not on anyone's side." He took a few steps forward. "But, if you get James's ghost outta here, Father Abram won't be so happy with Dinah."

Gabriel walked toward the door. Clementine reached her hand out, but retracted it.

"Gabriel," Clementine called. "Thank you."

Gabriel turned his face away.

"I'll signal you when it's safe."

He walked into the room, keeping the door ajar for us. I walked a little closer, peering through the crack.

"So, are we supposed to like him now?" I asked. "Because he tried to kill us a lot."

"Life's confusin', Ash."

Clementine and I kept one eye on Gabriel. Almost every Brother in Chicago was scattered around the room. I could hear little murmurs of their conversations, but everything seemed hushed. Even with me being almost a hundred feet away, I could see their reservations. Dinah stood tall over all the Brothers, but they hunched over, some with their arms around their legs. I couldn't tell the difference between the adults and the children.

I tried to squint and see if any of them had goggles on. A few members had something over their faces, but I couldn't tell if they were the goggles or just glasses. Gabriel started chatting with a few Brothers, his movements suddenly very fluid and lively. He bent down next to some of the Brothers, pulling down the things covering their faces. Gabriel then walked back to the room with James's ghost and left the door open behind him.

Clementine and I ran. We slipped through the door and sprinted toward the stairs to the catwalks. As we got closer to the Brothers, my heart raced and I panicked. At any moment, any one of them could have turned their head, stared at me, and sounded the alarm. Clementine grabbed my hand. Even with my shaking hands, she steadied them with her tight grip. Together, we scaled up to the catwalks and ran right above the Brothers' heads.

We practically fell down the steps when we made it past. I threw the door to the storage room open and slammed it behind us, locking it. I clutched the doorknob, breathing heavily. Clementine grunted and covered her nose. Clementine walked closer to the body. His feet still jutted out from behind the piano, still bloated and green.

Gabriel's brow furrowed. Clementine walked closer to him. She patted him on the shoulder. He didn't move. Everything about him looked defeated.

"I'm sorry we need to take your friend's spirit," she said. "But if we don't, dangerous things can happen."

"Bullshit," he wheezed. "Everything you ever say is bullshit." He pointed to James's body. "Just get my friend out of here and go so I can finally bury him. I still know this is all your fault."

The veins in my neck bulged. I grabbed Gabriel's jaw, slipped his goggles down, and made him look me in the eye. James's spirit could wait. I needed to teach that boy some manners.

"I've got half a mind to slam my knee into your nose right now." I clenched my fist. He winced. "If you say one more goddamn time that his suicide was my fault then I'm going to prove the entire Brotherhood right and drag you into Hell with my bare hands. You hear me?" I spoke through gritted teeth. "I had nothing to do with this!"

"Ash, sweetie." Clem's voice shook. "We ain't got time for this."

Clementine pulled my hand away from Gabriel's jaw. She grabbed my shoulder and nudged me toward the piano. James's cold feet made me shiver. The entire room seemed to pinpoint right toward his toes. Like blacktop on a hot summer day, the air around the piano warped and distorted the room. I shook my head and blinked. The distortion was gone.

I looked back at Gabriel, ready to fight back if needed. He limped over to us, pulling his goggles back up. I let down my guard, but kept my stink eye. Underneath his toughened exterior was a boy who had nothing and continued to lose everything. No mother, no father, and suddenly, without warning, no James. Outside, Dinah threatened to even separate him from everyone else, too. Gabriel's humanity was a problem. Everything about him was a problem and I wanted to burn him and punch him and hug him and save him from his shitty life.

"We can't hear ghosts." Each of his steps looked labored. "We can see them, but our earpieces don't pick up anything. When I found him, he was just—" he stuttered. "His ghost was screaming. For days, I had to watch him scream at me in silence. Do you know what it's like to watch your dead friend scream for help, and you can do nothing?"

Gabriel whimpered. I folded my arms, keeping my face as stone cold as I could.

"No," I said. "I was the one screaming."

The piano cracked. All three of us seized backward. Right down the middle, the cheap wood fissured. Splinters flew forward, narrowly missing my face. The distortion appeared again, this time warping the entire room. I knew I wasn't hallucinating. Something behind the piano was moving. A hollow, metallic roar came from behind the piano. Clementine shuddered. She turned to me and Gabriel, pushing us toward the door.

"Ash, you need to run right now," cried Clementine. "Both of you! Get out, now!"

The entire piano collapsed, filling the entire room with dust and debris. Clementine shoved Gabriel and me closer to the door. Even with her shoves, I kept my eyes on James's body. Another roar clanged through the room. As the dust settled, a horrible silhouette formed. A set of blackened eyes stared right at me.

On top of James's body, James's spirit writhed on all fours. No longer colorless and translucent, his spirit looked almost alive, but in no way human. His spine jutted out from his skin, convulsing around and reforming. It ripped out his rear, forming a long, centipede-like tail. His teeth grew and shoved his jaw forward, making his mouth three-times the size it should have been. His ears elongated and swelled out from his head. Thick black hair spouted out of his pores. The whites of his eyes disappeared and all that was left was black.

I opened my mouth to scream, but all that came out was a puff of air. Gabriel faltered backward until his back hit the wall. Clementine got between me and the creature and pushed me back again, this time with much more force. Every ounce of determination or courage was gone from her face. Only panic remained.

"Clementine! What the hell is that?"

"This shouldn't have happened," she muttered to herself. "It was a suicide. There's no reason this should have happened so quickly. The only way this could have happened was if—"

"Clementine!" I screamed.

"It's James, Ash! That's what happens when we don't take care of the spirits soon enough!" she exclaimed. "They become Revenants!"

"They wh—" Gabriel gasped.

James howled again, creating a horrible mixture of a human's scream and a rat's hiss. I took a few more steps back. Gabriel and I pressed ourselves against the wall, side-by-side, while the Revenant stared down Clementine. He didn't move and stayed perched on top of his former body. Clementine stood her ground and slowly raised her arms.

"James, sweetie," she whispered. "My name is Clementine Leigh. I want to help you."

Clementine took a few steps toward James. James lurched back and got into a pouncing position. He let out another horrible scream-hiss. Clementine stopped. James relaxed, but his body twitched. Another metamorphosis triggered and his fingers elongated and sharpened. Thick, frostbitten claws replaced his hands. Clementine took another step forward.

"Clementine!" I shrieked.

"Hush!" She turned back to James's Revenant and took another step toward it. "I know you've been told different, but Geist are the folks that help you meet Jesus." Another step. James's Revenant growled. "We make sure you don't have to linger too long, y'know?" Another step. "Please, come with Ash and me. We'll take you to Heaven."

Clementine held a shaking hand out to James. James's hissing stopped. The creaking in his bones slowed. My heartbeat stopped pounding up to my ears. Gabriel quieted his trembling knees. No one even breathed.

James craned his head closer to her hand. Somewhere lost between man and beast, it almost looked like he sniffed it. His spine straightened as much as it could, and he stood up from his former body. Even with his warped spine, he was still at least two feet taller than Clementine. His shadow eclipsed her and made her look barely a foot tall. I bit down on my lip so hard that it would have bled if I still had blood. Gabriel's stomach concaved from his tiny gasps of breath.

James's claws and Clementine's hands intertwined. For a brief second, Clementine's panic faded. She smiled at the beast.

The doorknob rattled. I stifled a gasp. Someone started pounding on the door. The rumbling of the Brotherhood startled James. He bared his giant front teeth at the door and grinded them, sounding like knives on stone. The pounding grew more severe, and Dinah screamed from behind the door.

"What the hell is that noise?" she yelled. "Open this door right now!"

James ripped his claws out of Clementine's hand. He struck her down into the remains of the piano, making a huge chunk of debris slice through her leg. Gabriel and I ran to the other end of the room as the giant Revenant raced for the door. James shot up another foot. His haggard footsteps slopped onto the ground as his feet doubled in size. He slammed his claw into the door and split it in two.

On the other side of the door, fear dawned on Dinah's face. Rosa grabbed her by the midriff and dove away from the door. James clawed at the walls and jumped out of the storage room. The screams of the Brothers were so loud they rattled my bones.

I stared at the shredded door. Another tiny fleck of wood fell to the floor. Another scream echoed from one of the Brothers. A smaller yelp came from a few feet from me. I turned my attention to Clementine. An entire splint of wood pierced her thigh. I ran over to her, grabbed her leg, and pulled it out of the splint. She didn't scream; she only gasped.

"You knew this was going to happen?" I asked, pulling her to her feet. "Every ghost is just a ticking time bomb that'll transform into a monster if we don't take care of it?"

Clementine looked up at me. Her eyes were foggy.

"Yes."

And just like that, everything made even less sense. Every time I felt like I finally got a grasp on life, something terrible happened. And each terrible thing was more terrible than the last. Morally, I could handle leaving my home to become a Grim Reaper. It made sense, in its own warped way. My fire powers made sense in the same way. But the fact that each dead person was waiting to turn into a giant rat monster was where I drew the line.

I reacted the only way a sensible person would. I grabbed Clementine's shoulders and shook her like a bottle of ketchup.

"These aren't the kind of secrets you're allowed to keep!"

A metallic roar echoed around us. Gabriel pushed past us. Clementine and I followed him. Outside, many of the older, stronger Brothers had already started zapping James with their gauntlets. One at a time, they ran up to him from different directions and slapped him with electricity. James barely registered anything. Each jolt just led to a twitch. Other members of the Brotherhood just stayed on the sidelines, screaming and tearing toward the exit. James didn't care who was attacking and who wasn't. He ripped through the crowd, lashing out at anything that moved. A girl who looked barely older than ten hid under a pew, trembling as James skittered around her.

Gabriel fidgeted on the sidelines. After five seconds of grit, he lost it again and stared at his Brothers attacking James's Revenant. With each passing second, the Brotherhood's ranks dwindled. More and more Brothers tossed aside their gauntlets and ran toward the doors.

"Stop!" shouted Dinah. "Stop running, you cowards! If you leave this room, that's it! You're unworthy to be in the Brotherhood of Eternity!"

Gabriel shook his head, then ran toward the girl under the pew. He grabbed the girl and carried her, ripping past James right as his tail flew above Gabe's head. Gabriel shoved the girl into the arms of another Brother and screamed, "Run!" Soon, only a handful of Brothers stayed in the room.

Dinah kept her distance. A large gash in her coat showed three thick cuts across her hip. The side of her coat was almost completely red. She clutched her hip, but the blood continued to seep through her fingers. She stumbled her way up the catwalk stairs. A thick trail of blood followed her up. On the penultimate step, she tripped. Her knees clanked against the grating, and she let out a loud, exasperated yell.

James's giant ears perked up. Just as one of the Brothers was about to attack him, James batted him away. The Brother slammed against the wall. The Revenant dug his front claws into the floor and skittered over to the stairs. None of the Brothers could keep up with the speed of the giant monster. A trail of frothy spittle streamed from his mouth, and each drop made the cement sizzle.

He collided with the stairwell, denting it. Dinah toppled face-first onto the catwalk. James attempted to climb the stairs. His massive weight bent the steel. Dinah crawled further along the catwalk. James roared again, saliva bubbling out of his mouth. He spat toward Dinah and splattered a wad of green spit onto her coat. The hideous coat almost evaporated like tissue paper. Screaming, she tore the coat off and threw it to the floor. It landed a few feet away from me before turning into a pile of brown mush.

"This is their doing!" Dinah pointed down at Clementine and me. "They know we've found a way to kill them, so now they've transformed your former Brother into a demon in order to kill us!"

"Oh my God! Just run, goddammit!" I screamed.

James shuddered at the sound of her voice. He stumbled up the steps on all fours, bending the steel along the way. Rosa and the other Brothers ran toward the stairs. James leaped up onto the catwalks. Two other Brothers grabbed James's boney tail and shot it full of electricity. With a powerful flick, James's tail knocked both Brothers down the steps and flat onto the wall.

The Brothers, without a second of hesitation, ran for the exit. James ignored them and kept walking toward Dinah. James, barely two feet away from the limping Dinah, backhanded Dinah across the face. Dinah flew off the catwalks.

Clementine ran under her. With a slight puff of wind, Dinah's fall slowed, and she landed on the ground with only a slight tumble. James wasted no time and jumped off the catwalks. With James plummeting right down to Dinah, Clementine stepped in between them. Clementine waited until James was barely a foot away from her face. Then she took a giant step back and slapped him right on his cheek. A colossal whirlwind pushed the Revenant upward, and James hit the ceiling.

James flew back to the ground, along with several huge chunks of the ceiling. He slammed back to Earth and created a James-shaped indent on the ground. The remaining Brothers crept over to Dinah. Gabriel joined his Brothers, but I stayed behind. Clementine reeled back. Looking dazed, she took a step toward James.

A hand grabbed her leg. Dinah whirled up and pulled Clementine by her ankle to the riddle-coated cement. Clementine's face hit the floor. Dinah flipped Clementine around and looked her in the eyes as she straddled Clem and wrapped her gauntlet around my best friend's neck. With blood streaming down her forehead, Dinah laughed. She strangled Clementine while shooting enough electricity into her that it lit the room.

"This is all your fault!" Dinah hysterically screamed. "If it weren't for you and that other demon, none of this would have had to happen!"

I ran. Nothing hindered my legs anymore. There was no fear. There was only rage. I shoved my way past the Brothers crowding Dinah and Clementine. Clementine's eyes rolled back. She lurched on the ground, helpless and shaking. Before I could help, Rosa grabbed my hair. She yanked me away from Dinah, and two Brothers kept their gauntlets around my arms, powered off but clenched.

"Dinah, stop!" screamed Gabriel.

"Shut up!" she screamed back.

"You goddamn nutcase!" I struggled against the Brothers. "Clementine saved your life!" I sneered. "She should have just let James have his way with you!"

The Brothers sent a little jolt through my body. I kicked at them, but Rosa pulled my hair again, and the Brothers sent another jolt through me. Dinah kept her grasp on Clementine's neck.

Dinah pressed a button on her gauntlet. The gauntlet tensed. She slid her hand out of it, but it stayed gripped around Clem's neck. Dinah stood up, her boots digging into Clementine's ribs, and then stepped over to me. She pinched my cheeks together and made a kissy face.

"Is that a confession, demon? You want all of us to die?"

Both Brothers let go of my arms and Rosa loosened her grip on my hair. Dinah grabbed the top of my head and pushed me down to the floor. My chin collided with the concrete, making my teeth almost shatter against themselves. Rosa put her gauntlet against the small of my back. Dinah cracked her neck. She knelt down beside me and pulled my head up to look at her. Several feet away, Clementine was still writhing in agony. I stared up at Dinah, dead in the eyes, and loogied into them.

"No. Just you."

Dinah punched me in the mouth. My jaw popped. It felt limp. I couldn't move anything. With another pop, it readjusted itself. Dinah stood up, kicked my face for good measure, and walked back to Clementine. She felt up Clementine's entire body, searching every possible hiding spot. She finally reached into Clementine's cardigan pocket. Inside was her father's watch. Dinah tossed it over to Gabriel. He caught it, clutching it in his gauntleted hand. My mouth went completely dry.

"Here's what's going to happen," she started. "That thing—" she waved at James "—is dead, which means we've got two helpless mice to play with. This bitch is dying as soon as possible." She tapped Clementine with her feet. Then she turned back to Gabriel. "But the one you seem so fascinated with? We're going to play some games with him. And, finally, when he's begging to die, we'll give him the privilege." She dug her feet further into Clementine's ribs. "But not before Father Abram makes a visit. Gabriel, break the watch."

Everyone looked over at Gabriel. He gripped the watch. I tried to move, but Rosa put all of her weight on me. Inside, my intestines burned. Everything felt hot, but no flames came. I was helpless, watching a man play around with my best friend's lifeline. My mind raced. I thought of anything at all I could do to help Clementine. Then I thought about what she said about how James should have had more time before he turned into a Revenant. I blinked.

"It's really convenient that James killed himself so you could set up a giant trap for us, huh?"

"Rosa, keep him quiet!" shouted Dinah.

"James was really excited about his birthday, and then after he got in a fight with you, he suddenly committed suicide, and then you made a master plan to lead Clementine and me into a basement where you gathered every Brother in the city to attack us." I clenched my jaw again. "Yeah, convenient."

"Shut your damn mouth," Rosa murmured. Tears were welling up in her eyes. "Don't you dare try to place the blame on someone else."

"You seriously think I was the one that did this?" I chuckled, then turned my attention to Gabriel. "Because of all the people in this room, who do you really think killed your friend?"

Gabriel stopped playing around with the watch. He stayed silent. Dinah's face twitched from me to him. Gabriel remained like a statue. Dinah stomped on Clementine again.

"Break the watch, Gabriel!" Her voice cracked. She screamed again, stomping even harder on Clementine. "These demons are the reason that James is dead!"

Gabriel tightened his clasp of the watch. Electricity pulsed through his gauntlet. My heart stopped beating. Instead, an intense heat burned my veins. It felt like I was in the car again, waiting to die. The heat around me burned my eyes. It hurt to keep them open, but I knew I couldn't close them for a second. The electricity waned from Gabriel's gauntlet. His hands shook harder. He looked around the room, resting on my face. Dinah took a step off Clementine and tried to make herself look as tall as she could.

"We've done everything for you! We've given you the home you never had! And you're hesitating? Do you understand what will happen if you don't kill them? You'll have nothing! Nowhere to go! Starving on the street!"

Gabriel glared right into Dinah's eyes. Without breaking away, he slid the watch into his pocket.

"I should have known!" she screamed "You weren't able to stop talking about that faggot ever since he died, and now you're on his side!"

Dinah shuddered and started walking toward Gabe, then back to me, then to Gabe again, until she just started pacing. Everyone's eyes were focused on her.

"People like you don't deserve anything! No friends, no home, nothing!" she stuttered. "You never deserved to be a part of this! If Father Abram knew that you second-guessed everything I did, he'd have killed you himself! He made me the leader, not you!" Her hands were shaking so violently, I couldn't even keep my eyes on them. "Shit! It should have been you in that bathtub with your wrists sliced open!"

Every word Dinah said only made the heat grow. Rosa inched away from my back. The concrete around me felt warmer. Ashes flew around me again. My clothes were burning. I was catching fire, and I no longer felt the heat. Gabriel looked over at me. I took in a deep breath, then looked over at the leader of Chicago's Brotherhood.

"Dinah," I finally said.

"What?" she snipped.

"Did you murder James?"

The same metallic roar echoed through the room. Rubble shifted. Right behind me, the Revenant crawled back to its feet. James's bones snapped. His tail extended another three feet. And his black eyes were fixated on Dinah.

"Dinah!" he roared. "Dinah, Dinah, Dinah!"

The Brothers scattered. Rosa and the other Brothers finally let go of me. Rosa ran to Dinah and Gabriel, staying in front of her superior and keeping her gauntlet ready. The other Brothers ran to the exit. Dinah screamed at them to come back, which only made them run faster. Only Dinah, Gabe, and Rosa remained. The Revenant crawled closer to the three last Brothers in the room and completely ignored me.

James jumped at Dinah. Rosa charged her gauntlet. As the Revenant flew through the air at Dinah, Rosa jumped and palmed his warped head. The gauntlet's shock went straight into one of his eyes. An explosion of black blood flew out of James's eye, and he collided with the floor. He arched his back, roared, and thrashed Rosa with his tail, sending her flying. She collided with one of the half-smashed pews, shoving it back several feet. She collapsed onto the ground. While she tried to push herself back up, she just fell back down, whimpering in pain.

With bleeding eyes, James whipped his head around and screamed for Dinah again. He clawed in every direction until he finally hit Gabriel. Gabriel soared across the room and slammed his head against a pew. The watch flew out of his pocket and skidded across the floor. Clementine's body lurched closer to the watch, but the gauntlet stayed latched to her neck. The gauntlet continued to pulse electricity through her body, and she kept on straining to breathe.

I tried to get to my feet. My shoes slid out from under me. Their soles were completely melted. I tried to catch my breath, but the air around me was so hot. Clementine was trapped on the floor with a gauntlet to her neck and her Memento MIA. James was rampaging through the Sanctuary and clawing at everything in his path. I needed to save Clementine. I finally got to my feet and ran.

My melting shoes squished against the floor as I ran to the watch. Dinah, with James only a few feet away from her, looked at me, then glared down at the watch. She dove for the watch. She laughed and tried to crush it with her fist. Then she stopped laughing. Her gauntlet was back with Clementine. She was so flustered, she barely noticed James staring right at her.

James slashed down. I skidded to a halt and shielded my face. Dinah looked up just in time to see claw collide with her stomach. With barely a flick of his giant hand, three claws pierced right through Dinah's torso. She didn't scream. She just looked down at the massive, crooked claws impaling her. Dinah's hands became limp, and she unclenched the watch.

Before I could even respond, James reeled back and hurled Dinah across the room. She flew through the air so quickly, it was almost as if she was shot out of a cannon. Dinah collided with the wall. The violent snap that resonated through the room was deafening. With barely a sob, Dinah fell to the hard floor.

James's rampage continued. He kept screaming "Dinah! Dinah!" even with her bleeding on the ground. I looked around for the watch. It must have slipped under one of the pews. Just as I crouched down to look, James started running toward me.

"Dinahhhhhhhhhh!" he growled.

My breathing became heavy again. I quickly kicked off my

scorched shoes just in time for James to get right on top of me. I ducked. James's boney tail slashed right where my head used to be. I lunged forward and slid right between his giant legs. I stumbled along the floor and made my way back to my feet. James bounded his way right toward me. I jumped onto a pew and hurdled from one pew to another. James, of course, was a lot less graceful and just crushed his way toward me.

I stopped jumping. Gabriel was prone on the floor right behind the pew I was standing on. He was desperately gasping for breath. A long, thick cut went from his eyebrow into his hairline and trickled blood down his face. He looked up at me, looking horrified, dazed, and above all else, miserable. James kept running toward me. The pews turned to dust under his weight. And he was heading right toward Gabriel.

I hopped down and grabbed Gabriel. I pulled him upright and tried to get him steady on his feet. Gabriel shook his head. He looked like he was having trouble getting adjusted, but I wasn't about to wait around for him to get his bearings. James was on a warpath and was about five seconds from being on top of me again. I slung Gabriel's arm around my shoulders, gripped his waist, and pulled him away from the pews. Within seconds, James's foot created a crater where Gabriel had been.

"Why are you helping me?" Gabriel wheezed.

"Because I'm an idiot."

Gabriel and I limped over to the wrecked stairs leading up to the catwalks. James kept barreling down the row of pews, but stopped almost mid-leap. He sniffed the air, then looked right toward us. My jaw clenched. James's remaining black eye glared right at me and Gabriel, and he started running again, still screaming out Dinah's name. I pushed Gabriel away from me and stepped toward the oncoming beast.

"Go," I said, not taking my eyes off of James. "Get that thing off of Clementine's throat."

"You're going to fight that thing?" Gabriel stumbled a bit and gripped the staircase's rusted guardrail. "Are you an idiot?"

"Uh, yeah, didn't I just say that?"

I ran toward James. James's breathing was heavy and almost ape-like. He was staring right at me. Gabriel was hobbling toward the still-screaming Clementine. Rosa was lost somewhere in the rows of pews. And Dinah was off in the corner, limp. I didn't know how long I had until Gabriel could free Clementine. I didn't know if I could distract him long enough. All I knew is that no matter how many times he clawed me, bashed my head in, or spit acid at me, I would survive. I lived through worse.

I reached into my pocket and pulled out my iPod. With a single flick of my wrist, I hurled the iPod right at him like a throwing star. The iPod soared right past him. But, for a split second, James's eye followed the iPod as it landed in the debris. He hesitated. And at that moment, I vaulted head-first into his stomach.

James inched backward. I also inched backward, not realizing that his stomach would be so damn hard. My eyes filled with fuzzy stars and I did my best to keep my footing. Shaking off my headache, I started hitting him as hard as I could with everything. My fists, my feet, my kneecaps, even a few more head-butts. He was barely budging. James swatted at me with both sets of claws. All ten of his jagged nails ripped across my chest. I screamed and fell to my knees, but I stood right back up. I knew the pain would disappear as quickly as it came. And once I was back on my feet, I hit him again.

A clanking sound came from behind me. James's head instantly pointed in its direction. Gabriel had accidentally knocked aside several pieces of debris as he limped over to

Clementine. James took a step toward Gabriel, his mouth starting to secrete the same acidic fluid he shot at Dinah.

He took another step toward Gabriel. He hunched over, almost looking like he was ready to leap right at Gabe's head. My heart stopped. I glared at James. And, suddenly, I felt the heat again. It coursed through my entire body. I reached out toward James and palmed his one good eye.

"Hey!" I screamed. "Eyes on me, jackass."

His entire skull spontaneously combusted. The matted hairs on his head caught fire and he roared in agony. A long, pained roar that shook my bones. The blue flames spread along his entire body until he was one giant inferno. One giant inferno reeking of burning rat. He blindly flailed around until he fell right to the floor, twitching violently. The flames spread to the debris around us. Before he could try to get up, I stomped my foot onto his long, burnt muzzle.

Gabriel finally hobbled his way to Clementine. He put his hand in Dinah's gauntlet, shut off the electricity, and pried it off Clementine's neck. Clementine's eyes rolled forward, and she gasped for breath. Tears rolled out of her eyes, and she pulled Gabriel closer to her. Gabriel shuddered as she dug her nails into his back for a giant, desperate hug.

James whimpered in pain again. Clementine shot to her feet. She shoved Gabriel behind her. Clementine ran toward the prone Revenant. Before he could try to roar again, Clementine pulled all the air out of James's lungs. James's stomach collapsed. His breath flew around him, picking up all the splinters in the room. A swift wind current formed in the room. Whatever tatters of a shirt I had left flew off in the wind. Clementine formed a miniature tornado around the Revenant. All of the blue flames in the room died. My feet shifted from under me, and I hopped off of James's muzzle. Clementine stood her ground. The twister shifted. It expanded, shortened, and pulled in all the air around it.

The twister became a bubble of air, caging the giant Revenant. Clementine pulled the bubble closer to herself. The huge bubble flew up to her and rested itself right on top of her fingertip. The Revenant stayed still. The room was finally silent. Clementine looked back at me, balancing the bubble like a giant basketball. I would have laughed if I weren't so exhausted. Instead, I fell to my knees. After the mini cyclone, Clementine's watch slid right by my feet. And only a few inches away from it was my trusty iPod. I picked both of them up, and neither had a scratch on them.

"Ready to go, hon?" Clementine said as I slid her watch into her pocket.

I wanted to say "Yes." I wanted to scream "Get me out of here now!" But a movement caught my eye from the far end of the room. For a second, I thought it was Rosa. But when I looked harder, I noticed that it was Dinah. Not her body, but her spirit. Dinah's ghost, transparent and dressed in a white robe, stared at me with such contempt in her face that I could almost see the red in her eyes. She tried to storm over to me, but she couldn't make it too far. Her real body was holding her back. I got up and started walking toward her. Clementine followed, only a few steps behind me. We were trained for this.

"Looks like it's time, Dinah," I said.

"No, it's not!" she screamed, swatting her fist at me. I was well out of striking range. "Don't you dare even look at me!"

I kept looking. It was so weird to me how someone who was such a threat barely a minute before looked so small and frail. I almost wanted to pity her. But I knew better.

"So," I said, getting my face as close to her without having to worry about getting slapped. "Why'd you kill James?"

She sneered and looked over at Gabriel.

"Because your boyfriend wasn't home, so I had to improvise."

I clicked my tongue and took in a deep breath. I looked toward Clementine.

"Should we put her in the air bubble?" I asked.

She nodded. "Yeah, let's put her in the air bubble."

I grabbed Dinah by the waist. She tried to kick and punch me off of her, but I just hoisted her up and tossed her almost weightless spirit into the air bubble with the man she killed. Or the man that killed her. Same thing. All of her screams were deafened by the wall of wind between us. I tried to hide my smile. Finally, she shut up.

"Hey, Clementine. Hey," I nudged her. "I know we see a lot of dead things, but I never thought I'd see a Dinah soar."

Clementine started walking toward the exit.

Before I could catch up, Gabriel started limping toward us. Clementine looked back at me and gave me a knowing nod, and I cringed. The nod was way too knowing. Clementine carried Dinah and James away from the wreckage, passing Gabriel along the way. It looked like she said something to him, but it was too quiet to tell. I walked up to Gabriel, grabbed his arm, and sat down with him on one of the only untouched pews in the room. Gabriel and I kept our faces blank. I had a lot of things I wanted to scream at him, and I was sure he had similar things to scream at me. But we were both tired, beaten, and all-around done. I crossed my arms, looked away from him, and sneered.

"Thanks for not killing Clementine," I scoffed. "It's a damn shame I have to thank you for that."

Gabriel looked toward Clementine. Both his former superior and the monster that his friend became still floated above her. He loosened his gauntlet, letting it slip off his hands and fall to the floor.

We sat in silence for a while. He refused to look at me. Instead, he kept his eyes on James. I could have comforted him, maybe said some inspirational quotes to get him through his friend's death. But nothing helpful came to me. I was burnt out.

"I was wrong. We were all wrong about you." He shoved his head into his hands. "I'm—I'm so sorry." He slumped further down in the pew. "Nothing makes sense anymore," he whispered. "What do I do now?"

Gabriel turned to me. His eyes were red, and a good bit of blood was running down his face and arm. I sighed and wiped some of the blood away from his eyes. He shuddered, and I paused. I felt the heat of his skin against mine. He looked me in the eyes, my mouth dried, and I stood back up. I knew Gabriel needed help. But I was not the person to give it to him.

"Quit the Brotherhood, that's a good start. And you still owe me a present."

I turned my back to Gabriel and tried to walk away. Something stopped me. My heart stopped beating as if to tell me it wouldn't start again unless I turned around again. Clenching my jaw, I looked toward Gabriel again. His beautiful face was still covered in dark blood, but I could see the pain in his eyes.

"This isn't your fault." As much as I wanted to sound strong, all I could muster was a whisper. "None of this is."

Gabriel looked to the floor and nodded. From the way he scrunched his eyes shut, I could tell I struck a nerve, and I knew I needed to stop talking before I made things worse. I started walking away just in time for Rosa to stagger to her feet. Gabriel rushed over to her. He whispered something and tried to help her get her bearings, but she slapped his hand away, disgusted. I shook it off. That was a problem for another day. I turned away and didn't look back again.

I rejoined Clementine. She wrapped her arm around my shoulders, and we limped toward the door. With the ghost and the Revenant trapped, we exited the Brotherhood's former hideout. The mist outside cleared up, giving us a perfect view of the crescent moon above us. The air was clear. We could breathe again. And we began our long trek home.

Chapter 15
My Tomorrow

It didn't take long for us to get back to normalcy. Within a few days, Clementine and Johanna were back to patrolling the city, Jesse was back waiting on Clementine hand-and-foot, Vee was back to smoking whatever she could get her hands on, and I was back to pouring all of my emotions into a pot pie. In the days since we brought James and Dinah to the portal, we hadn't seen any sign of the Brotherhood or any Revenants. Life became quiet.

Clementine and Jesse were off having a nice dinner together, leaving me alone with Johanna and Vee. When I brought dinner to the table, Johanna whispered "thank you," then started her silent prayer. Vee didn't even look at what I put on her plate and kept on drinking her second beer of the hour. I sat down and prodded my pie with my fork. I looked at the discontented faces of Johanna and Vee. That was it. That was normalcy.

My new normal: sitting in a spooky mansion, tired and beaten, with a bunch of women I barely knew. "Friends" would have been a liberal word to describe Vee and Johanna. "Co-workers" would have been better. Clementine, my best friend, hid almost a hundred years' worth of secrets from me. Together, we collected souls before they could mutate into horrible monsters, but only a few of us knew that last part.

On the upside, I actually pulled apart the Brotherhood. Or, at the very least, the Chicago branch. So, I had a reprieve from a scary organization I knew nothing about, who still thought we did the devil's work and who had mysterious technology to see us. Not to mention a shady leader who was partially to blame for my death.

For some reason, I didn't feel good about it. My gut knew something was off. I reached my goal. I stopped the Brotherhood, and they weren't going to bother Clementine or Jesse or the Maison girls ever again. And I had no idea why I felt so empty. Deep in my mind, I knew it was because I was still dead. But suddenly, I was dead and without a purpose.

Johanna sat up from her seat. She wiped her mouth with her napkin, then started walking toward the door. Her pot pie was only half finished, but I wasn't about to call her out on it. Especially since Vee hadn't even touched hers.

"Thank you for the meal, Ashton," she murmured. "If you still wish to wait on starting up patrol, I am sure we can wait as long as you need."

I said thanks, even if I didn't know what to really say. Of course, I didn't want to patrol. Patrol sucked. But the tired, weak tone of her voice made her sound almost disappointed. Johanna headed upstairs. Vee trudged away from the table, too, leaving her untouched plate for me to clean up. She opened the door to the basement, tossed her empty cans into the abyss below, and headed upstairs with Johanna.

Honestly, I wasn't in any mood to eat either. The incident with James was still ruining my appetite. I cleaned the table and made sure to box up Vee's leftovers, since she was probably going to reheat them at midnight after hotboxing her room. Then I just slumped down on the table and rested my head in my arms.

The front doors opened. Clementine's delicate footsteps clicked through the foyer and got louder until they stopped right next to me. I tilted my head upward just as Clementine placed a ratty plastic bag onto the table. She sat down next to me and crossed her legs. Jesse almost sat down, too, but after seeing the look Clementine gave him, he just put their leftovers in the fridge and headed upstairs. Once he was out of earshot, Clem turned her attention back to me.

"Ran into your friend on the way home."

It took me a second to realize who she was talking about. "He's not my friend," I scoffed.

"He's your somethin'." She started fiddling with the bag, but didn't open it. "We had a nice little talk. He told me to give this to you."

I stared at the bag for a bit. It wasn't ticking, so it probably wasn't a bomb. It had better be my goddamn present. My hands twitched toward the bag, but I kept them planted on the table. Clementine grabbed my chin and moved my face to look her in the eye.

"You really helped that boy. I hope you know that. You helped all of us." A quivering smile grew on her face. "And we're all so grateful to have you in our lives."

Clementine hopped up from the table and turned around before that quiver could turn into something messier. She left the ratty bag on the table and walked toward the stairs, no doubt heading straight for her workshop.

"So, I don't wanna see that frown for at least another week, because it's my turn to bake you somethin' sweet." She waved goodbye. "Might not be as good as what you make, but I'm sure I'll get to your level. I've got forever to learn."

I let out a long, deep sigh. A little smile crept along my face. I grabbed the bag and got up from the table. Gabriel's present rattled with every step I took. As I headed to the foyer, I thought long and hard about what to do. Not right then, but in general.

Clementine was wrong. We didn't have forever. We had immortality. If we wanted to, we could have lived in Zinda Mansion for thousands of years. Watching generations of people be born and die, countries form and fall, maybe even watch the human race go extinct. Just sit and watch the sun burn out.

But we had a finite amount of time with people. Eventually, my parents, or Faye, or Yvonne would die. And even the Geist would leave, with or without the Brotherhood. Nothing I could do could stop these immortals from eventually stepping through the portal. I only had a finite amount of time to spend with everyone, and I wasted so much time already.

I headed upstairs to my room. Johanna was at the top of the stairs. As I ascended, Johanna descended. We both stopped on the middle step, our bodies facing different directions but our eyes matching.

"You going for a walk?" I asked.

"Only a small one."

She continued to descend. The sleepless woman headed straight for the front door. My foot tapped on the marble. A "small walk" meant that she was going to patrol for me, even after what the Brotherhood did to her. And I knew I needed to be better than that.

"Johanna!" I called. She turned around. "I'm going out tomorrow. I know this means you'll have to mess with everyone's schedule again, but I'm ready. And I'm sure Vee's gonna be happy that she gets to work less." I waited for a reaction. She gave none. "And when I get back, maybe we could go on another walk together?"

She kept her spine stiff. I wondered if she even breathed. Finally, she nodded.

"That would be wonderful."

Johanna left the building. I went back to climbing the stairs. When I passed Vee's room, I noticed her door was wide open. I stopped to look, and Vee was slumped at her desk, drinking another beer and flipping through an album of what looked like yellowed news clippings. She slid some empty cans into the overflowing recycling bin next to her desk. She noticed me, and instead of screaming at me to leave, she just pushed aside the album and snarled at me, showing off her pronounced canines.

"You actually volunteered to go on patrol tomorrow?" she asked, eyes half shut.

"Yeah," I shrugged. "It's kinda my duty now."

"What's the damn point? Johanna's just gonna clean up after you anyway. You're just wasting time." She leaned onto her desk and buried her chin in the nest her arms made. "Everything's just a waste of time."

Vee went back to drinking. I left her doorway and headed up to the next floor. I went to my room, sat down on my bed, and ripped open Gabriel's present. The first thing that caught my eye was a CD in a paper sleeve.

"You've got to be shitting me," I mumbled.

I pulled out the CD. If it was a goddamn mixtape, I was fully ready to leave the mansion and kick him in the dick. I pulled the CD out of the sleeve and put it around my finger like a ring. Gabriel must have been broke if he was using technology from 2003. On the front of the CD, written in the worst handwriting I'd ever seen, Gabriel had written the mixtape's title.

My music's good. Eat a dick.

I laughed at his lie. Another thing caught my eye. Inside the bag, hidden under the crappy mixtape, was a familiar yellow box. My hand shot into the bag and ripped out a package of lemon drops. Just seeing the candy made my mouth tingle. Of course, Gabriel personalized the gift. The logo had a big X written over it in black marker. Right above it was, in giant black letters, *A DICK.*

I never laughed harder in my life. Both the box and the CD fell to the floor as I clutched my stomach. There was no reason to really laugh that hard. It wasn't too funny. And I was much funnier than he was by a long shot. But I was still laughing, stupidly and violently enough to shake my bed. Even with my self-awareness, I was still laughing with complete sincerity. And I hated it.

I jumped off my bed and picked up the candy and the CD. I grabbed an ancient CD player from the music room. Then I headed over to Clementine's workshop. She was sitting at her sewing machine with her head resting on an unfinished dress. Jesse was sitting at a desk parallel to hers, typing away on an ancient typewriter, with his tongue sticking out to show he was deeply, deeply concentrating. Daisy skittered along the floor in a little hamster ball, and I did my best to avoid her as she weaved around my legs. I tapped Clementine on the shoulder. She jumped and went right back to work as if she totally wasn't napping.

I plugged the CD player in, put in the mixtape, and pressed play. I sat down next to Clementine, stretching back in the chair, and kicked my feet up. I ripped open the pack of lemon drops and tossed Clementine and Jesse a few. Clementine popped one in her mouth, and her entire face puckered. Jesse stopped typing and started howling with laughter. It even sounded like Daisy was laughing. The look of betrayal on her face made the chaos of the day seem so far away. A gentle guitar riff pumped out of the CD player, and Gabriel's smooth voice filled the room.

"We sing to you, our Lord, our God, to find our way back home…"

"Well, at least it's not ska." I rolled my eyes.

Clementine turned her head. "Thinking about addin' this to your little music player?" she chuckled.

"Not a chance in Hell." I smirked.

I stretched again. I smiled at Clementine, at her dress, at

Jesse's lame poetry, even at the CD player and the emo gospel music coming out of it. I plucked a lemon drop out of the package and shoved it into my mouth. My mouth tingled, and I started to giggle.

I stood up, got behind Clementine, and wrapped my arms around her shoulders. She cooed, patting my arms with her free hand. I buried my head in her hair. I didn't want to think about immortality. All I thought about was spending time with everyone else. Somewhere in the city, Winona and Farrah were probably planning another honeymoon and Teresa was planting some lilies in her greenhouse. The lives of Geist revolved around death, but it was no more than a job. The very fact that I was hugging Clementine meant that I was alive.

I lost a lot along the way, but it was better than the alternative. In many ways, it was a blessing. On that terrible day, right before I died, I was gifted with something, and that was a guaranteed tomorrow. And, for the first time in a while, I was looking forward to my tomorrow.

About Mark Kelly

Mark Kelly is an avid gamer, wannabe model, and occasional podcaster. He has been writing novels since he was five years old, but most of them are not exactly publishable. After receiving a BFA in Creative Writing from Bowling Green State University, he's tried his best to actually make it worth the money he spent on it. Originally from Cincinnati, he currently lives in Atlanta with his husband, Matt.

More From Deep Hearts YA

Mark of Ravage and Ruin
Jacyn Gormish

Trapped in the Asylum and destined to become an assassin, Barli wants nothing more than to escape and return to the arms of her girlfriend. But when the moment arises for possible freedom, she learns that a friend is to be killed—and only Barli can save him.

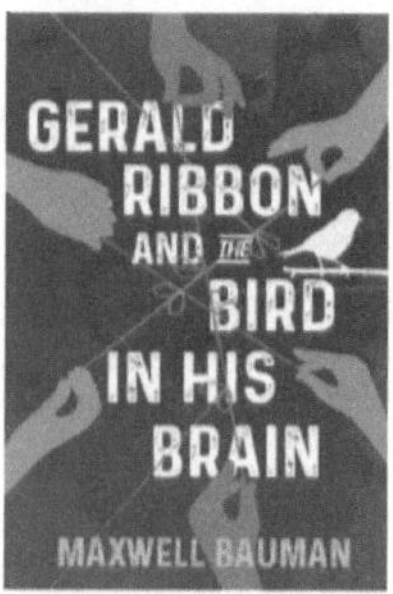

Gerald Ribbon and the Bird in His Brain
Maxwell Bauman

Gerald Ribbon has a habit of ruining his love life, and the bird in his brain that gives him terrible advice certainly isn't helping.

The Mixtape to My Life
Jake Martinez

Justin has always been comfortable in his skin, even if the world around him wasn't. A junior simply counting down the days for when he can leave for college, Justin's life is thrown for a loop when the one thing that helps him feel like himself suddenly slips away from him. But an unexpected blast from his past puts summer on a new and exciting path, one as random and unexpected as a mixtape.

www.ingramcontent.com/pod-product-compliance
Lightning Source LLC
Chambersburg PA
CBHW021303190726
48288CB00003B/661